The Waterworks of

Clearwash City

Book 1

Timothy J Waters

Copyright Notice

Book Dedication

- -

To my wife Julia and my daughter Josephine.
It has often been said,
"Many a truth is spoken in jest,"
which is why this book, in places, is so daft.
However, daft as it is (amongst its jests)
it contains many a truth.
I hope that you can find them.
Your loving husband and father.

- -

"Like a snarling, growling lion or a stampeding, furious bear,
(doing whatever it desires) so is a fiendish sovereign who rules over a
helpless, troubled and downtrodden people."
The Book of Proverbs – The Bible

- -

Assorted Book Review Snippets

- -

"I was captivated by this book from the first chapter! A very clever, funny and brilliant portrayal of the age old battle of Good vs Evil (literally!). Appropriate for children and adults, I loved the creativity, careful thought and attention to detail that have gone into bringing this world and its characters to life. The descriptive writing opens up your imagination to the surroundings, sounds and smells – could make an excellent film! Would highly recommend this fascinating book."

"The author has created an original story full of gentle humour that readers, other than its target audience, would enjoy. His writing flows, the dialogue is realistic and his characters are delightfully batty."

"Brilliantly descriptive and imaginative, amusing too ! Made me want to keep turning the pages to find out how things ended. A really good read."

"An engaging start to what promises to be a clever story. Unique fascinating characters. Awesome world building. Good descriptions."

"The style in which this story is written is engaging and entertaining. I was gripped by it from the start, and thoroughly enjoyed the twists and turns. The outcome was not at all as I expected, which increased the pleasure. This is clearly aimed at children; mine have grown up and moved out, but I would have loved to have read a few pages with them each night at bedtime. Having said that the book was aimed at children, I couldn't put the book down, and read it in a day, so no worries about being bored. I understand that there is another book in the pipeline, and I am looking forward to its release. I can highly recommend this book; it is an excellent original story well told, a regular page-turner."

"I smiled at all of your humour in the story. Made me smile a lot."

"You use great descriptions for this story. It's well-crafted and readable."

"This book is an awesome read! Full of adventure with characters that become to feel like family. Exquisite descriptions of settings and characters make the story come alive. The struggle between good and evil, which is a constant throughout the novel, keeps the reader guessing right to the very end. Lady Pluggat (heroine) was a favourite of mine. I definitely recommend it. Enjoy!"

"I love this story. It has lots of detail, so you can just picture exactly what it's like."

"Having not read anything by this author before I wondered what it would be like but was not disappointed. I look forward to further stories."

"A novel solution for tyranny. The likes of Hitler, Mussolini et - al, all meet their Waterloo. The author's confidence grows as he delivers a flushing success. A good omen for the future."

"Hello Tim. Your book is incredibly imaginative and it made me feel as if I was a little kid again and this is a great thing."

"Certainly one of the most original stories I've come across and that's no small thing."

"Wow! This book is absolutely amazing! I have been reading this book to our children, aged up to 18. Although I confess we started slowly, we found that the more we read, the more captivated we became. We are all desperate for the sequel, and LONG to see it made into a film, as it would be spectacular. We have found "The Waterworks of Clearwash City" INCREDIBLY funny, and I often had to stop reading so that we could all roll over laughing! The story is completely unique, and to start with, was a little slow due to our 'suspension of disbelief'. However, as one gets to the core of the story, one finds the book rather difficult to put down. The book seems somewhat 'ageless' as it appealed to all the family, who appreciated it on different levels of understanding. All our family can unanimously say is:
'Read this Book: You won't regret it!'"

- -

A Quick Note from the Author

The idea for this book came from a drama script that I wrote in 2001/2002 for children aged 7-12 years who were attending an annual 'custard slinging' summer club, run by my wife and myself. The storyline was wacky, funny and at times ridiculous. It so captured the imaginations of our young audience that I decided to turn it into a book. During this process, the book became a little more serious than the original tale and it now spans a much wider age range, mainly for teenagers and adults, though I have had one primary school teacher read it to her year 4 class and they all loved it. Despite this growing up of the storyline I have, however, tried to retain at times the basic feeling of 'daft fun' that gave the original script its birth.

To any children reading this book...

...the prologue and introduction sections are quite long and perhaps a little difficult to understand. (They're mainly for adults like me who like to think a lot!) You don't actually have to read either of them as the story stands by itself. If you really want to know about the background ideas behind the story, however, you're free to have a good browse through and see what you can pick up. If you're not into prologues and introductions then just turn to chapter one and get on with reading and enjoying the tale; you'll quickly find out what's happening and soon see what it's all about. I hope you have as much fun reading this story as I did writing it – Tim Waters.

Thank You and Contact Details

My thanks to everyone who has helped me with this book – to my wife and daughter who have given me the space and time to write it (and who have put up with me chatting on many an occasion about the storyline) and my thanks to anyone who has given me valuable feedback.

My thanks to all the schoolchildren who have sent in drawings inspired by the book – they look great.

Contact the author using the following address:
Email: authortimwaters@gmail.com

This book is available in a variety of formats. You can find out more at: www.clearwashcity.com along with all purchasing details.

It would be a great help if you could please leave a review of this book on Amazon where you purchased it.

If you enjoyed this book then please consider supporting the author by either lending or purchasing an extra copy for someone else who you think will also get pleasure from reading it.

Book Illustrations

The illustrations in this book have been created by myself, the author. They are a combination of iStock purchased images combined with royalty free images downloaded from the Unsplash.com website. My thanks to all of the contributors to Unsplash: in my opinion it is one of the most useful photographic resources on the internet. I have used my computer skills to merge images together to create the final illustrations that depict the different events in this book.

Contents

Preface – For Grown Up Readers

NOTE: If you are a young reader, just miss this part of the book out and get on with reading from chapter one as this section is for adults and you'll find this bit really boring! ;-)

Some might think it bizarre when I say that this book is all about liberty, sovereignty, free will and restraint. Together these four heroes of truth seem like extraordinarily strange and unequally yoked travelling companions - who, if left to themselves, would surely wander off and find their own particular and uniquely lonesome path. For what does liberty have to do with restraint or sovereign power with free will? How can the fullness of the one be met in the fulfilment of the other or how can the balancing of the one be set off by the inequalities of the other?

I want to share with you, to argue through the pages of this lightly humorous and at times oddly peculiar story, that all four of these wonderful realities must not only be allowed to be, but must come together and actively, jointly, live in mutual adoration. They must not just co-exist and survive as agreeable bedfellows, giving a nodding recognition to each other's presence. They must become one, woven and pulled together into and through every fibre of the fabric of life. Anything else falls short. For one without the other, or the putting of one before the other, amounts to nothing more than a humanly botched and misassembled ideological pretence.

In the end, it will prove to be more than a deceitful trail or blind alley. It will slowly grow to manifest into a most beautiful, even seductive, false lover and companion. She will parade herself as a bastion of freedom whilst becoming an all demanding and treacherous friend, full of feigned promises and deluded hopes. The cure for which is, at least in this short preliminary note, more profound than I can say.

Introduction – What do you dream of?

NOTE: If you are a young reader, just miss this part of the book out and get on with *reading from chapter one as this section is for adults and you'll find this bit really boring! ;-)*

You know it doesn't matter how many times you try to hide and conceal them, camouflage, cover, shroud, or disguise them. In the end you just have to sit back, reflect and admit, that there's one thing you simply can't do. You can't get rid of them. You can try and squash them, quash them, quench and quell them, subdue them, soothe them, charm and harm them; all to no avail. You cannot throttle them, muzzle them, gag or muffle them; tread them down, string them up or drown them out (to be sure all such methods fall on deaf ears). They will not be teased or appeased. They will not be bottled up, packaged up and sent far away on a long holiday. You can't call them to heel or get them to kneel. And you know what? No matter how hard you try and no matter how often you do it, they will always be there; loitering, lingering and waiting for that unprepared moment to pop up and show you just how much alive and well they really are.

What am I talking about? Well of course I'm referring to those ancient scripts, those divine writings of truth - expertly inscribed and yet scrawled, all over the walls of the innermost chambers of your heart; the poetry of faded truth, blueprinted across your soul. You know, the things written (but rarely read) that together make the person called you, you. Collectively they make up the sum of your purpose-filled vocation. They pervade and invade the "Book of your Conscience" and they never, ever, quite go away. Moreover, once you close those tired eyes of yours at the end of the day, to enter that time of slumber and rest, they will always be there, stirring and rousing themselves to life. It is there that they find their prophetic voice, whispering into the depths of your deepest dreams.

Maybe you've never taken the time when awaking from your subconscious shutdown to use those sleepy moments to reflect and ponder that our dreams reveal to us our longings, our yearnings and even sometimes our highest callings? I have often thought that it is in these great stirrings of the soul, mysterious and unfathomable, that we are reminded of some higher and more lofty, eternal purpose. For many of our most noble heroes and awesome world changers have been, at heart, dreamers. Dreamers who dared to imagine a world different to that in which they found themselves born. Who would not let go of the inescapable calling they felt within and who, despite many a discouragement, kept the inner

1

flame burning; so that in the fullness of time they could rise up and take their place in history.

So what about you? How do you dream and what do you dream of? No, I don't mean dreams of entering puzzling lands with enchanted forests where animals speak and spells must be broken; defeating ogres, dragons, goblins, giants and trolls. That's just a sign of too much cheese the night before. And, I don't mean dreams about rivers of gorgeous, delicious, adorable, rich chocolate pouring in and through every crack and crevice of your tingling, exhilarated mouth being slurped up with a euphoric tongue and spreading an elated satisfaction through every fibre of your being. Or, if your taste is a little different, of hot, steamy puddings swimming in seas of creamy custard with lashings of juicy rosy-red, strawberry jam. For those of us with full stomachs those kinds of wants and dreams are just surface desires when our tummies begin to rumble. No, I mean the dreams that are an echo of our race's beginnings and declare to us who we are. Where we find, to some measure, the purpose of our existence and where truth, justice, correctness and the unshakable rock of doing what is right, burn deep within.

For each individual soul, their dream is very secretive and very much their own; a closed door on a personal chronicle that shuts out the intrusions of the outside world. A place where no one can enter and say, "That's mine," or "I've been there before." Where your own thoughts create a unique world into which only you and your desires tread. Yet it is here, in this very place of exclusive seclusion and solitude that we find ourselves strangely at one with each other. For, in and amongst our corporate slumbering, appear shared threads of common thought. These together are like a giant weaver's puzzle, which - once stitched, pulled and entwined - form a great and awesome tapestry where each strand is joined and sewn by an accomplished hand.

Put all of the dreams and desires together and, like the fibres stitched and interwoven at the heart of a great masterpiece, the picture is complete. What appears in our joint sleepiness is an enormous, communal, spectacularly coloured, informative and illuminating work of art – a storyboard of callings; held together on some vast, dreamy loom. Some would call it a comfort blanket, an emotional prop to tickle the minds of delusionary romantics, but for those of us 'in the know', it is a beautifully written and intricate prophetic tale - only realised by the divinely led; who find themselves in the time of their timidity, waxing brave and bold.

On this subject of togetherness the people of Clearwash City are not too dissimilar from the rest of us. Yes, they too dream in different forms and various ways - but it is specifically the object of their dreams that unites and draws them collectively as one. For there is a single focus of desire, a shared longing, that continually appears in

2

their rest. All of the people in Clearwash City dream every night of one thing. They dream of soap!

Yes, you heard me correctly, they dream of soap. Their night-time thoughts are made up of nothing but the imaginary sensations of clean fresh water being sprinkled onto their dry, parched faces and at the same time smelling those soft and gentle fragrances from abundant soaps that appear all around in huge masses, filling up every part of their fantasy. They dream of lying back in a tub of hot, bubbly water, sinking into and amongst the sweet smelling oils and bath salts that will infuse their tired and worn out bodies. They fantasise about rubbing those gentle, soft, lathered suds over their toes, their knees, their chins, cheeks, ears and nose; lavishing it around their necks, arms and legs as they bask in the sunshine of bubble mania.

"Soap!" I hear you protest. "What's so special about soap?"

Well, nothing really. Soap is, in itself, just soap. But consider this. Have you ever desperately wanted a wash? I don't mean just felt a little icky and in need of a bath or a quick scrub up over the bathroom sink! I mean have you ever smelt so bad, felt so gunky, been so sweaty and messy from the top of your head to the tip of your toes that you've yearned to rub even the smallest amount of cleansing cream onto your stained and grimy skin?

Moreover, how do you cope when you suddenly wake up from your bathing dreams to find yourself still grubby, dirty and smelly? It's like being truly, truly, hungry and dreaming you're indulging yourself in a most wonderful feast; only to wake again and find that the craving is still there, unsatisfied and crying out for attention. So it is with the people of Clearwash City who wake morning by morning to dashed hopes of cleanliness.

"But," you complain, "Why are dreams about soap so different from dreams about custard and rumbly tummies?" Well, to my knowledge, no one has ever outlawed 'being hungry' and turned it into a crime. So, what if it was against the law to have a wash and be clean? If just the smallest amount of scrubbing would get you into such trouble that you could lose your job, your home, your friends, your family and even your life. What would you be prepared to do? What risks would you take? To what lengths would you go, just so that you could feel clean again?

This is the story of a small group of dreamers who lived beyond the mere whims of pleasure: who went beyond their surface desire to be spotless and their right to embrace the luxury of soap. They did not so love their own lives as to shrink back from the task in hand and merely dip their toes into the bathtub of freedom. No, they took a great deep breath and, after plunging in amongst oodles of bubbles, lotions, foams, bath salts and sweet smelling oils, found themselves in the timeless company of those many battle scarred and 'soaked to the skin' heroes who had gone before them - and of course, a great big rubber duck!

Book Characters

Chapter 1 – A National Celebrity

Across what looked like the beginnings of a pleasant evening sunset, multiple plumes of billowing smoke ascended into the crimson heavens. Together these columns of rising dirt saturated the air with a nasty smelling and discoloured smog, swallowing all that stood in their path. It was like watching the encroachment of a company of troops on parade, a marching detachment, who trudged through the firmament, stamping their mark in the atmosphere and leaving behind a trail of muddy tracks. This dirty military machine had one objective, to eat away at the great expanse, block out the sun, and so establish a canopy of darkness over the city. Up, up it all floated, a collective gathering of airy filth that unfurled a foul and grimy stench as each column of choking death staked its claim on the open sky.

This attempt at blockading the last rays of the day's sunlight would have no doubt been a quick and successful campaign if the smoke had not been suddenly met, swept up, and carried off by a persistent north-westerly breeze. This blustery wind, offended by the foul reeking invasion, wafted and drove the brown cloudy effluences here and there, around and above the city rooftops. With a final exhale that emptied its lungs, it then blew and propelled the polluted stench beyond the city walls; out into the vast expanse of the great beyond, the desert, where it finally dissipated. Over and over this process repeated. The air would fill with smoke until it choked, then be rescued and made clean once more by the breeze - that is pending the moment when the wind itself ran out of breath and took time to inhale. In those moments of windless calm, the polluting would start all over again.

Tall, blackened lanterns, dotted throughout the great metropolis, were the main culprits who fed the air with this gloomy contamination. Burning their smoky-red haze into the moist and sweaty air, they filled the atmosphere with a powdery soot that tasted of charcoaled fine grit. This relentless leakage of murky and misty vapour contributed greatly to the quickly darkening sky, making the sunset dusk a little more sinister than usual. It was as if a dark curtain was being drawn at the end of a long day and the casting of this early shadow spoke prophetically of the events to come.

Each cluster of toxic gas, exhaled by the numerous lanterns, was saturated with the heavy and overpowering smell of phosphorus, irritating the nose, the eyes and back of the throat. This odour was strangely mixed, however, with the sweet-scented aroma of homemade rum punch, being served from large, elevated bathtubs on the edge of a great market square. The crowds that had assembled there were, as usual, in more than a drunken stupor. Loud whistles, cheers and jeers accompanied the raucous noise of their laughter and chatter.

"Citizens of Clearwash City!" bellowed a loud voice. "We are overjoyed at your jovial presence here tonight and look forward to an evening of fun, frolicking and high adventure."

The greeting came from a set of aged and rusty loudspeakers, attached to a begrimed and burnt-out clock tower which belonged to a grand, marbled palace; its variegated walls and high stately rooms towered into the evening sky imposing a majestic and noble presence. In front of the palace was the large, cobbled marketplace into which a vast and euphoric crowd had assembled. Surrounding them were the many walls, streets and lofty buildings that together made up the jigsaw of what was once a great city. A vast and dirty capital, its crumbling houses, tired assembly halls and closed factories told the story of a prosperous time long gone.

"Are we ready?" cried the megaphoned voice, and the crowd responded with a cheer.

"And to any stragglers out there who've not yet arrived – here's a special reminder as to why you should come to the highlight of our summer festivities."

The voice droned on and on, talking about the immensity and grandeur of the event. Its sound echoed and bounced through the city's maze of weary streets, drowsy lanes and derelict avenues. The enthusiastic invitation to the forthcoming party felt quite hollow and out of place. For even though the voice knocked on a multitude of unopened doors, behind each one was nothing but a worn out building or an empty home. Music finally flooded the air as the announcer finished off his introduction to what he called the evening's 'great theatrical performance' and launched into announcing the main event.

"The authorities of Clearwash City proudly present for your delight and blissful entertainment the next pitiful, pathetic and wretched victim who, through his own deplorable stupidity, will now give us all great pleasure by having to endure the techno-magical, techno-tragical, 'Free Flowing Foamy Flusher Machine'! We welcome you to feast your eyes upon this most marvellous event and to inhale the joy of our soapsud extravaganza."

A roar of applause rang out from the people whilst a green uniformed brass band began to play a happy, sprightly tune.

"And now," continued the voice, "I give you your host for this evening, the one and only Mr Erepsin Ville of Clearwash City. I give you Mr E!"

From somewhere behind the magnificent palace vast emissions of hissing steam suddenly erupted like an explosion of dense fog. The dank, mushrooming vapour quickly engulfed the palace building and everything in its immediate vicinity. It drifted out over the streets nearby, right across the market square, and settled upon the on-looking crowd, hanging in the air like a moist, watery shroud. The people jostled with each other, trying to brush aside the white mist whilst peering intently through the smog to see what would happen next. From the epicentre of the cloud bomb an object inflated - just like the expansion of a large balloon or a ship's sails. Whatever it was, it was hefty and huge. The people fell silent, standing in awe and holding their breath. Mechanical grinding sounds followed, as if trying

7

to start a motor, and then more spurts of bulbous gas discharged into the wet haze. Engines roared, gears cranked and slowly, out of the cloud, a great vessel emerged.

Similar in shape and size to that of a sailing ship's keel, its vast, streamlined body glided gracefully through the air. Attached to the ship's underside were three noisy propeller devices that kept it afloat; helped by an elongated hot air balloon from which the craft was suspended. Gradually gaining momentum, it tacked from side to side following its pointed nose like a pirate boat on the prowl. Out towards the crowd it sailed, taking a course that curved around the edge of the palace building. Then, once enroute for the market square, it surged straight ahead. With columns of smoke continually erupting from its flanks, the ship's propeller engines wound themselves up and the mighty craft rose into the air. The crowd of onlookers shrank backwards, hands over their ears, as the ship soared above their heads.

Cheers, whistles, whoops and much applause accompanied the ship's ascent. Up and up, it zoomed, constantly rising skywards and navigating its way through the invisible airwaves. After reaching a great altitude the magnificent boat turned, pointed due west, blew out a blaze of fire from its engines and sailed out towards the setting sun. The crowd screamed with pleasure as the vessel sped away from them at a tremendous velocity, racing across the skyline of the heavens and leaving streaks of steam in its wake.

At the ship's bow stood a lone, solitary man; his slight and slender frame now silhouetted against the backdrop of the twilight sky. Placing his hands firmly on his hips and bulging his chest with pride, he rode out across the firmament like a conquering captain of the high seas. Gusts of the airstream blustered about him, running its invisible fingers through his long milk-chocolate hair. Enjoying this caress, he closed his eyes, held his head back and let the breeze continue its loving touches. Once it reached the outskirts of the city the mighty vessel gracefully tilted on its axis to make a full turn before lunging back towards the market square, navigating its way along a weaving and winding path. Then, without warning, the craft's engines turned themselves off and fell silent. The ship glided under its own momentum and then, with a hiss of steam from its front to break its forward motion, slowed to a gentle, quiet halt. All was still and a hush came over the spectators, who waited below in expectation.

The man on the ship's bow took hold of a steel cable (one end of which was secured via a locked metal wheel to the ship's mast) and ceremoniously attached the other end to a belt around his waist. Stepping up onto the ship's cathead, he pulled some eye-goggles from his back pocket and put them on. After putting his long hair into a pony tail, he stretched out his arms into a 'v' shape above him and leant over the ship's side. Dangling above the void he could see the crowd filling the market square below. A rush of delight and merriment went through the people as their hero came into view. Bellowing and shouting, they hollered with rapturous glee their dissolute enjoyment at the man's recklessness (and even

8

possible demise). Their corporate throng of noise rang out in wave upon wave of cheer and applause.

Leaning further still, until the wire behind him was rigid and taut, the man wavered over the gap and let the sound of the pleasure-seeking mob rise to a crescendo of gratification. For a few more seconds he just let himself sway in the nothingness, feeling the wind in his face and an inescapable call to his oncoming glory. His veins and heart pumped with bliss whilst his ears rang with the people's praise. Then, wishing to swim right down into it all, he flipped a switch on his belt that remotely unlocked the wheel on the ship's mast and, with the cable now running free, raised himself up onto his tiptoes, tipped his head backwards and dropped overboard. Down, down, down he fell, like a fallen angel plummeting to the earth. The musty smells of the city's foul air rushed about him as he tumbled through the atmosphere; a moment of exhilaration. Out of control. No boundaries. Free-fall.

At the same time that the man began his sudden descent, the ship from which he jumped opened up a series of small holes along its sides. A string of forty-eight cannons poked their noses through and sent out a succession of booms and bangs. Each explosion propelled a small object which travelled for a few seconds and then, BOOM! detonated into a mini firework display. The crowds stared in wonder as they looked up at their champion. It took their breath away to see him dropping out of the sky to the backdrop of smoke, fire and awesome fizzing colours.

Using the remote device on his belt (which controlled the wheel back on the ship to which his cable was attached) the man finally altered the speed of his decent to something more steady and at the same time adopted the immortal pose of a superhero flying in mid-air. The devoted multitude cheered with delight, raising their half-filled punch glasses to toast their host's arrival.

Finally the figure on the wire slowed to a halt above a large, wooden stage, situated in front of the assembled crowd. Then Mr E, as he was called, took hold of the cable and unhooked himself, dropping gracefully onto the timber platform. He stepped forward a few paces and bowed graciously to warmly greet his audience. A skinny gentleman of average height, he was bony faced and lean. Dressed in pinstriped trousers and a waistcoat, he handed his jacket and goggles to an assistant, exchanging them for a cane and a leather top hat. Swaggering up to a standing microphone he just stood there, arms stretched out, hat and cane held aloft, and receiving everyone's rapturous applause. Like a national celebrity he remained motionless, a statue, simply nodding his head with a wry smile and lapping up every succulent moment.

"My, my, my," he called into the microphone, "is this not a devious, deceitful, dastardly and defiant crowd of revellers I see before me? How delicious!" Great laughter, howls, hoots and hollers came from the throng who pushed and shoved themselves forward, wanting to get a better look at Mr E; only held back by a small fence and a row of nervous armed guards who stood poised, tense and ready for action. "My most noble and loyal subjects," called Mr E again. "It's flushing time!" The crowd went wild with excitement. "Let us now savour the moment," he continued, "as we deal with a sham of a man who has proved himself a liar, cheat, swindler, fraudster, rogue and charlatan. A twisted and warped individual, he has loved nothing but the wages of self-pleasure, decadent amusement and egotistical gratification. He is a man full of his own imaginary magnitude and who now, as you shall shortly see, amounts to nothing more than a pathetic, blundering wimp. So let us indulge our appetites by beholding our lawbreaker who stands accused and condemned. Ladies and gentlemen I give you, the once so wise and so noble, Sir Frederick James III."

Mr E pointed his cane towards the ground in front of the stage.

"Ivan," called Mr E, "music!"

Towards the back of the wooden stage stood a large, steam-powered church organ and at it sat a short, plump, balding figure; dressed in a bulging black leather jacket. On his head he wore (slightly tilted on one side) an elongated top hat which, I might add, enlarged the height of his not so tall frame. His short, stubby fingers ran up and down the organ's keys blasting out a terrible din. Then, as Ivan's music soared to a dramatic crescendo, the ground in front of the stage slowly opened up to reveal a gaping pit. From somewhere inside that yawning hole came the metallic noises of clunk, clank, clatter, clatter, clatter and clink, clunk, clank, clunk. The sound of each mechanism, each cog or gear change resonated across the market square. Cogs turned, chains rattled and out of the ground emerged a large, rusty, cast iron machine.

Chapter 2 – Oh How Delicious!

The bizarre, metallic contraption that came into sight looked like an enormous, corroded metal box with a polished, domed lid. Rising out of its top and sides were various pistons, pipes and rubber tubes sprouting in all directions like the hairdo of a mad professor; each of which juddered and shuddered as pressurised steam whizzed its way through them, sending high-pitched shrieks into the air. Across its front sat a large glass pane, through which lots of frothy, bubbly water could be seen churning over and over, like the insides of a giant industrial washing machine. This window was surrounded by numerous buttons that continually flashed on and off in a bright display of twirling colours. At the foot of the machine were several large levers, pedals and switches. All around the machine's base were small interlocking wheels that turned in rhythmic unison. Round and round and round they went as the machine rose out of the ground.

To the left of the machine stood a small room made from pure crystal glass; very expensive and obviously made by a master craftsman of some kind. It shone somehow, radiating an inner light that brightly illuminated its surroundings. Sticking out of the glass cubicle's top was another large pipe which bent back and re-joined itself onto the rusty machine's lid. Inside the glass room stood a sad, lonely figure - his head bowed low and his hands hanging limp at his sides. Taking several quick intakes of breath, to give himself some composure and strength, (for nerves clung to every part of his trembling body, making even standing difficult) he slowly lifted up his head to look out at the heckling crowd. A weak, embarrassed, smile appeared on his pale, pastel-shaded face to try to defy the mob of onlookers - showing them that all was well. At the same time, however, his legs wobbled and quivered with fright.

As soon as the crowd caught sight of Sir Frederick the throng of onlookers jeered, booed and hissed. Almost as one man they hurled their glasses of rum punch high into the air and within moments they came raining down, crack, smack, crash and smash; a sudden hailstorm, a plunging tidal wave of glass clattering and shattering onto and around the glass room. Together they created a carpet of splintered shards across the market square's cobbled floor. The machine finally stopped rising and sat humming its dull, melodic tune. Mr E gently raised his hat to welcome his victim. This gesture was accompanied by a broad cheesy grin across his amused face. He giggled and chuckled to himself. His chuckle then turned into a chortle and his chortle into a hearty laugh - which grew until it boomed into a loud flood of cheer, doubling him over with absolute hilarity.

"Ha!" he cried, "Got you at last!"

Mr E leaned forward on his cane and, through a blue tinted eyeglass which popped down from somewhere in his top hat, peered at Sir Frederick.

"Ladies and gentlemen," he said. "What is this we see before us? Have we ever seen in our midst such a pathetic and pitiful picture of despondent lonesomeness? And all this from a man who has portrayed himself as a proud pillar of promised freedom. Clearly you can see that today he is nothing of the sort; just a short-lived fallacy, a cloudy, hollow delusion to the minds of the weak-willed and feeble. Ladies and gentlemen, I wish to crown this most delicious and juicy moment that we find ourselves sharing today and to rename this ruffian and rebellious turncoat. Ladies and gentlemen I give you 'Sir Frederick the Fainthearted'!"

"Frederick the Fainthearted," the crowd jeered back.

"You – you - you won't get away with this," stammered the man from inside the glass room, his lips trembling with fright. "I'm telling you. This is not the end you know. You can't stop - stop all of us. We'll get you in the end!"

Mr E just continued to laugh as his merriment overflowed into a little dance which he jigged across the stage.

"And now!" cried Mr E again, through the city loud speakers, "Let us commence with our little ceremony of delights to cheer our hearts at the end of this bright and hot summer's day."

With those words he grabbed the microphone, leapt off the stage and positioned himself next to the glass room. Pointing his finger at Sir Frederick inside he cried, "This man has chosen a crooked path, a warped and perverted way that is full of shame, deceit and wayward self-gain. He has preyed upon the imaginary and delusionary needs of others, leading them on to his own advantage. This sham of a man, this hoaxer, this dishonest snake of a friend; an innocent dove he at first appeared to us but what a viper we have found him to be!"

Pulling a scroll from his inside waistcoat pocket, Mr E exchanged with Ivan his hat for a judge's wig and relaxed into a large oak chair provided by a couple of the guards. After ceremoniously setting the wig upon his head, he unfurled the scroll and read.

"My most noble and loyal subjects who are gathered here today, let me recount for you just some of the long list of offences committed by this crook. Sir Frederick James you have:

1) Broken law 1447 section B - 'collecting rainwater without a permit.'

2) Broken law 19622 - 'conspiring to sell rainwater through an underground, unofficial trade route to weak-willed, disobedient inhabitants of this city.'

3) Broken law 44792 by seeking to guide others into 'washing without proper authority.'

4) Broken law 352 version 14c by 'creating a kind of soap', made from cow's milk and pondweed, which could be used for 'washing.'

5) Broken law 6792 by not having upon yourself the 'required lotion smells provided by the state'.

6) Above all things you have finally sealed your fate by breaking law 1579-e in conjunction with law 62274, as you have used the banned substance called

'toothpaste' and applied it to your teeth using a common clothes brush. Not only have you used the aforesaid brush and paste in this way, but you have also persistently tried to clean your teeth on strictly 'non-brushing' days.

For these and other serious crimes which are too many to be listed here, you are today to endure the Free Flowing Foamy Flusher machine, as everyone can now see."

The crowd reacted with great hollers and howls of laughter or jeers of displeasure as each crime was read out. Then, "Flush, flush, flush, flush, flush, flush, flush," they all began to chant.

An elated Mr E got up from his judge's seat and handed his scroll to Ivan. Walking over to stand near Sir Frederick, he made a show of reaching for a large set of keys that dangled from his belt and shook them to jingle out a sound that signalled Sir Frederick's demise. Slotting one of them into a keyhole in the Flusher machine's front, he rotated it twice and placed his thumb and index finger on either side of a large dial, ready to give it a twist. Then, turning to face the crowd he cried,

"It's time to say goodbye. Goodbye to a betrayer of the state. Goodbye to a false friend. We shall not miss him and we shall not regret what we most nobly now do. Let us cleanse this city of all that is vulgar and wayward. Let us rid ourselves of disloyalty, dishonesty and distrust. Let us bring our citizens to a new place of openness and uprightness by purging from amongst us those who would be like

13

this betrayer and double-dealer. Let us be bold, bright and brave and finish the job by sending him on his way!"

With these words he twirled the dial between his fingers, pulled down two levers and the machine at once began to tremble and shake. Its inner engines stirred themselves into life. The delighted uproar of the people rose into a crescendo of high-pitched pleasure as the lights across the machine's front beamed brightly. With a grinding, a hissing and a deep mechanical cough, cough, cough, its inner workings jolted together and finally formed a rhythmic tune. Whoop, whoop, whoop, an alarm shrieked as water bubbled up from beneath Sir Frederick's feet and the room gradually started to fill with water.

The small wheels on the outside of the machine whizzed around at a tremendous speed. First one way and then the other, back and forth for nearly half a minute, until they all abruptly stopped. Then, from a speaker built into the side of the Flusher machine, came a deep electronic voice.

"Flushing traveller, prepare for new destination. Direction downwards, lowest level and out," said the machine. "Have a nice trip."

"Whoooooooooopee," shouted the crowd as one voice together, and then laughed. This was clearly something that they had all done on many an occasion and were quite adept at making the noise simultaneously and in joint harmony.

Sir Frederick turned deathly pale as he placed his sweaty, sticky hands flat against the cold glass walls of the room to brace himself. With desperation etched across his face, he looked out into the assembled horde, his eyes anxiously scanning this way and that, searching for any comfort and compassion. Amongst the people he could see, here and there, some onlookers who were not happy with what they were watching. They were just individuals dotted throughout the mob who stood quietly observing the events as they unfolded before them. His gaze finally rested on a very well-to-do looking lady who stood at the edge of the great assembly. Tall and elegant, she raised her head and returned his stare with a look of gentle, kind-hearted pity. She briefly placed her fingers on her lips and gestured with her hand as if to almost, but not quite, blow him a kiss goodbye.

"Goodbye M'lady," said Sir Frederick, under his breath.

"Goodbye," she mouthed back to him.

Gaining some strength from this brief encounter, Sir Frederick turned to face Mr E. "We'll get you for this!" he shouted. "I tell you Mr Erepsin Ville, you'll be standing where I am one day. May the heavens above bless the day when we have our just reward and everything you've done to us is paid back double into your own lap."

"Oh, how delicious!" responded Mr E. "I love it when they go down fighting. Doesn't it make our little event so much more gratifying?" he said, looking out at the crowd who replied with more taunts and laughter.

"We'll get you for this!" shouted Sir Frederick again, banging his fists on the sides of the glass room - but the clanking of the cogs and the grinding, clunking

14

mechanical melody of the machine had already begun. The small glass room slowly began to turn round and round and round and round. Clunk went another cog. Clunk, clank and then clunk again, taking the room into a spin. Faster and faster it went, speeding up with every turn. From the glass room's ceiling the large pipe poured down bubbling soapsuds and from holes in the floor the water now gushed and spouted upwards, causing Sir Frederick to lose his footing.

Soon the small room was spinning and humming at high speed with a whirlpool of water inside. Faster and faster it went, gathering speed with every turn. Somewhere between the splashing water and the soapsuds, parts of Sir Frederick could still be seen; every now and then an arm or leg would briefly appear against the glass walls before vanishing amongst the frothy bubbles.

"Help!" he shouted, but no one responded to his cry.

The machine whizzed and whirled the little room until the high pitched sound of its spin echoed across the market square, bouncing off the walls and buildings in the city. Mr E stood with his head up, eyes tightly closed and his arms spread out towards the sky. He took in every moment, every second of the event with sheer, unadulterated pleasure. Finally he opened his eyes, cleared his throat, and held his cane aloft like a conductor's baton. Beginning to conduct the crowd they all chanted together:

"Round and round and round we go,
Faster and faster the water does flow.
It gushes and froths with pure delight,
It swishes and sloshes till flushing is right!"

Mr E skipped over to the end of the flusher machine and, taking hold of a large chain that dangled from the top pipe, swung on it with all his weight. There was a heavy clunk followed by a great gurgling noise which echoed through the air, just like a giant plug had been pulled from a bath. Then a swilling, a swirling and a great sluuuuuuurrrrrp; the descending water gurgled and the glass cubicle emptied itself, flushing everything inside away. The glass room decelerated and then just sat there, very clean and very empty.

"And off Sir Frederick goes!" cried Mr E.

The crowd broke out into rapturous applause as Mr E removed his judge's wig and threw it into the throng.

"Well that was a good one," he added. "Loads of bubbles that time don't you think?"

Everyone laughed.

"So we say goodbye to our dear friend," he continued, taking his key out of the machine. He received back his top hat and carefully placed it onto his head (and at the same time, I might add, used the shiny walls of the glass room like a mirror to admire his reflection). "We're not missing you already - Sir Freddy!" he said. "Bye, bye now, bye, bye. Be good and say hello to that dear brother of yours for us, won't you?"

Ivan unlocked the door of the glass cubicle and briefly peered down the plughole to make sure that Sir Frederick was gone. Then he pulled a couple of levers and twirled some dials on the Free Flowing Foamy Flusher's front panel and the machine descended again into the ground from which it had come.

"Now that's what I call entertainment!" cried Mr E, who then took a bow, now that his job was completed.

The crowd responded with cheers whilst Mr E sauntered and half danced back up the steps of the wooden stage, dragging the microphone behind him. Then appeared a sudden change over his demeanour and his maddened eyes went dark with rage.

"And let that be a lesson to you all," he shouted into the microphone. "No one, absolutely no one, is allowed to have a wash in my city and anyone caught by the sniffer squads not smelling of the said authorised odours will follow where you see this most noble gentleman has gone today. Let this be an example to any of you simpletons who think that you can get away with doing the same. My laws in this time of water scarcity are the highest moral wall of defence against the foes of unfairness, prejudice and injustice. Anyone breaking them will end up as Sir Frederick today. Now be off with you, I don't want to see any more of you until tomorrow!"

And with those final words the countdown to the night-time curfew began. Police balloons quickly ascended into the sky and the heavens were once again filled with their droning presence. With searchlight beams dancing around them, the crowd dispersed, shuffling out to leave the market square empty and bare.

Chapter 3 – An Icy Moment

Some went off that evening happy and amused, whilst others stole their way home, quickly seeking refuge from the event. The posh lady stood at the edge of the square and watched everyone leave. Dressed in a long expensive coat and a jet-black pillbox hat, with a half net veil dropped across her powdered face, she looked a picture of noble propriety.

Finally, as if to acknowledge that the event she had witnessed was over and gone, she let out a deep sigh; lines of pain etched across her distressed brow. Turning to talk to a scruffy fellow who stood beside her, she said, "Come on Scrub. It's time for us to go to our homes."

"Yes M'lady," replied the shabby companion.

She escorted the young man out of the square and together they made their way up towards where he lived.

"M'lady?" said Scrub, as they walked along.

"Yes," she replied, in a tired tone.

"Where did Mr E get his Flusher machine from?" he enquired. "And why does it talk about 'going down' when it gets ready to flush?"

"I don't know where the machine came from," replied the lady. "He says he made it himself a long time ago but I don't believe that for one moment. In my view he doesn't have the intelligence or technology to put together such a contraption."

"Oh," said Scrub, a little surprised. "Anyway, why does the machine talk when it's about to flush someone?" he added, seeing that his second question had not been answered.

"Now please Scrub," she said, a little impatiently. "I've really had enough of today and Sir Frederick was…" she suddenly stood still without finishing her reply. Then, after taking a moment to compose herself, walked on in silence with Scrub trying to keep up with her now quicker walking pace.

"Well at least he's clean now," said Scrub, carrying on the conversation and seeking to console his companion. "Sir Frederick, I mean. He's clean and isn't dirty is he, not like the rest of us."

The elegant lady briefly scowled at Scrub but quickly replaced it with a calm and gentle countenance.

"Just because we can't wash doesn't mean we can't be clean," she replied. "And just because some people use water on the outside, doesn't mean that they're clean on the inside."

Scrub thought about this, glancing up at her face. Beneath her veil he could see a layer of makeup that was applied so thickly it was almost like tribal war paint. Still a little confused, he thought it best not to continue their chat and so decided to keep quiet.

After dropping Scrub off at his house, the lady walked on through the city streets. Different people acknowledged her presence as she went, with greetings or gestures that honoured her rank as a lady of the realm. Visiting several people that evening, she didn't linger at anyone's door and refused to go in, but preferred to briefly chat on each doorstep. She enquired after the welfare of everyone she called on and gave assurances to them that solutions would be found to any problems they had.

Eventually she found herself just wandering alone through the city streets, her heart sinking to the depths of her soul – feeling keenly the loss of her friend. Her purposeful walk had gradually turned into a tiresome meander, aimless and pointless. Her legs kept moving but her heart and mind had drifted into a numb nothingness that did not care where she was or where the journey would end. Turning here and there, as the whim of the moment dictated, she went up and down flights of stairs, through market squares, across small bridges that spanned dried up canals, down cobbled alleys and along winding roads. Briefly sitting on a park bench and momentarily closing her eyes, she tried to relax, but couldn't shake off the images of Sir Frederick's demise and so moved on.

Finally entering a small disused orchard, full of thirsty and gnarled apple trees, she ran her fingers over the dry, crisp bark of each tree as she wandered between them. No fruit, and no promise of any, yet there was something reassuring and comforting about their presence despite their obvious distress from drought. It was just nice to be surrounded by living things rather than the hard stone of the city walls and the harsh cobbled ground under her feet; to hear something different from the droning din that the numerous vending machines made which were dotted throughout the city, delivering useless goods to the people.

Sitting down with her back resting against one of the wilting trees, she took off her coat, kicked off her boots, and relaxed the back of her head on its trunk. Her mind and heart spun dizzily from the evening's events and, wanting some solace, she looked up at the canopy above. Gazing at the mass of twisted, knotted branches, she set her will to imagine them transformed. Branch by branch and twig by twig, she chose to see them not as tired and dry, but as beautiful, in blossom and fragrant with life. Descending further into her daydream, in her mind's eye she mentally renewed every tree in the orchard from desolation into a consoling bloom. The thoughts seemed to somehow soothe her pain, so she willingly kept up the fantasy.

Closing her eyes tightly she fell deeper and deeper into the self-induced vision; being calmed by its drug-like denial of reality. Her pretence filled the air with a perfume, emitted by the tree's abundant blossom.

She tried to sniff, to inhale deeply the aromatic bouquet of her surroundings. Multitudes of tiny petals fell from the branches above and settled onto her face, each one a gentle kiss to say that all was well, a shower of clean goodness to wash away the events of the day (which were obviously only a temporary blip to be denied and forgotten.)

In her mind flowers grew at her feet. One by one they sprouted and spread out, scattering across the orchard floor; a carpet of rich vegetation, a mass of swirling colour, an artist's mixed pallet, all gently swaying in the evening breeze. Listening hard for the bird song, she enjoyed its chattering and calling amongst the brightly coloured green leaves and the buzzing bees that flew back and forth over her head; all of this to the backdrop noise of fresh running water that flooded the nearby canals. Children played alongside them. She laughed to herself, enjoying in her mind's eye the fun they were having, splashing each other until they were soaking wet. Then she cherished the images of their mothers lovingly wrapping them up in warm, fluffy towels, smiles on their faces and not a care in the world to chase their happiness away.

"In the fullness of time…" she whispered to herself, quite dreamily.

Who knows how long she sat there in her delusional mental escape, but she was rudely awakened by a blast of warm air and a shower of dust pollution that fell through the tree canopies all around. In the sky overhead a droning flying machine screeched to a halt. Down flashed a searchlight onto the road next to the orchard. From there it scanned the area, swishing this way and that, searching the locality. Quickly coming to her senses, the lady pulled on her boots and coat, leapt to her feet, and scurried to the other side of the orchard. Within moments the place where she had sat was under the spotlight as the beam continued to leap from place to place. A thick, wiry hedge bordered the grove and she quickly grasped the reality of her entrapment. Moving from tree to tree, she began to trace the orchard's edge in order to make her way back to where she had entered and then out onto the road. She stopped, however, when four static lights suddenly illuminated the entranceway, shining down from the flying police patrol and so making escape impossible.

Dodging, ducking and diving, the once elegant and refined woman found that she had to leave all of her gracious mannerisms behind in order to keep herself from being discovered, as the light continued to search the grove. It became a game of guess and move, or just wait whilst the light glided past her - sometimes only a couple of feet from her position. A second light appeared from another police balloon ship and it also began a sweeping search. Not knowing how to deal with two lights she found herself standing still, frozen with her back against a tree, watching the lights chase each other around the orchard. She knew, however, that standing still wasn't the answer. It would only be a matter of time before she was discovered. So, breathing in deeply to renew her courage, she watched for an opportunity to move.

At the back of the orchard was a wall of coarse, tough hedgerow. It was overgrown, slightly wild and so filled with thorns that it was not something anyone would want to get close to – but there were slight gaps in the bush's growth and the lady knew it was the only way out. After securing her hat firmly in place, she began counting the swaying motions of the searchlights. She watched and waited. "One, two, three, four and one, two, three," she chanted under her breath to find the pattern of each swaying beam. Pulling her fists inside the sleeves of her thick coat to protect her hands and wrapping her arms around her waist and face, she hesitated in anticipation of making her escape. Voices on the road suddenly appeared as the night-time watch took up their positions across the city.

"Don't panic!" she whispered, through gritted teeth. "Wait, wait, wait, wait, wait!" she mentally commanded herself, ordering her emotions to stay calm and her body to keep still.

Soldiers entered the orchard on the opposite side of the grounds and began to spread out, joking and laughing as they went, not taking their job very seriously. The lady just focused on the spotlight beams and poised herself for the dash. Finally the gap between their sways opened and she made good her escape. Running towards the hedge, she single-mindedly focused on a small gap in its growth and sprinted with a determination to breakout. Tightening every muscle in her body to prepare for impact, she launched into the hedge; at the last instant dropping her head down as she entered its prickly belly. Seconds later, splayed face down on the ground in and amongst what felt like a thousand tiny fingers all grasping and pinching at her, she felt her lip bleeding and her shoulder numb from knocking through several sturdy branches. As expected the soldiers on the far side of the orchard heard the sound of her exit and called to each other to try to locate the source of the sound. She couldn't wait, however, to discover if she was hurt or to try and keep the sound of her departure quiet; to get away was the main thing. So, pulling her knees up to her chest and putting her hands over her head to hold her hat in place, she forced and pushed her way through the thorny bushes. Her progress was like being lashed with whips as the thorns and twigs pierced her outer coat and snapped around her, scraping at her arms and limbs. She didn't stop, however, but found that licking her fingers as she moved helped to dull the pain.

Back in the orchard the soldiers eventually found the newly made hole in the hedge and were busy shining their torches into it, but weren't able to see very much. The branches had already half closed in around the temporary gap and the city guards, not wanting cuts and bruises themselves, were not keen to enter the thorny scrubland. They signalled to the patrol balloons to shine their lights in their direction. It took a good few seconds of frantic yelling, however, before they gained their attention - but by then the lady had forced her way through the undergrowth. With almost a yelp of pain she heaved herself through the last few of its branches to break away from the hedgerow's embrace, falling out onto her knees and leaving the orchard behind.

She found herself on a small pathway, flanked on either side by tall, wild grasses that stood proudly to attention and gave brief nods as the evening wind rippled across them. After glancing over her shoulder, she scrambled to her feet and hurriedly followed the narrow trail; picking up the folds of her long coat and dress as she ran. The path wound this way and that and finally stopped at the edge of a dried-up riverbed. Glancing back again to see that the police patrol lights were still sweeping over the orchard and surrounding hedgerow, she dropped herself into the dusty channel where the river had once flowed. Trailing its meandering path, she walked and half jogged for a few minutes, each footstep crumbling through a thin top layer of hard baked soil amidst the multitude of other footprints already there.

Eventually there came into view a large pipe, sticking out from the side of the river's red earthen bank. Without hesitating she stepped in, bowing her head slightly to keep her hat from scraping along the pipe's dirty roof. She walked on and on into the dark passageway. Many times, in the course of her journey, the tunnel divided into two or came out briefly into the open air where there were more pipe entrances to choose from. Through tunnel after tunnel she went, deciding quickly which way to go and which pipe to walk in, following a very familiar route, until she arrived at an open mouth again where the pipe maze ended. Briefly poking her face out the other side, she scanned the sky above and her surroundings left and right. Once happy that all was clear, she dropped out of the pipe. On her right was a concealed stone stairway, hidden behind an overgrown hawthorn bush. Having climbed the stairs, she stopped at the top to open a small gate and then went through into a highly cultivated garden.

Along a neatly kept gravel path she now walked to the crunch, crunch sound under her feet. After navigating a small maze, made from neatly clipped hedged walls, she finally walked out onto a long, broad lawn. Making her way across the grass, she removed her shoes and walked in a more relaxed manner, sinking her toes into the mossy ground as she went. On her left were the iron gates which guarded the entranceway to her large country estate and on her right, up a long driveway, was her home, a great mansion residence for the rich and wealthy.

"Well my dear, you nearly got caught for being out too late tonight," she said to herself, in a rather casual, almost jovial tone. She laughed briefly at her own comment and then stopped.

"Stop it," she said, correcting herself. "Oh Georgiana, why do you..." but she didn't finish the sentence.

Having made her way across the grass and then up her long driveway, she looked back from the front of her very wealthy home and felt in her heart like a pauper. The evening's events suddenly came flooding back to her, the flushing of Sir Frederick and then her walk through the city, which had been so lonesome and grim. The dirty capital was usually a dull place but tonight it had seemed especially bleak and grey. She remembered the silence that had followed her as she meandered her way through the streets and the wind that had whistled around her ankles and then on, chasing its echoes down the deserted cobbled boulevards and nearby lanes.

"Oh Dad!" she said, almost to herself as if referring to a rock in her life that was gone but to which she still clung.

She let her tearful eyes roam across the expanse of the great city, a place where so many people dwelt but where nobody lived; a grey, stoned shell in which a population was kept prisoner to false hopes and long forgotten dreams. Taking in the shabby, grey silhouettes of the derelict factories and abandoned streets, she tried to see through the mess and dirt to remember some dim and distant childhood memories of what once was. "Look what we've become," she sighed.

Taking in a long, deep breath, she strengthened both her posture and resolve.

"We'll see your end Mr E...," she said, in a bitter tone, "...in the fullness of time. There are those of us who are not satisfied with sipping to subsist, or with sampling to survive. We want to drink deep and live. Your scarcity is illusion and our forced dependency is defined as you doing us a favour. Your divide and rule has become to us deprive and ruin."

She shivered. Mid-summer it might be, but keenly feeling the absence of Sir Frederick's company brought a tinge of winter into her normally cheerful and generous heart. Struggling to stay warm, she wrapped her arms around herself and rubbed her shoulders; wondering where her next comfort would come from. The chill of the night air from the desert had drifted in, but tonight it felt especially cold. It's always an icy moment when you lose a friend.

Chapter 4 – In The Reign Of The King

Just outside the walls of Clearwash City lay the great expanse of a vast, arid desert. Stretching itself out towards the horizon it played host to the blackening backdrop of the night. The sky had turned a deep, blood-red in preparation for the setting sun's departure and this canopy of dark crimson seemed, in some way, to reflect the deathly nature of the lonesome wilderness. Amidst the dehydrated terrain of sand dunes and rusty-brown, weather-beaten rocks, multiple gusts of dusty winds skipped and danced their twisting, turning, waltz-like movements across this territory called 'No-Mans-Land'. Scurrying here and there, these swishing and swirling breezes continually chased their tails, playing a never-ending game, whilst wafting great piles of swelling lifeless dirt into the air.

To any onlooker the wind's behaviour was perhaps a warning, a show of strength, demonstrating just how far and wide this inhospitable domain stretched. This was a waterless and thirsty wasteland, friend to no-one and predator to the misguided or ill equipped. A prowling beast, she lay in wait for the unsuspecting traveller or the intrepid explorer, to take captive, devour and digest any who might seek refuge within her borders.

With night-time swiftly approaching, the wilderness rocks and barren stretches of parched land found themselves swallowed up by the long drawn out shadows of the surrounding hills and mountain peaks. The sun slipped beneath the skyline and the desert owl, swooping this way and that, looked for its first meal of the night whilst the wild coyotes howled in the oncoming darkness.

On a ledge, near the summit of a tall mountain peak, two figures stood in the shadow of the rockface; peering through a telescopic instrument and gazing out towards the horizon. Like statues, they neither moved nor spoke, apparently mesmerised by what they saw. One was a man with a stern, weather-beaten face and the other a girl, nearly but not yet into adulthood. Completely still, they kept watching and staring off into the distance, whilst the wind pulled and tugged at their grey cloaks that flapped in the night breeze.

Over the mountaintops, in the direction the figures were gazing, ten thousand lights danced and sparkled as the last rays of the setting sun bounced off the numerous windows that belonged to the white marbled towers and buildings of Clearwash City. Like a great stony creature settling down to sleep for the night, the city was quiet and covered in shadows. Flags flew from every tower and lofty edifice whilst between its turrets guards could be seen walking along the top of the great wall that surrounded it. High in the sky the motorised police balloons gently sailed through the evening air. Beaming down their circular lights from these floating vantage points, they systematically searched the city back alleys and side streets, trying to catch any stray residents who might be in parts of the capital that were off limits to ordinary citizens.

Through the eye of their telescope the two figures had watched the flushing of Sir Frederick James and then followed the dispersion of those who had gathered in the great square to say goodbye to the city authorities' latest victim. Now their gaze rested upon Mr E as he skipped and hopped his way back into the city palace. He was gleefully happy, now dancing on his tiptoes, now throwing his bright silver cane into the air; at times he flapped his arms like a bird and crowed like a cockerel at the top of his voice.

"That man gets more ludicrous and bizarre by the day," sighed the young woman.

"Yes I know," replied the man. "He's completely mad."

"The people aren't ready yet, are they?" the young woman commented, a tone of sadness and disappointment in her voice.

"Well," replied the man. "It's still difficult to tell. Things can change very quickly. Right now some are, some aren't and some never will be. I just hope that as many as possible can come over onto our side before we send out His Majesty's herald."

Their final few minutes were spent peering intently at the palace clock tower and in particular at the central flagpole, from which a large golden standard flew with a red letter 'E' emblazoned across it. Around them, the last glimpses of light said goodbye to the evening and finally disappeared from sight. It was night and all became quiet and still.

"Nothing to report then," said the young woman, stretching after coming to the end of a long day.

"No," replied the man, "nothing today. We'll come back here tomorrow morning for the early shift and then that's us done until next week."

"That's *you* done until next week," she replied. "The day after tomorrow I have city infiltration duties."

"I wish you hadn't volunteered for such a thing," he said.

With those words they both dusted themselves down, packed up their equipment and pulled a scarf loosely across their faces.

"After you Mr Tremblay," said the young woman, gesturing with her hand.

"No, after you Miss Tremblay," came his reply.

"Age before beauty," she said.

"Wimpy youth before stalwart age," he said.

"Stalwart!" she replied. "What's that?"

"You know," said Mr Tremblay. "To be unwavering, unfaltering, resolute, persistent, committed, dedicated, unswerving, determined, courageous, daring, fearless. All the things that my generation are and that today's wimpy youth aren't."

"Oh Dad!" she sighed, with a smile in her eyes and walking on ahead of him. "You're impossible."

"No, not impossible," he teased. "Stalwart. That is bold, fearless, daring, valiant, brave, stout-hearted, even perhaps audacious. Do you know what audacious means?"

"I'm not listening to you Dad," she said, sticking her fingers in her ears as she walked.

"Now Anna," he chuckled with a grin. "When did you ever?"

Carefully they made their way down the side of the ridge and followed a path until they came to the edge of a rocky crevasse. Beneath them was a deep drop off the side of the mountain into bottomless darkness. Ignoring this apparent danger, they briefly fingertip-touched hands at arm's length to ensure there was enough space between them. Then, lifting and draping the bottom front edges of their cloaks across each opposite shoulder, leant forwards over the wide expanse and together dived into the abyss below. Dressed in grey from top to bottom, with their cloaks tightly wrapped around them, they plummeted straight down for a few seconds and then flung open their capes. A wind caught underneath them and - snap! - their cloaks became rigid by a thin metal frame that clicked into place as they fell. Gliding through the night air, they flew down and finally landed gracefully onto the dusty, red earthen floor at the foot of the mountain.

Walking on for a short time, they turned aside into a gorge and came across a large wicker basket that sat behind a pile of fallen boulders. The basket was twice their height and just as wide. Taking hold of a dangling rope ladder they climbed in and disappeared from view. Moments later, four large mechanical legs popped out of the basket's corners and pushed upwards, raising the wicker frame off the ground. At the same time a large balloon began to inflate from just above the basket's top. Up it went until it hovered directly overhead, held in place by four large chains attached to the basket's corners. Anna and Mr Tremblay appeared directly under the balloon, obviously standing on some unseen platform inside. Holding up a small night-time heat-seeking device, they used it to quickly peer into the darkness around them, scanning the night air to make sure that no one was nearby. Jets of steam billowed out from beneath each of the basket's metal legs and the hot watery air flooded and mushroomed all around. The basket temporarily shook for an instant and then, whoosh, up it zoomed high into the atmosphere. Up, up they climbed, higher and higher, their speed accelerating all the time. The evening wind caught them and their cloaks swayed and swished in the night breeze. Woven onto the chests of their tunics was a royal red, gold and blue crest. On the crest were the pictures of a great lion and a prowling bear, standing opposite each other underneath the wings of an immense soaring eagle. Boldly written above the crest were the words, 'In the Reign of the King.'

"Home in a few minutes," said Anna.

"Rhubarb pie for supper," replied her father, with a glint in his eye.

Soon they were miles high and quickly disappeared into a cloud.

- -

Back in Clearwash City Mr E had taken a long time to settle down before retiring for the night, his buoyant mood had kept him up for hours. First he ate a hearty meal. Then he watched some dismal short plays, put on by the catering staff in the small theatre at the back of the palace. Being quickly bored by their theatrical attempts, Erepsin decided to join in and made himself the star of each show – inventing characters that were not part of the original script and forcing everyone to spontaneously act around him. Once the dreadful events were over and the 'actor extraordinaire' (as the audience of eleven people had called him) had left the stage, he finally went to bed in high spirits. After dimming the oil lamp that hung on the wall next to his bed, his head sank into his delightfully soft and luxurious pillow. The room fell into semi-darkness and his eyes closed; a satisfied smile finished the day.

Hours later, however, as his dreams deepened, his shallow and happy mood fled away. A shadowy gloom crept across his face whilst his countenance darkened. Juddering movements erratically shifted his limbs from side to side; trembling here and there and quaking from inner fears. Whatever it was he was seeing in his minds-eye, it clearly made him distressed. He mumbled a few times and grumbled some complaints about his people's behaviour and lack of loyalty. Through gritted teeth he almost growled out his displeasure at anyone that he could see in his dream. Then, thrashing his head from side to side, he suddenly bellowed out in a husky, harsh-pitched yowl, "They're all traitors, the lot of 'em."

His agitated tone barked the words into the surrounding darkness, but the hush and silence that filled the bedroom's atmosphere quickly swallowed them up and they were gone without a reply. This non-response to his words only served to irritate his dream induced hallucinations. "Traitors, vagabonds and rebels!" he shrieked again in his sleep and then hesitated, waiting, listening for someone, anyone to reply. The stillness and shadowy-gloom that surrounded the bed now matched Mr E's mood. Feeling bereft and alone, Erepsin loudly licked his lips whilst his uneasy breathing pattern turned from a deep gasping into a repetitive wheeze. Perhaps he was now exhausted and out of breath or perhaps it was just the lack of comeback from his imaginary audience that distressed him – it was difficult to tell. Eventually he calmed and, having paused to wait for something (but couldn't quite remember what) he continued his mumbling and random chattering.

Words began to tumble out of him in a troubled manner; a rambling and murmuring that meant very little to any sensible listening mind. This went on for some time until a new, sharper discourse emerged amongst his many confused utterances. The words he spoke became critical and severe; harshly spat out with a scornful, spiteful contempt.

"I've never trusted 'em," he yelled in a deep throaty voice, "never will," he added in a quieter, menacing manner. "There's nothing you can do to change my mind. It's completely made up you know. I know what they're up to! They're all just waiting. Waiting, waiting and waiting they are; all the time waiting for me to slip up, trip up and fall into one of their rotten snares. I shan't be taken in, not me. I'll not be hoodwinked. I know what they are; deceitful conspirators, ready to shut me down and run me out!"

Again Erepsin paused to listen. In his mind's eye his words rang in the ears of his captivated audience and he waited patiently for an answer. The audience however, (who were meant to be listening to his address) were obviously not impressed and the noiseless room gave him no encouragement, no comfort, no comradeship. He stammered a little, not at all sure what to say next or why his lively speech was met with such an icy contempt. After a time he stirred himself, picked up the conversation, and continued.

"Keep 'em down, that's what I say! Put 'em right under your thumb. Squash 'em, till they're as dead on the inside as dirty they are on the out. Servitude, that's what they need. A rod for their backs and a whip for their heels; that's what the likes of them understands."

"No! That's not true." replied a quieter, almost whispering utterance in objection. The soft voice seemed to appear from somewhere within Erepsin, as if someone else inside him, a conscience perhaps, had been listening all along and didn't want to talk but had finally been provoked into action. "They're not that bad," it added.

The husky voice from inside Mr E seemed momentarily jovial that he'd finally got the conversation he was looking for. He echoed the last words of his friend.

"Not that bad?" he curtly enquired. "They're all rotten, through and through."

"You leave them be," retorted the soft voice from within him. "What have they done that you hate them so?"

"Done!" came the gruff reply. "Done! I'll tell you what they've done; rebels, the lot of 'em. Ruined my city they have, that's what they've done. Just look at it! Mess, grime and filth! Who could live in such a place?"

The darkened room went quiet for a few more moments, the soft voice perhaps pondering what had just been said whilst Erepsin's uneasy respiration was the only sound breaking the surrounding silence. The lattice at the window shook and rattled from a strong wind that howled outside. With the moon briefly appearing from behind the clouds, for what seemed only an instant, a stream of dreary light flooded in. In those few seconds of semi-illumination, the richly ornamented bedroom was once again revealed. Within its highly decorated walls were several armchairs, an open-hearth fireplace, a large sink, a four-poster bed and a golden 'tick-tocking' clock, which sat on the mantelpiece above the hearth. Then, just as quickly as it came, the light faded and the semi-darkness returned.

"You don't know 'em like I do," said the gruff voice through Erepsin. "Trickery, that's the word. Tricksters and fraudsters. Always scheming! Always up to something they are! Never happy with their lot!"

"What have they got to be happy about?" replied the softer, whispering tone. "It's all your fault. You got them in this scrape. You get them out again."

This question seemed to hit a raw nerve in his grumpy friend who thundered his response at the top of his voice.

"Who do they think I am?" he cried. "Some kind of happiness puppet to keep them entertained no doubt! Stroppy and thankless - that's what best describes 'em."

Again, it went quiet.

"You're lonely," retorted the patient and gentle voice, once the atmosphere had quietened. "Not quite what you thought it would be is it, being number one?"

"Shut up!" snapped the gruff voice. "I know where your loyalties lie. Always been with them you have, right from the beginning. It's their side that you're on. Traitor!"

"Don't call me that," pleaded the soft conscience from within Erepsin, clearly intimidated by his friend.

"And why not? Should have had you flushed years ago."

To this there was no answer. Seeing that he'd scored some kind of success the harsh mannered speaker carried on the conversation.

"So, whose side are you on then? About time you made up your mind it is. Lost your sense of fun you have. That's what your problem is; lost your stomach for *proper* entertainment. Proper fun requires guts."

"I don't want anything to do with it!" came the unsettled reply.

"You can't handle it!"

"No, I just don't find it funny anymore."

"You mean you've lost your backbone, you spineless wimp!"

"No, that's not true," replied the soft voice.

29

"Round and round and round we go...," taunted his crabby friend.

"Stop it!" he objected, quite upset. "Just stop it!"

"Ha!" came the hollering reply, "Told you, you've lost it."

The argument continued until the wind outside ceased it's howling and the light rain that fell ended as the storm clouds broke. Bright moonlight returned and within minutes the room received a gentle luminosity. On the bed Mr E's contorted body was sweating so profusely that the sheets on which he rested were beyond damp. Thrashing his head from side to side, his face grimaced and twisted as his tormented thoughts continued to rush through his mind.

"Where has my waterworks gone?" demanded the gruff voice. "It's gone! It's gone!"

"It's not your waterworks," he quietly replied to himself. "Never was."

"Yes it is!" he bellowed back. "It's mine, given to me before the dawn of time it was."

"Now you're just being silly," he gently said.

"No I'm not!" he snapped.

Erepsin began to writhe from side to side on the bed. Shuddering, trembling, his limbs almost jumped uncontrollably as some terrible emotion ranted and raved inside and was bursting to get out. Gripping his fingers into the mattress and bed sheets he began to cough. Each movement of his chest was accompanied by a pant for air, and each gasp of air brought a surge of pain. Then gulping, swallowing and choking, he lay in this quaking state for about half a minute, struggling to inhale. Finally he cleared his throat and took in several deep gasps to breathe more easily; his body calming - sinking back into the mattress to become quiet and still.

"He is coming you know," he eventually said in the gruff voice.

"I know," came a soft reply from within him rather timidly. "In the fullness of t..."

"Not far away now he is", interrupted the grumpy personality. "The ruin of us all will he be."

"You've got to stop him," said the second soft voice. "I-I can't do it; haven't got the courage like you."

"Stop everyone I will," said the gruff voice. A broad smile came across Erepsin's face. Then he laughed to himself and added, "I've got a surprise you know. Do you want to know my secret?"

Erepsin was about to reply when, Ding! The clock on the mantelpiece chimed out. Ding! Ding! Ding! (Four o'clock in the morning.) At this he sat bolt upright.

"Oh, my!" he said, wiping his hand across his face. He looked at the measure of sweat on his palm and then pulled at his shirt, sodden with perspiration. After spending some moments to clear his head, he swung his legs over the side of the bed and staggered to the sink. Filling it with water he splashed his face, ran a sponge around the back of his neck, and then stared into the mirror opposite. The harassed reflection gawped back at him and, for a brief instant, he found his head in his hands - where he sobbed until he realised what he was doing. Pulling the sink's plug and wiping his face with a towel, Erepsin walked over to the window. Peering through the lattice he looked down onto the streets of Clearwash City. All of the doors to every house and home were closed and the people were out of sight.

"Come on Erepsin," he said to himself. "Get it together." He glanced over to the bed but immediately refused the idea of returning. "Time for a quick bath?" he thought to himself. He shook his head. Quickly exiting the room, he moved purposefully down the corridor at an almost running pace. With the palace staff all asleep, he went undisturbed through door upon door till he entered one of the study rooms at the far back of the palace. It was a place which used to belong to the head waiter years ago. Erepsin had been familiar with it since childhood – often being sent there as a boy by his mother when she was fed up with him. The room was far from anyone, a lost corner for a lost and lonely person or a refuge for a recluse who was happy with his own company. Later on in life Erepsin had made the room his own private study, a place of withdrawal from his immediate world. He now rested for a while, relaxing in the arms of a broad leather-backed chair; an old friend, crimson red and spoilt with stains and the wrinkles of age. Despite it being old it was still comfortable and its smell brought back memories of boyhood. He dozed for a few minutes till a gust of cold wind caused him to awaken and shudder.

The draft blew in from two large air vents set into the wall on his right. Each vent was square, about three foot tall and just as wide. Together they looked like doors to a magical cupboard with their lattice of crisscrossing iron bars hiding the secrets of the palace's cooling system behind them. He stared hard at the rusting metal network for a few moments, wondering if a childhood adventure lay somewhere beyond. Then, after locking the door to the study, he walked over and pushed on each vent so that they swung backwards. Behind them, a narrow gap that he could still crawl through and beyond that a slight slope down to a low winding tunnel. This Erepsin entered and followed the passageway as it turned left and then right, going slowly downhill all of the time. Each step took him closer to a watery bubbling, chattering sound. Around one final bend he went and entered a small stone chamber (a place he'd visited many times before). Moonlight streamed into it from a series of drainage holes in the roof above, showing that he was underground somewhere just outside the palace building. Through the chamber a gentle river flowed, babbling along its way in a happy manner. It flowed at a good pace, finally exiting underneath the far wall and disappearing from sight. On the opposite side of the chamber, there it was, a small gurgling fountain that danced to a sprightly tune. This was the source of Erepsin's private water supply – from which he kept the city population alive.

Mr E sat down next to the river and put his hand into the flow. The water was cool and ran quickly through the gaps between his fingers. There was always something soothing about its movement and its sound. He had often sat there for long periods to calm himself after mood swings or bad dreams in the night. Now he relaxed his tired limbs and, feeling safe again, let the allurement of deep slumber come back to woo him into sleep once more. Lying down on his side next to the river, he let its babbling chatter fill his ears whilst his hand swished in the icy current. For a moment everything else in the world went away and he was free again to just be himself. He closed his eyes and lay on his back to rest. His mind stopped spinning, peace flooded in at last and a hope arose of better things to come. Nothing to disturb, no distractions, all was finally at ease; even his breathing sounded clam, calm in comparison that is to the nattering brook that continually ran at his side.

"What a chore," he thought to himself as the water's talk filled his ears. "Having to continually chatter and jabber without any rest!"

It made him feel positively tranquil, whilst his manic friend rambled on its continuous and never ending conversation.

The first moments of deeper sleep were nearly upon him when his left eye suddenly received a spat of water from the river. It may have been that some dirt had fallen from the ceiling to cause the splash and so sprinkle his face, he couldn't tell, but Erepsin's response was to jump out of his sleep and wipe the water from his flickering eye. He then wiped his hand across his face and found himself staring briefly upwards. On the chamber roof he saw something that he'd almost forgotten was there. A small royal crest, painted beautifully, made up from the figures of a great lion and a prowling bear, standing opposite each other underneath the flight of a soaring eagle. Above the crest was written some words that had faded and couldn't be read any more but beneath it was the phrase, "In the fullness of time." Something deep within Erepsin immediately snarled at the image. He rolled onto his side, sat up, stuck his hand in the river and, in defiance of what he was looking at, splashed the water as high as he could make it go. Disturbed and upset by the crest, he then got up and walked out of the chamber, wishing that he'd never revisited it.

Chapter 5 – Scientists Not Chefs

On the streets of Clearwash City not a person could be seen. Its narrow, cobbled, twisting, winding lanes all merged themselves together into a maze of deserted, lonesome roads. Doors now shut, windows tightly closed and lights, if any, were hidden behind drawn curtains and closed shutters. Everything was completely quiet and still and, except for the occasional drone of the motorised police balloons swooping through the night sky, not even a whisper was to be heard.

On the night air however, to the attentive ear, a low muffled sound could sometimes be detected when the wind blew in a certain direction. None of the guards on the wall heard it and no one in the houses and buildings did either, but it was there, like a persistent echo in the night. Chatter, chatter, it went or perhaps a clatter, clatter. Sometimes it went a clunkety clunk or whoosh, whoosh, or a mixture of them all. Time and again the sound rose and fell on the gentle breeze. Moving away from the city centre, towards the less inhabited areas, the sound became a little clearer but was still muffled and difficult to make out. It could only be heard properly from inside a small woodland wilderness, located on the outskirts of the city, just inside the boundary of its western wall. The mechanical tune hummed its way through the branches and leaves of the trees, singing it's clattering, chattering, thumping, grinding melody. In the middle of the small wood, a narrow path wound through the dense foliage until it met and ran parallel to a low wall that marked the edge of an overgrown garden. Inside the garden stood an old oak tree and behind it a small, concealed stairway that descended into darkness. This was the darkness that kept hidden the entrance to a secret underground bunker and it was from this bunker that the sound came.

A door opened briefly at the bottom of the dark staircase and out darted a young gentleman who rushed up the stairs spluttering, choking and coughing. Dropping to his knees next to the old oak tree, he coughed some more; thumping on his chest with a clenched fist whilst gasping for air. Eventually a smallish, pink substance dislodged itself from inside his throat and he spat it out. Then, taking a few more deep breaths, he exhaled to steady himself and put his head between his knees. Finally, he lifted up his face again, replacing what was once a panic-stricken countenance with relief.

Swivelling around to sit down, the young man lay back on the grass to take a short breather. Light-headedness, nauseous sickness and a sleepy faintness momentarily flooded his heavy head and limbs. Feeling like dizzy-lead, the man found himself pinned to the ground for the next minute or so until the sensation gradually left and a calmness settled. Then, letting his hands run over the moist, damp foliage growing about, he stared up at the star-studded night sky.

As the moments passed, the man's eyes gradually closed away from the starry host. Dreaming he was somewhere else, he sank into the illusion of being on a nice sandy beach with a splashing sea and plenty of drinks under a sun-scorched sky. He had hardly settled himself, however, when the door to the bunker below opened again and a voice called out.

"Come on lazy bones, we're not done yet. You can sleep in the morning."

The voice belonged to a young woman who stuck her head around the door and saw the feet of her slumped colleague dangling over the edge of the stairway's top step.

"Having forty winks are we?" she enquired.

"Go away," said the man on the grass.

"Come on," she replied, "we've got a schedule to keep to."

"Go away!" repeated the man, in a disgruntled manner.

"Our schedule," she called back in a colder tone. "Time is going by!" and with that the door closed again.

The young gentleman groaned and grumbled to himself, protesting that his belly ached and muttering something about 'hard labour'. He pulled himself to his feet and descended the stairs again mumbling, murmuring and complaining his way down each step.

"Time is going by," he said, sarcastically to himself. "Time is going by, time is going by," he chanted.

He unlocked the iron door using a key that dangled on a chain from his belt and then pressed a button just to the right of the lock. An electronic voice from small speakers in the doorframe asked him to place his hand flat against the door, which the young man did.

"Time," said the young man again, in a more reflective manner. "In the fullness of time," he added, as if quoting a well-known mantra.

A thin strip of light ran across his fingers and palm, scanning them for identification.

"In the foolness of time," he said mockingly. "Everyone's a fool who works here."

The door swung open to reveal a misty room and, reluctantly, he stepped in.

In the dimly lit bunker swirls of hissing vapour floated and drifted across the room, hanging in the air like a dense, thick fog. The walls ran wet with condensed moisture whilst the stifling heat fanned the clouds of gas that enveloped and shrouded everything. Through this smog the young man walked, passing many people who, like him, were all dressed in white. They were engaged in frantic activities, quickly running to and fro amongst rows and rows of long wooden tables. On these tables, many weird and wonderful robotic machines performed their pre-programmed duties; together they made a terrible din. Some machines hammered, sawed and squashed whilst others shook themselves violently, rattling and mixing up their contents. Many had shiny drills that whizzed and whirred. Others heated up fizzing elements that sparkled and crackled, shooting sparks into the air like mini fireworks. There were mechanical gadgets that whisked and mashed whilst others

34

pulled, twisted and stretched different gluey, rubbery substances. Tall pulleys, suspended from the chamber's ceiling, sped up and down and cranked the long arms of pumps, which in turn stirred pots and pans full of boiling, steaming liquids.

The young man walked tentatively around the room, guided by the lights of many table-top gas burners which flared brightly in the steamy mist. All ablaze, they sent their orange and blue dancing flames licking up at the feet of different sized test tubes, held in racks down the middle of each table. The various mixtures in them continually bubbled and spluttered whilst spaghetti-like tangles of brown rubber pipes ran from table to table, joining the experiments to each other. At times he had to bend down, duck, squeeze under, through and in between these pipes and experiments to get to where he was going. (A complete health and safety nightmare – but somehow that kind of thinking wasn't important in this bunker). He coughed again. In the air hung a lingering, smouldering smell that was so strong he could taste it and, as usual, it seemed to stick to the back of his throat.

Fastened across the four walls were a variety of charts, drawings and graphs. Near the far end of the room was a huge oval, chamber that stood by itself separate from everything else. It had gas pipes entering it on both sides. Red and yellow lights flickered and flashed across its front panel and, near the middle of this machine, a charred and blackened grill revealed a burning fire inside. The machine spewed out a constant flood of smoke from this vent and across its front, written in red, were the letters J.E.N.N.Y.

The young man quickly passed J.E.N.N.Y. (putting a hankie over his nose as he went) and finally arrived back at his desk where his colleague was waiting for him, along with what looked like a plate full of small pink canapés. He looked at them dubiously, remembering the problem that one of them had caused him a few minutes ago. Then he looked out across the room again to mentally prepare himself. The four walls of the underground chamber, sodden with the damp and heat, continually echoed with the clattering, rattling, shaking and bubbling noises of the experiments as all of the sounds mingled together like a chorus of swarming insects.

Very gingerly he took up one of the pink items, glanced at his friend and popped it into his mouth.

"When it's your turn, I hope *you* choke," he said to his grinning friend. Then after a few more chews he pursed his lips and blew so that a pink bubble began to protrude out of his mouth. It grew and grew until it burst back onto his face. Strangely enough, the man didn't wipe the pink substance off but just stood there.

"One, two, three, four," the other colleague began to count, with a chuckle in her voice, whilst looking at him with a wink and a smirk.

Walking quickly around the bunker, the other people moved between the tables continuing their frantic activities and looking after the experiments and the bubbling liquids in their pots and pans. Many of them wore large goggles to shield their eyes and some had donned hardened bowler hats to protect their heads. Underneath their outer science gowns, glimpses of bow ties and stiff collars could be seen peeking through amongst multi-coloured suit jackets. Looking at their dress you couldn't be sure if they were meant to be having a good night out, going to work in an office, or employed on a building site. Everything in the bunker, however, seemed to be running like clockwork with everyone knowing exactly what they were supposed to be doing.

On the opposite side of the room sat a man perched on the edge of a table. He had a stained yellow and white beard along with curly, white hair and bushy eyebrows to match, which sat under a wrinkled forehead. He wore baggy brown trousers and underneath his blemished white jacket was a brightly patterned waistcoat. On the end of his nose was a pair of gold-rimmed and very thick lensed glasses and behind these the man's eyes danced from side to side. He kept watching his workers who laboured on, toiling throughout the night, clearly they were on a mission to save the world and time was more than running out.

"Well, there's no denying it, that's a good night's work nearly finished and done, even if I say so myself," shouted the white bearded man over the constant din of the machines. He jumped up and walked over to a worker nearby who was mixing a paste in a pot. "Use the other one," he said, pointing to a box of lime green powder that was on the end of the table. "Just use the cleaning agent by itself."

The man walked slowly around the room, peering at each experiment as he went. He stopped at another table and pointed at a blue paste laid out on a glowing red-hot metal plate. "Very good," he said to another worker, "now slowly, very slowly, mix this in with the bubble gum powder and then we can put it into the freeze chamber. We'll be needing some later."

36

"Yes, Professor," the assistant replied.

"Now, how's that other bubble gum coming along?" he said out loud to himself, and with that he walked down the long room and stopped by a tray that had a bright pink substance on it. Two assistants joined him and began at his instruction to pull and twist and tug the pink gum in all directions.

"Pull harder," he said. "Pull harder."

The Professor watched how the gum twisted and stretched and then, taking some of it into his hands, examined it very carefully; running it through the tips of his fingers and then rolling it into a ball.

"Hmm," he said, after he had prodded it and given it a quick smell. "George!" he called, "George, where are you? I need you again."

Another assistant came over to him from the other end of the room. He was average in height, thin with bright, short ginger hair, had a longish chin and a thinly buttoned nose. His tired sunken eyes showed little sign of life, deep shadows framed them, a bulls eye target declaring a severe lack of sleep.

"Bubble gum test time again," said the Professor.

George dropped his shoulders, let out a sigh and bent over towards the Professor, standing very still with his eyes tightly shut. The wrinkled expression on his weary face showed that he was expecting something bad to happen. It did. Taking some of the bubble gum that was in his hands, the Professor squashed it flat like a pancake, licked it twice to add his own saliva and rubbed it all over George's face. At the same time another assistant began to slowly count, "One, two, three, four..."

"Oh," said George, taking a gasp of breath as the gum was rubbed onto his skin. "It's really cold!"

"Oh don't be such a wimp," said the Professor, still rubbing the gum into George's cheeks and chin. "This gum's been out of the freeze chamber now for a good two to three minutes. You don't know the meaning of the word cold. I remember when I was your age; the Senior Professor had me standing in a barrel of iced tea for half an hour whilst chewing on deeply frozen ice cubes after I had drunk fourteen cups of extra chilled milk. You kids today don't know how good and easy science life is."

"Twelve, thirteen, fourteen," said the other assistant, still counting slowly.

"So don't you worry about a little cold gum on your face," continued the Professor.

"It's not just the cold," said George, spluttering the words out between his trembling lips. "It's what's in the gum. I really don't like the thought of it."

"Oh, don't be such a wimp," said the Professor again. "We're scientists not chefs. It's not as if we're going to be eating the stuff!"

"Eighteen, nineteen, twenty," said the other assistant.

"Right," said the Professor. "Let's quickly get this gum off."

The Professor helped George peel and scrape the bubble gum from his face, which came away remarkably easily and all in one piece. He then held it up to the light and examined it. Pulling out a mini gas lantern from his pocket to help him see more clearly, he inspected it again and then George's face in fine detail, poking and pulling at his skin as he went.

"Hmm," he said again after a few moments. "The gum's not quite ready yet. Another four or five minutes of pulling and twisting and then we'll heat it through in Jenny. After that it should be finished."

He patted George on the shoulder. George's face now looked quite clean but a little red and sore. "Well done lad," said the Professor.

George managed a weak smile in return and then hastily made his way to the back of the room to carry on his work.

"Right, carry on as you were both of you and be quick about it," said the Professor to the other two assistants with him. "It's turned morning outside and we're running out of time."

The two assistants, wearing industrial rubber gloves, began pulling and stretching and twisting the gum again whilst the Professor cast his eyes over the room to see what else was happening.

"Fantastic," he said to himself, glancing at the different experiments. "Well, I think that this time we may well just manage it. Oh, it's just fantastic," he said, rubbing his hands together with delight.

He felt that the moment of truth for him was finally at the door. Not only was his current experiment drawing to a conclusion, being the fulfilment of months of work, but it also represented a lifelong dream to be a successful, even famous, scientist; one of the greats who made their own unique difference in the world so that the world would never be the same again. For him, a new day was about to dawn; a day when he would be able to make his own stamp on history and leave behind an impressive, personal legacy. Clearing his throat, he called out over the din of the experiments, "Our night's work is nearly over and done everyone. The ever rolling ball of scientific invention bounces on today past new boundaries of knowledge." He began to strut his way up and down the room, feeling confident and successful. "What a new day this is going to be," he continued. "I shall..."

The Professor, however, didn't finish what he was speaking as there came a loud Knock! Knock! Knock! from the bottom end of the room on the bunker door. All froze and looked at the Professor, who in turn stared back at everyone. "Was anyone expecting a visitor?" he eventually asked. They all shook their heads. Knock! Knock! went the door again. "Oh dear," he said to himself. "Well it's too late to hide all of this stuff now."

Chapter 6 – Bubble Gum Soap

"Switch these off," said the Professor, pointing in the general direction of the experiments. His assistants quickly moved between each of the long tables and within a matter of moments the machines were quiet and still, except for the odd splutter from a bubbling pot or test tube. Feeling sick in the anticipation that it was the city police outside, the Professor swallowed hard and made his way through the entanglement of wires and rubber tubes that were scattered across the floor. Down to the iron door he went and, with a tentative hand, took hold of its handle. He paused. "Er, who is it?" he said.

"It's me," came a woman's voice in reply.

A sigh of relief came out from everyone.

"Er, please place your hand on the door for a final security check," said the Professor.

The door itself seemed to hum as if scanning something and then a mechanical voice from a speaker in the far corner of the room droned out:

"Palm scan complete. Data verification of individual concluded. Identity of personage confirmed as: Lady Georgiana Pluggat-Lynnette."

The Professor unlocked and opened the door. There, in the doorway, standing at the bottom of the steep stairway, was the very well-to-do looking lady. Removing her hat, she was tall and slender with neatly curled, brown hair, a slender nose and a broad smile that touched a slight dimple on either side of her cheeks. Wearing now a very expensive morning dress, a pearled necklace, bracelets on her wrists and bright shining rings on her fingers, she looked very decorous and correct. Surprisingly, however, over everything else she wore a see-through plastic mackintosh.

"Oh, Lady Georgiana," said the Professor, with the sensation of relief still flooding through his veins. "You had us all on edge. We weren't expecting anyone from the resistance to visit us this morning. We thought we were about to be arrested."

"Oh, I am sorry," said the lady, gently waving her hat through the air to push the steam aside so that she could see to whom she was talking. "The council heard that you might be having a break-through on something new and sent me over. Is that right?"

"Yes M'lady," said the elated Professor, looking very pleased with himself.

He pulled up a stool for the lady to sit on and enthusiastically brushed the dust off its top with his dirty handkerchief. Then he pulled one up for himself. They both sat down and the Professor carried on.

"And when we have finished," he said, "everyone, absolutely everyone, will be able to have a wash without the city authorities knowing about it!"

"Really?" replied Lady Georgiana, looking surprised and pleased. This was news indeed. "And how would that be?" she enquired.

"Well," said the Professor, taking his glasses off and cleaning them on his lab coat as he spoke. "As washing with water in the city is now against the law, we need another substance to wash with, right?"

"Er, yes, that's true," said Lady Georgiana, quickly glancing around the room to try and see what they were all up to.

"And," continued the Professor, "we therefore need to disguise this face washing substance as something else, right?"

"Well yes, I suppose so," she replied.

"So," said the Professor, "it must be something that is often seen in public to ensure that no one suspects anything. And what better, therefore, to disguise this substance but as bright pink chewing gum!"

"Chewing gum?" she repeated.

"Yes, chewing gum," said the Professor, with a cheery smile.

"Oh dear!" said the lady. "I never chew gum. Disgusting habit if you ask me. Sounds terrible!"

"No, not terrible, incredible!" continued the Professor, throwing his hands up into the air as he spoke. "Everyone knows that gum is sold in the city. It's not difficult to get it and we can all easily chew it."

"Correction Professor!" said Lady Georgiana, sitting up very straight. "Some people easily chew gum, but it's a habit that I personally have never tried and do not intend to start."

"Well you won't have to chew it for long M'lady," said the Professor. "It would only have to be twice a day at wash time. Let me show you how it works."

He shot off his stool and fetched a large handful of gum from a nearby table.

"All you do is put this new super-duper, super-stretchy bubble gum into your mouth and within a jiffy you'll be able to blow a bubble as large as your head. Then simply pop the bubble and it will squash back onto your face."

"But that's disgusting," said the lady, putting her hand to her mouth in horror at such a thought. "It'll get all tangled up in my hair and stuck onto my eye lashes. Really Professor, I think this time you have gone too far!"

"No M'lady," said the Professor reassuringly, "there's a lot of anti-stick properties added to this gum that means it comes straight off your face. The gum itself has cleaning agents and creams in it that will cleanse and moisten your skin at the same time. Just rub it all over your face and the gum will come off into your hands, containing all of your facial dirt. Even more importantly, the city authorities will never know."

Lady Georgiana sat and stared at the bright pink gum that was in the Professor's hand but said nothing. Everything within her, her noble upbringing, her education, her position in the city, taught her to revile the substance that was before her. The Professor could see that she was thinking very hard about the gum and that she didn't like the idea at all.

"Look," said the Professor, "I'll show you how it works. George, where are you?" he called, looking down the room, but George was nowhere to be seen.

"Er, I think he's just gone to one of the back store rooms sir," said one of the assistants, who at the same time was trying to look inextricably engrossed in his own work.

The Professor looked over his shoulder and saw that, for some reason, most of his assistants had quietly left the room.

"Oh," said the Professor, looking a little disappointed. "Oh all right," he said, "I'll do it myself," and with that he popped the gum into his mouth and began to chew, at the same time smiling reassuringly at Lady Georgiana.

"I would at this stage normally just lick the gum and then rub it straight onto my face," he said, between chews. "But I think that as I'm demonstrating this to your very good self I'd better show you its full effects. If the gum is chewed, as I am doing now, then the saliva in my mouth works with the dung beetle powder to release a stronger cleaning agent. All I have to do now is to blow a big bubble."

"I'm sorry Professor," said the lady, already feeling a little off colour. "Did I hear you say, 'dung beetle'?"

But the Professor was already blowing a very large, bright pink bubble which he promptly popped with his finger and rubbed the gum all over his face and beard. Lady Pluggat just stared at him with an 'I'm going to be sick' sort of expression etched across her countenance.

On the Professor's face sat the gum, like rippling lumps of runny ice cream. It began to bubble in places making a squidgy and squelchy sound as the different chemicals reacted with each other. The Professor called for a mirror and a small hand-held one was handed to him. He looked at his reflection, admiring the gum with great pride and pleasure as it worked to clean his skin.

"My greatest achievement," he thought to himself.

He then smiled and beamed at Lady Pluggat like a veteran soldier wearing his honorary medals.

"Does it hurt?" Lady Georgiana eventually asked, looking concerned.

"Not at all," replied the Professor. "It does have a far more dramatic effect though when you chew it first."

The Professor picked a little of the bubbling gum off the side of his face and held it out to Lady Georgiana.

"Here," he said. "I'll pop this onto the palm of your hand and you can see for yourself."

Lady Georgiana hesitated, not sure that she actually wanted something squidgy that had been in the Professor's mouth put in her hand, but she finally forced herself to receive the sample. It sat there on her skin bubbling away; the gum was warm and tingling and felt like a thousand tiny mouths sucking and nibbling on her palm. The Professor was right, it didn't hurt, but all the same it was a very strange feeling.

Once she felt that she'd allowed the gum to remain on her hand long enough to show some measure of respect for the Professor's experiment, she hurriedly brushed it off and examined her palm. Now there was fresh clean skin showing through and the sight of this was quite surprising.

"Now all I need to do is to count to twenty and then to remove the gum," continued the Professor.

"Why to twenty?" she replied, in a cautious tone. The gum on the Professor's face had now turned a deep purple and the sight still made Lady Georgiana feel quite nauseated.

"Well," he said, trying to find just the right words, "we have found that at around twenty the gum must come off otherwise... there can be complications."

"Complications?" echoed Lady Georgiana, now beginning to feel quite unsettled and that this absurd experiment was unquestionably flawed.

"Oh, nothing to worry about," said the Professor, smiling sweetly and brushing the comment aside as if it was of little importance. "We'll have it fixed quite soon. All that happens is that after a count of twenty the gum's anti-stick properties do tend to start to reverse; a chemical U-turn which creates an unexpected and unwanted glue-like effect. Rather annoying really. It took us quite by surprise when it first happened, but we've recently made some good progress and though it's not altogether conquered, I think we'll have it fixed soon, I hope."

"You hope?" echoed Lady Georgiana again.

"Well true science is always full of obstacles, holdups and surprises, don't you think?" replied the Professor. "There are always hurdles to get over if we are to complete the course - and risk, adaptation and modification are just part of the process to get there. And, as I said to George when we first came across this particular gum sticking problem, 'George my lad' I said, 'Who needs eyebrows anyway?'"

The Professor then turned to look at his assistants, to see if anyone else was laughing with him from his last comment, but when he found no-one had joined in his bit of fun, he then asked, "Well, who's counting and what number are we up to?"

The remaining assistants looked up from their work and then at each other. Seeing nothing in each other's faces they just stared blankly back at the Professor.

"Well," he said again. "Who's counting?"

But the assistants had nothing to say.

"What!" exclaimed the Professor, when he saw their vacant expressions.

"Well don't just stand there," he added, springing to life and beginning to scrape at the gum with his fingers. "Quick, help me get this stuff off."

And with those words all the remaining assistants stepped forward to take hold of the gum. They pulled and tugged and pulled and tugged, but it wouldn't move. It was solidly stuck, fastened like a limpet; glued to the Professor's forehead, chin, cheeks, ears and nose.

"Oh my!" said the Professor, wondering what on earth he was going to do.

Twenty minutes later Lady Georgiana's polite smile was getting a little tired around the edges whilst the Professor continued his pursuit of facial freedom from his gummy mask. Urgency had steadily turned to panic within him as failure followed failure each time something new was tried. His bid for freedom had involved a variety of methods from dipping his head into bowls of various liquids, designed to loosen the gum, to mixing together anti-stick pastes and applying them around the mask's edge. He'd then spent time heating the gum up with jets of steam so that it would expand, whilst wedging ice cubes under it in the hope that the mask would simply slide away, but it still wouldn't peel off. Time and again he applied different substances and techniques, but all to no avail.

The panic and anxiety that steadily pumped through his veins finally caused him to just grip the gum with his hands and to spend the next couple of minutes falling over chairs, rolling under tables and generally scrambling about the room, trying more and more different ways to get rid of it. Sometimes he hopped from leg to leg and other times he bent down and waddled to-and-fro, like a mother duck going out for a country walk, yanking at the gum as he went. In the end he finally stopped, out of breath, with the gum still firmly fastened onto his face and beard. Now the gum was smudged right over his glasses and he couldn't see at all!

Then, in a moment of absolute desperation, he got down on all fours, put his head between his legs, stuck his bottom in the air and squashed his knees into the gum mask. Lady Georgiana looked away, not wanting to witness the sight of the Professor in this very undignified position.

Using his knees to anchor the gum in place, he carefully positioned his hands on either side of his head and dug his nails into the sides of the bubble gum mask. He began to rock backwards and forwards. He shook his head from side to side and wiggled his bottom up and down. Then, using every muscle in his body, he pulled and twisted to lift his head away from the gum. Soon he was surrounded by a horde of assistants, all trying to prize off the offending face mask.

"Ah," cried the Professor in pain, as everyone tugged together. "Someone's got hold of my beard. Let go, let go, let go, everyone let go!"

Then, with the help of a single assistant, he tugged and pulled at the gum over and over again.

"Ah!" he shouted again in pain. "Ahhhhhhhhhhh, ouch!" he cried, as his head finally shot back leaving a perfectly moulded piece of hardened pink gum between his knees, which was the exact shape of his face and beard. Little strands of white hair stuck out from it in all directions where significant bits of his beard and eyebrows had been left behind.

"Oh!" said the Professor, staggering to his feet and catching his breath. Finding his balance he leaned on a nearby table and blinked several times, trying to re-focus his eyes. He rubbed his fingers over a now very rosy-red face to make sure that his nose and beard were still mainly in place and then carefully peeled his glasses from the gum mask. Placing them back onto the end of his nose he noticed, with great annoyance, that one of the lenses was now cracked, making them useless. After giving his assistants a very irritated glance, he gave the hardened pink gum to one of them and cleared his throat.

"We'll talk about this later," he said. Then, taking in another deep breath, he walked back to his stool opposite Lady Georgiana and sat down.

"Sorry about that," he said, still scratching his beard and looking a little stupid. "We should have that side of things sorted soon but, as you can see, my skin is completely clear of dirt."

Lady Georgiana looked at the Professor, whose face now looked as if it had been left out in the sun for several hours on a hot day and she gave him a nod and a very slight smile, in order to stop herself from laughing.

"And," she asked with a glint in her eye and a slightly cheeky smile on her face, "what about having a bath? How would you do that with this super-duper gum of yours?"

"Well," said the Professor, looking a little surprised. He hadn't expected the question. "I suppose if you wanted to have a bath, you could just blow a really huge bubble whilst standing in the shower and then rub it all over yourself. It would have exactly the same effect."

"Really!" said the elegant lady, not sounding at all convinced. "Well I must say that that's a very unique idea! That would be a real incentive to help you get up in the morning," she added, with a hint of sarcasm.

"Yes", said the Professor, regaining his composure and looking very pleased with himself again. "It would bring a whole new meaning to the word 'bubble bath!'"

"Hmm," said the lady. "Yes, quite."

The Professor took out his handkerchief and began to wipe his face. He could feel his skin stinging and throbbing.

"And how long will it take before you know if you have had success or not?" asked Lady Georgiana.

"Well," he replied, "we're just about to put our final test gum into Jenny now."

"Jenny? Who or what is Jenny?" asked Lady Georgiana, in a cautious tone.

"Jenny is my newest and finest machine," said the Professor, proudly pointing to the large oval chamber on the far wall. "Jenny stands for 'Joint Explosive Nuclear Nutronic Yielder'. She is the only machine in the city that can heat things up to more than one thousand degrees in a matter of minutes."

"Hmm," said the posh lady again, feeling a little uneasy.

"Well, we're about to fire her up and feed her some super-duper expanding bubble gum. Would you like to stay and put on a fire suit with the rest of us? It's good to be around when we make something new in the world."

"Actually I think that I will leave you to it Professor," said Lady Georgiana. "I wouldn't want to get in your way. Anyway, morning is here and I've got Scrub waiting for me upstairs. It's nearly time for his medicine so I had better go and let you get on with it."

"Very good, M'lady," said the Professor. "I shall look forward to giving you the news of our success very shortly."

Lady Georgiana smiled weakly, got off the stool and went quickly back up the stairs she had come down earlier.

"Very good, Lady Georgiana," called the Professor again after her. "I'll bring you the good news as soon as I can." He then closed the door and turned to look at everyone. "Well that was a resounding success for sure," he said, confidently stroking what was left of his beard and feeling more than contented with himself. He locked the door and addressed his workers. "Right, let's get on with it everyone. Get your fire suits on. Get me some frozen gum. Get me some fire starters and open up every gas tap on Jenny. This is going to be sticky, tricky and exceedingly dangerous. Now, where is George?"

Chapter 7 – Never Say Bubble Gum Again!

In the early morning air, above the Professor's secret bunker, sat a scruffy little fellow who was keeping a look out for anyone passing by. He wore a tatty, chequered shirt (half tucked in on one side) brown trousers (badly worn at the knees) and scuffed brown shoes to match (with untied laces). His full name was Stephanus Cadmar Roberto Uriel Bannerman - but no one used any of those names when talking to him; in fact everyone just took the first letter from each of his names, put them together and called him 'Scrub' for short and by that name he had been known for many years. Scrub's eyes were a bright blue, a little like Lady Georgiana's. His uncombed, mossy hair seemed to have a mind of its own, standing up to attention on one side as if he'd recently awoken from a heavy night's sleep. The only thing keeping his hair in order was a soldier's helmet, which he wore at all times – though he could never explain to anyone why this particular hat accompanied him everywhere he went.

Scrub was always thinking about things. He would spend days and days thinking about the same thing over and over again. Nothing important to the average person, but to him his thoughts and perceptions were the very pinnacle of life itself. He'd often share his thoughts after a time and be surprised that no one showed much interest in them. He would, however, on the odd occasion come out with something quite remarkable; like finding a beautiful diamond in a deep, lifeless coalmine.

He sat on a small patch of dirt peering intently around him; first at the ground, then the woodland, next the grassy meadow, up into the sky and then back to the ground and woodland again. To his left was the well-hidden flight of stairs that went down to the bunker.

"Scrub," called a voice from the darkness somewhere down the stairs, "Scrub, it's me. Is it safe to come out?"

"Oh, Lady Pluggat," said the scruffy young lad. "Yes it's all clear."

A few moments later the posh lady came up to the top of the stairs, smiling at Scrub as she arrived.

"No one has passed by," said Scrub. "Not one person. I have seen four rabbits, three blackbirds, fourteen sparrows, a fox and four hundred and twenty seven ants, but no people. I think I might have counted some of the ants twice though, cause they're really difficult to tell apart you know and they keep moving."

"Oh Scrub," laughed Lady Georgiana, quietly to herself. "When I said to keep a lookout for *anything*, I only meant humans."

"Oh," said Scrub.

"Never mind," she replied. "Let's get back to the city circle."

Lady Georgiana removed the plastic mac from over her dress and, after carefully folding it, placed it inside the crevice of a nearby rock for use on her next visit. Together they left the walled garden, taking great care to pick their way through the bushes and shrubbery that had overgrown the path. Looking left and right, they quickly stepped out of the bushes and onto the small winding trail that would take them out of the woods and into the lifeless city area again.

"Lady Pluggat?" enquired Scrub, in a cautious tone of voice that acknowledged the subject he was about to raise was potentially an off-limits conversation.

"What is it?" she replied.

"Can I ask if the Professor has finished his experiment?" said Scrub.

"Not yet," she replied. "I left him when it began to get dangerous."

"Oh, can I go and see?" said Scrub, turning to go back and hoping that his positive attitude would gain him access to the professor's bunker.

"No!" said Lady Georgiana, catching his arm to stop him. "You know only too well that you are banned from that bunker after the trouble that you caused the last time you were there. The Professor would go nuts if he saw you in there again."

"I like nuts," he quietly said.

"Don't be impertinent!" she rather sharply replied.

They walked on a little further but Scrub's mind was still on the experiment in which the Professor was currently engaged. He imagined him in a dazzling white coat with a smile behind his dazzling white bushy beard, surrounded by enormous test tubes, long wires and twisting cables. Bunsen burners shot jets of billowing flames up into the air and the room was filled with the echoing sound of multiple bubbling liquids. He saw how, with his helpers surrounding him, this great Professor was doing extraordinary things with powders and gum that magically changed colour or blew up to create great clouds of smoke. Scrub longed to be with him. To him the scientific process was so fascinating. Not dull or laborious, but impressive and awesome. To be involved in such a life of experimentation, innovation and invention was a hallowed thing, almost a religious high calling in fact. A calling that was to Scrub so sacred that, to be entrusted with any of its many tasks, was nothing short of being part of a pilgrimage of unfolding truth; a daily walk, a continuous journey that step-by-step caused the unlocking of treasured secrets for the greater good of all humanity – the process of which, for those involved, amounted to nothing less than the ingenious actions of remarkable discovery.

"Will he finally manage it this time?" said Scrub, a few moments later. "I hear that he's using bubble gum."

"He might do," said the posh lady, "though I'm not sure that this time I actually want him to succeed. Washing with bubble gum isn't my idea of a civilised life."

Scrub was about to reply with what he thought would have been a witty comment but Lady Georgiana saw his mouth open to offer the verbal banter and held up her finger to stop him in his tracks.

"I don't want to hear it, whatever it is," she said.

After a couple of minutes of walking, however, Scrub found that his mouth was once again engaging in the subject that would not go away.

"What are they doing right now?" he asked.

"They're heating up the bubble gum," she replied. "I'm led to believe that it is very dangerous."

"Oh the Professor will be all right," said Scrub, a sound of confidence in his voice. "He knows what he's doing."

Lady Georgiana just muttered a quick, "We'll see," in response and quickened their pace in order to leave the conversation behind.

The two of them continued to walk down the path towards a pair of iron gates that were set into the inner city wall. The wall, covered with ivy and other foliage (all mingled in with each other as every plant jostled and battled for its own space) was old and crumbly - you could argue that it was the foliage that kept the great stone boundary standing and not the bricks and mortar! The gates, left slightly ajar, stood to weary attention; stained brown from years of rusty neglect, they were in themselves symbols of the kind of welcome that lay beyond. As they reached them, Lady Georgiana turned to speak to Scrub.

"Now Scrub," she said, with a stern face. "What do you say if someone asks you where we have been?"

"Err, I say that we have been for a walk in the country to look at the wildlife M'lady."

"Well done Scrub," she said, looking quite surprised. "And you can truly say that, as that is exactly what *you* have done."

"Yes M'lady," said Scrub. ". As I've already said, I have seen four rabbits, three blackbirds, fourteen sparrows, a fox, four hundred and twenty seven ants…"

"Alright, alright," she interrupted before Scrub got into one of his verbal flows; from which it was difficult to escape once the verbal dam had burst and the river of words had begun to gush forth. She gently put one finger over his lips to quieten him and then looked him in the eye.

"And if someone asks me the same question I shall answer them in such a way as to not let them know that I have been to see the Professor. Is that clear?"

"Err, yes Lady Pluggat," replied Scrub again.

"So," she continued, "when we are speaking to any guards that we may encounter on our way home, you don't have to interrupt me with information that you think that I have missed out, do you?"

"No M'lady," said Scrub.

"Right," said Lady Georgiana, a tone of relief in her voice. "That's sorted then."

With that she took hold of the gate, but before she could open it there came a sudden rumble that sent a tremor through the ground beneath their feet. The rumble was followed by another and another. Scrub and Lady Georgiana both looked back towards the woodland garden from which they had just come. Then, BOOM! There came a sudden and very loud explosion. It shook the ground so violently that they clung to the iron gates to keep themselves from falling over. A few seconds later smoke slowly rose into the sky from the vicinity of the Professor's bunker.

"Oh dear," said Lady Georgiana.

"Oh dear what?" said Scrub.

"I don't think that was meant to happen," she replied.

"Really?" said Scrub.

"Yes, really" said Lady Georgiana.

"Do you think that noise was the sound of the bubble gum exploding?" asked Scrub." If it were, then I could always give the Professor some of mine to use."

"No, I don't think that will be necessary," she replied.

"No?" said Scrub.

Lady Georgiana shook her head, "No."

They stood there for a few seconds, trying to decide what to do next.

"I really could give him some of my bubble gum," said Scrub, trying to be helpful and with some hope arising in his heart that he may get the chance to go back into the Professor's bunker again.

Lady Georgiana shook her head again and Scrub's heart dropped.

"In fact, I think that it may be wise," she added, "when you're talking to the Professor in the future, to never say bubble gum again. Come on, let's go. We have to be quick. That noise will bring out the police patrol balloons and we don't want to be found here when they arrive," and with that she turned and exited through the gate with Scrub following.

Chapter 8 - You Only Wash Twice

Out in the desert a dilapidated, weather-beaten bus carefully made its way along a twisting, winding road. Up and over and down and around it went, following the sides of the hills and mountains. The bus looked like a long metal grey tram which moulded at its front into a pointed nose. Spluttering out a greasy liquid from its underside, it hummed a steady tune as it chuntered along, leaving a trail of wet oil in the dust.

On board were an assortment of people, fat bellied retired businessmen, artists seeking new horizons, news reporters after a story, families beginning their summer holiday and individuals who just wanted to go somewhere quiet and secluded, to get away from it all. The general feeling amongst them, however, was not relaxed or friendly. It had been a long journey and the holidaymakers were beginning to wonder what sort of summer break they had embarked upon and when, in fact, it would actually begin.

"Are we nearly there yet?" asked one of the passengers. "It's been nearly three hours now in this hot, stuffy tin can. This wasn't mentioned in the brochure you know. Where is this city exactly? Is it in the middle of nowhere?"

"Don't you worry," replied the bus driver, wiping his handkerchief across his hot, sweaty forehead. "We're a lot closer than you think."

"I should think so too," said another passenger. "Why on earth do people in this Clearwash City like living so far away? Don't they ever miss living close to anyone else?"

"Well," said the driver cautiously, "some managed to, well... I mean, some left the city a couple of months back but, on the whole, most people stay where they are. Of course, Mr E does get rid of around one person from the city every month for one thing or another. He does get upset a little easily these days."

"Mr E?" said a passenger, "who is Mr E?"

"Ah," replied the driver, "Mr E is the person who is in charge of Clearwash City. Since he, err," and for a moment the bus driver paused to choose his words very carefully. "Since Mr E rose to power, the city authorities have kept things very much in order with everything running smoothly and with great efficiency; which is quite a difficult thing to do since I hear that the people can sometimes be a bit of a handful."

The passengers looked at each other a little uneasily. "What do you mean?" a news reporter asked, whilst getting out his notepad and pen.

"Oh don't worry," said the bus driver, "you won't be coming into contact with too many people face to face and you'll be quite safe. There isn't anyone bad in the city as such. It's just that Mr E does have a few strange rules for the people to live by and sometimes the odd person gets caught for breaking them. Anyway, your holiday is to look at the ancient buildings that are in the inner circle of the city where only a few people are allowed to go. You're all staying in the presidential suite at the palace you know."

"Presidential suite?" said another passenger. "That sounds nice. Is it very grand?"

"It is for Clearwash City," said the bus driver. "You'll have enough running water for a wash on the first and third days of your stay and, if the weather's right, on the final day of your holiday you might even get enough for a bath, if Mr E is feeling generous!"

"What!" exclaimed several of the passengers together. "You've got to be kidding. You only wash twice!"

"Oh don't worry," said the driver again. "I'm sure that you'll enjoy your stay. There really are some magnificent buildings and ruins to look at you know. The city is very old and I hear has a fascinating history. Anyway, you'll soon see for yourselves, it's not long now. Shortly Clearwash City will be in sight and when we get near I'll stop the bus so that you can all have a good look before we finally go in."

This comment was met with various mutterings by different passengers, not quite sure what to make of the bus driver's remarks. A few moments later, however, they rounded the corner of the last hill and then they could all see it. The bus stopped. There, in the valley below them, was a grand city. Behind its high outer wall sat beautiful towering white buildings, all dotted across the expanse of the great metropolis. There she was, a great champion of architecture, culture and elegant civilisation, resting like a large mother hen, basking in the morning sunshine and waiting for her chicks to come home.

The passengers gazed in wonder at the varied buildings, built in row upon row of terraced landscapes and elegantly seated side by side. Across these, thousands of lights glinted and danced on the numerous windows that belonged to those magnificent constructions. On the many towers that were dotted throughout the metropolis, red and gold flags flew, flapping in the persistent northerly breeze. Everyone sat and stared in silence. What a wonderful sight! Somehow the streaming, dazzling rays of light from the rising sun, coming up from behind the city, blurred out the dirtiness of the great capital and a vision was revealed of what it once was, a city clothed with a mantle of golden glory.

"Beautiful, isn't she?" said the bus driver. "Absolutely beautiful. Never get used to this sight when we're coming in on the first run of the day. It takes your breath away it does."

After a short time, the bus started up again and made its way down to the city entrance.

"You'll be in for a treat coming into the city at this time of day," added the driver. "Quite spectacular is the atmosphere at the mo. They call it rush hour."

The bus went through the city gates and suddenly there were people everywhere, pushing to and fro as they made their way along the narrow paths and cobbled roads. The noise was deafening. People called, yelled and shouted, even from windows high up in the towers to those down on the streets below. Others raced along the road, in front of the bus at times and then darted off into the small side streets.

"A busy place is Clearwash City at this time in the morning," said the driver. "Never quite figured out why it happens this way, but it's always the same every late afternoon and the start of every morning. The place just comes alive. Folks appear from nowhere to talk and shout at each other. You won't get a moment's peace in the outer circle of the city now for a good half hour; then things will suddenly die down, as quickly as they started up and everywhere will seem quite deserted again. Very strange, very strange indeed, but then you'll find quite a few things strange in this place."

"What are they all wearing?" said one of the passengers. "I can see a letter 'E' on many people's clothes."

"Oh," said the driver. "That's just the sign of Mr E. In theory everyone should wear one at all times. It's his way of reminding everyone that he's in charge. I believe it's one of his more recent laws that he's trying to pass and enforce at the moment, though not everyone conforms to it."

The bus continued from street to street, dodging the people as it went, until it arrived at a large archway; flanked on each side by armed guards. After showing some papers to a sentry, the driver was permitted to take the bus through into the great square. Large enough to be a market place, it was surprisingly empty of people. The brakes squeaked and the bus stopped in front of a wooden platform. Everyone collected their belongings together.

"I'll be back here to pick you all up again five days from now at eight sharp in the morning," said the driver. "Have a nice time and thank you for travelling with 'Miles in Minutes Buses'. Enjoy your free holiday."

With that, the bus doors hissed open and everyone got off.

The first thing to come to everyone's notice, apart from a strange musky smell floating in the air, was the large and majestic palace that stood opposite them. It was a very grand building with tall columns and many narrow crystal windows running along its front. Right in the centre of the palace was what once would have been an impressive clock tower, from the top of which a large flagpole protruded. It had been badly damaged by fire and its clock hands, face and mechanisms were blackened and rusted from neglect and exposure to the elements. More gold and red flags flew from the building's roof and, printed in the right hand corner of each flag, was a large capital E. At the entrance to the palace grounds were two tall iron gates, set into a high wall, with armed guards at either side. Anyone could see that this impressive and imposing building was the city's centre of power.

The second thing that came to everyone's attention was a brass band, standing impatiently on the wooden platform, thumbs twiddling and feet tapping from their long wait. They suddenly began to play a very fast string of almost out of tune (and definitely out of time) notes as the passengers assembled themselves at the front of the stage. The band members, dressed in a deep green uniform with black hats, only performed for a few seconds, stopped, picked up their instruments and walked away, a sign that they had been waiting for ages for the bus to arrive and just wanted to play and be off.

Behind where the band had stood was Mr E. He was dressed in a long, dark blue coat, a brass buttoned cavalry top, jeans, a bowler hat and a large brown pair of cowboy boots; certainly an odd sight to the eyes. Under his bowler hat his long, shoulder length coffee-coloured hair was combed neatly backwards and tied into a ponytail. Placed carefully over his left eye was a tinted blue monocle and, bizarrely, a large fan was placed just a few feet away from him which blew a continuous, strong gust of wind in his direction.

He stood very still, leaning on his golden cane with his coat flapping in the fan's breeze, as if stuck in the middle of a dramatic film and displaying in freeze frame, the image of a superhero about to save the day. Waiting until these newly assembled holiday makers were as still as he was, he simply moved his slightly narrow, sunken eyes from side to side, looking over each one. Then a small grin began to appear on his face above his whiskery chin. The group of visitors began to shuffle as he gazed at them and the seconds ticked by without anyone saying anything. More time passed with nothing being said and the newcomers now began to exchange worried glances, not knowing quite what to do. Then, without any warning, the fan stopped blowing and Mr E came to life.

"Honoured guests," he said, stepping forward with a smile. "So glad you have arrived," and with those words he gave them all a welcoming bow. "I hope," he continued, "that your journey was pleasant and that your holiday will be most enjoyable." The passengers nodded out of uncertain politeness. "So," continued Mr E, "I say to you welcome; welcome to Clearwash City, a wonderful, vibrant, happy place full of bubbly people who are overjoyed to be a part of the marvellous history of this great place."

Again, Mr E stepped forward a little closer to the group.

"Who am I?" he said. "Well my name is Mr E and I am a part of the distinguished Ville family who have been resident here for many generations." At this, he gave another gracious bow. "My mother", he continued, "who was a noted politician and scientist, decided to call me Erepsin and with such a name I was christened, Erepsin Ville. No middle name was given me and probably this was just as well. Not liking the name Erepsin, however, I like people to call me Mr E for short, Mr E. Ville, but often I'm just called 'Evil'...ha!"

Glancing at each other, the bus passengers looked a little uncertain, not quite sure what to make of the last comment, but they didn't have time to say anything as Mr E stepped even closer to them and said, "So here we all are in Clearwash City. A strange name you say, Clear-Wash City? Well once you're here it's very clear for all to see, or should I say smell, that nobody, but nobody who resides in this city

54

ever has a wash! You'll probably have noticed by now that odd odour in the air, a rather musky stench that gently fills and irritates the lower part of the nostrils. Don't worry, you'll get used to it, most people do."

"I", said the excessively thin man, "am the master of Clearwash City and so I should be with the brainless folk who were here before me. I am in charge of this place because I control the water supply to the city. I give enough each day for people to drink to keep themselves alive, but not enough to wash with. Can't be wasting it now, can we?"

At this point the crowd of visitors saw a shortish man appear from behind a long curtain at the back of the stage. He walked with a very straight back and with his head held high, pointing his nose straight out in front of him as he went. In his arms he carried a cardboard box. Mr E saw him and said, "Ah, may I introduce my Prime Minister and Clearwash City's official organ player, Mr Ivan Robert Ritant, through whom I execute, err or rather I should say, introduce my plans for the city."

"Very good, very good Mr E," said the little man. "I've brought the 'E' symbols as you requested."

"Oh, my good fellow, you're so dependable," Mr E replied. "Please take an 'E' everyone before you start your holiday. It is important to wear it at all times whilst you are resident in this city. It means that you are under my protection and, like everyone else in this great city, enjoying my hospitality."

Ivan went amongst the holiday guests making sure that each one put an 'E' symbol on. The fabric of each symbol seemed to have a sticky back to it that clung to the clothes of the wearer wherever it was placed.

"Anyway," continued Mr E, "enough of this little chit-chat. I hope that you enjoy your stay here in Clearwash City and that you catch the spirit of this wonderfully sticky, sweaty place. And now," he said in a rather over dramatic voice, "I must leave you. I have, err, matters of state to deal with. Come Ivan, there is work to be done. Oh, being a tyrant is such a tiresome thing," and with those words Mr E and Ivan abruptly turned on their heels and left the stage.

The crowd of newcomers looked very puzzled. They stood casting their gaze about them, like people who had gone on a journey, taken a wrong turn, and had just realised the immensity of their mistake! Rush hour was beginning to die down in the streets outside the square and the noise was steadily falling away as people went back into their homes. On the far side of the market square a group of dirty children suddenly appeared, dropping out of the windows from a long, narrow building. After sitting on the cobbled ground to form a circle, whilst two of them lay on their tummies in the middle (pretending to be the hour and minute hands of a clock), they all chanted together:

"In the fullness of time,
The clock does chime,
Ding, dong, clap, clap, clap.
Tick-tocking a mechanical rhyme,
Ding, dong, clap, clap, clap.
Time is ticking, nearly gone.
Who will you be hiding from?
See the hands move to and fro,
Hear the silver trumpet blow!"

Then the children put their hands to their mouths, blew the sound of a trumpet and laughed. The guards at the market square entrance, irritated by the children's behaviour, ran across the marketplace to meet them. However, before they could arrive, the scrawny and scraggy band of kids slipped back through the windows from which they had come. Then, with laughs and giggles (and after briefly placing their faces against the glass and pulling faces at their chasers) they disappeared.

Not quite knowing what else to do, the small party of bussed-in newcomers walked towards the palace, carrying their cases and bags across the square to begin their holiday.

"Well," said one of the passengers, "I think that this is the last time I'm ever going to go on a free mystery holiday. Remind me to never again enter my name in any more competitions, especially if they're put on the back of washing powder packets!"

Chapter 9 - Lotions Are Forever

The wind had picked up later that morning as Lady Georgiana Pluggat-Lynnette made her way across the market square and walked towards the palace; her right hand firmly pressed down on her hat, keeping it in place. She paused near the wooden platform, glancing at the place in the ground from which the Free Flowing Foamy Flusher machine had emerged the previous evening. A shadow of grief passed briefly over her face as the memory of her friend momentarily filled her mind but, remembering where she was and that she was probably being watched, she forced herself to move on. Quickening her step, she passed through the large iron gates at the front of the palace grounds and hurried up the steep flight of stairs that led to the main palace entranceway.

The sentry guards, standing either side of the great oak doors, gave her a nod of recognition as she approached them and waved her through. Crossing a marbled, shiny floor, she began to ascend a broad, velvet-carpeted stairway that led up to the public library. On the stair she hesitated, just for a short time to gather her thoughts. It had been a busy day for her so far. Earlier that morning she had made her way to the great market square to pick up her daily state allocation of drinking water from Mr E's store; as usual just enough to drink to keep you healthy but not enough to wash with. Then, along with the rest of the important people of the city, she'd been required by the state authorities to visit the palace law room where Mr E had ranted on about some of his new and updated laws. These laws had been printed onto rolls of wallpaper and were to be sent out to the homes of all the city residents.

"And may I remind you that these rolls of wallpaper are to be put up on everyone's living room wall before sundown today," said Mr E.

"I'd rather put this stuff up in my toilet, or even better, use it in my toilet," the Professor had whispered to Lady Georgiana.

When that long meeting was nearly over, Mr E finished it off by bringing his flusher machine into the law room and flushing five more people out of the city. He'd caught them the night before in one of the city's wild meadow gardens holding a so-called meeting of the 'local wildlife club'. At this meeting they were experimenting with a set of brand new and specially designed plastic hedgehogs – each one having moisturising gel carefully concealed in-between its fake spines. These the group were using as hairbrushes to clean and condition their hair – highly illegal, breaking law 4461c which clearly states:

"All citizens must not engage in such activities that will nourish, oil, moisten or dampen any part of the head in order to obtain a look or feel that is not designated and approved by the state's department for fashion, style and general appearance. Façades created by so-called vogue fads and trends, that create all manner of custom-made tastes and likings for false sophistications and refinements (pertaining to erroneous delusional elegances) are forbidden. All tastefulness and constructions of decent-looking hair styles and facial features – beards, moustaches, eyebrows etc. and the manufacture of facial 'looks' in the city are to be defined by the city authorities alone."

Suspicions about the wildlife group's activities had been aroused when one of them had picked up a real hedgehog by mistake. The loud yelp of pain that followed had alerted the secret police and it took only a few moments to locate them, then the game was up. All five were flushed at the end of Mr E's law room meeting. Then, once the dreadful flushings were over, Lady Georgiana had to visit the market square to listen to Mr E talking about his latest lotions for everyone to wear.

This had been a particularly dreadful event, far worse than it normally was. To the right of the stage the green uniformed brass band had been playing a variety of cheerful tunes whilst Lady Georgiana had stood with Scrub near the front of the crowd alongside a stout, ginger-bearded man. The stout man was dressed in a slightly bulging tweed jacket, green trousers, a brightly coloured red and purple shirt and polka dotted bow tie. Anyone looking at him would have thought he was quite wealthy but struggled to match colours correctly.

"Well Basil," Lady Georgiana had said to the ginger bearded man, "Here we go again. I just hope that this lotion selling business passes by quickly. I do hate it when he tries to behave like some kind of super famous celebrity, acting as if he's doing us all a favour."

"Yes I know what you mean Georgie," Basil replied, "and those smelly lotions of his are getting worse and worse."

"I quite liked the last one," said Scrub.

"Oh, do shut up Scrub," said Lady Georgiana with a sigh.

"Sorry, M'lady," said Scrub, "But it was quite nice I thought."

You thought did you?" she replied. "Then Scrub if that's the case, can I suggest you just stick to the things in life that you're actually good at and try not to do the things that you can't."

"And what can't I do?" asked Scrub.

"Well thinking doesn't seem to be one of your strong points, so I'd try and stay away from that if you can," she retorted.

"All right, M'lady," said Scrub, doing his best to stop thinking.

Basil cast a sideways glance at Lady Pluggat to say that her last words to Scrub weren't quite appropriate but she didn't see as just then the Professor stepped out from the edge of the crowd. He limped over to them, clutching his leg as he went and finally took his place alongside Basil. He was now quite beardless; having given up all hope of successfully rescuing the remaining hair on his chin from where the bubble gum mask had ripped so much of it out. It would take him a long time to re-grow such a splendid thing again, but for him that was the price you paid for science.

"Good morning to you again," he said in a tired and almost sarcastic tone. "I tried to slip out of the city inner circle a few moments ago to avoid all this but as usual the guards are everywhere. The last hour and a half in that law room has completely done me in and I'm not sure I can take any more today. Have I missed anything?" he said hopefully.

"No, I think they're just about to start," replied Basil.

"What a shame," said the Professor, feeling deflated. "I can't stand going through this ritual you know. It really seems to somehow spoil my day."

"Yes," agreed Basil, giving the Professor a knowing look.

"I could make better smelling lotions than he does in just ten minutes in my laboratory," continued the Professor. "I'm sure he makes them smell bad on purpose."

"I quite like them," said Scrub.

"Shut up, Scrub," said Lady Georgiana, with a withering look.

"And the worst thing of all is that he expects us to pay for them," added the Professor.

Just then, the city Prime Minister Mr Ivan Robert Ritant arrived. He appeared from behind a large curtain that hung at the back of the stage. Crossing the wooden platform, he stood at the stage's edge, next to a standing microphone. In his hands was a cardboard cut-out of a green bottle, which he held aloft. Taking a large handkerchief from his inside jacket pocket, he dropped it over the cardboard bottle which seemed to disappear. Then, removing the handkerchief, a real glass bottle was revealed balanced on his palm. Very pleased with his own magic trick he beamed with pleasure and said, "Welcome, everyone welcome. It's my favourite part of the day. It's lotion time!"

A corporate sigh went out from some brave souls in the crowd whilst the majority gave a tentative applause that petered out as quickly as it started; it was an event that all were required to attend but few enjoyed.

"Welcome," he continued, "to this morning's feast of aromatic delights. Sniff and see how attractive you can be. A splash of lotion and you'll be aroma in motion; now for your host for this morning I ask you to welcome the incredible, invincible, unbelievable, the very one and only Mr E!"

Lady Georgiana put her fingers into her ears and looked at Basil who was doing the same. The Professor, now wearing a small pair of ear mufflers that he had pulled out from his jacket pocket, frowned at Scrub who had fetched two very dirty handkerchiefs from his pockets. Taking an end in each hand he stuffed one into each ear. With the wind chasing its tail that morning, Scrub's hankies flapped in the strong breeze making him look like he had the floppy ears of a Labrador puppy - but Scrub didn't care about his appearance.

From somewhere high in the firmament a balloon machine descended out of the sky. Attached to its underside, on a long chain, was a thin iron box that swung and spun gently in the breeze. Down the box plummeted and eventually rested

with a bump in the middle of the stage. Mr Ritant briefly opened the side of the box to show it was empty and then, throwing a large sheet and magic dust over its top, there came loud explosions of gas and steam on all sides. BANG! The box fell apart revealing the figure of
Mr E, dressed all in black like someone off to a solemn occasion. The brass band played a long blast of notes whilst Mr E rushed to the stage's front and, like a TV game show host, gave everyone a most gracious bow.

The crowd applauded, some because they wanted to and some because they thought it best to just fit in with what was happening.

"Thank you, thank you," said Mr E. He cleared his throat and shouted into the microphone, "Can I smell you?"

"Yes you can!" the crowd chanted back.

"And now ladies and gentlemen, boys and girls" continued Mr E, "it's lotion time! Such wondrous fragrances are here for us to treasure. They bring joy and happiness without measure! Oh taste the sunshine and the dancing rain and with these lotions you'll want to splash them on again and again and again. Never has so much love and attention been poured out on these masterpieces of invention. So hurry up and bring on the pleasure, for my lotions are forever! Ivan, bring in the bottles."

The brass band played another cheerful tune whilst Mr Ritant went to the back of the stage and brought back a silver tray holding three different shaped lime green bottles. He paraded the tray across the stage three times holding it high above his head as if he were carrying a great prize. Finally, when his proud one-man procession had come to its conclusion, he put the tray on a table near the front of the stage and selected a bottle from the collection.

"Can I have a volunteer from the audience?" said Mr E, pointing to the nearest person. "You madam, yes, you. You look like a good volunteer," he said. "It's a wonderful job for you, to sniff a good smell or two! So come on up and see, just how smelly a lotion can really be." At this, there was another blast of music from the brass band. The volunteer, helped by some guards, made her way to the stage and ascended the stairs, looking more than a little nervous.

"Just sit there," said Mr E, pointing to a chair next to the table on which the bottles were set. Once she was sitting down, Mr E stood next to her and bent over so that his nose was just inches from her own. He continued, "Now we are going to set before you a selection of the most wonderful lotions and potions. All you have to do is choose which one we're all going to wear. Is that clear?" The volunteer, dry mouthed and nervous, simply nodded.

"And I must say," said Mr E, glancing at the crowd with a cheesy grin on his face, "that we're selling it at an unusually low price today." At this comment everyone in the crowd looked at each other, not convinced at all that Mr E was doing them any favours.

Mr Ritant held up the first bottle to the crowd and said, "Our first bottle is a surprising little number made from an unusual collection of items found in the farmyard, specifically made for those of us with a great appreciation of the more piggy aspects of life. Its name is 'Piggiest, Porkiest, Dungiest', that's Latin you know."

"All right Ivan," said Mr E, "stop showing off your foreign language skills and get on with it."

"That was actually your cue Mr E," said Ivan.

"Ah yes," said Mr E, "'Piggiest, Porkiest, Dungiest, for the girl who likes to waft the smell of the outdoors wherever she goes; which is just as well because if you wear this no one will ever let you come inside again. Bottle number two Ivan, please."

Mr Ritant fetched the second bottle, went again to stand in front of the microphone and held it up for all to see.

"This one I have called 'Stinkus de la toilet', that's French you know. This aftershave is evocative of the smell in your bathroom," said Mr Ritant, "after Uncle Jack has been to stay for a week."

"Ugh!" sighed the crowd together; all seeming to know for some reason who 'Uncle Jack' was and, more to the point, what the smell would be like.

"It's an aroma," continued Mr Ritant, "that has the particular ability to hang in the air and to follow you throughout the day and the night and in the morning you'll feel even sweatier, I mean even sweeter and bright."

Mr E took the bottle into his hand, smelt it and quickly put his head away to one side.

"Ah," he said, "the perfect aroma for the bathroom boy who wants to impress. Wear this lotion and no one will forget you, even if they wanted to. Bottle number three Ivan."

"Our next and final offering," said Mr Ritant, holding up the third bottle "is called 'Drego los Pipo los Drainos' – that's Spanish you know."

"This is a fermentation of the most delightful collection of ingredients taken from a nearby drain. Especially designed for the person who wants to demonstrate that 'has-been washed out' feeling."

"Ah yes, my favourite," said Mr E, holding the bottle high into the air for all to see. "We should wear this one all the time. It gives one a sense of mystery. Wherever you go you would hear people say – 'What can that be? Is it a waft of waste? Is it a smell of grace? Is it a sniff of delightful drain or just the gentle pong of stale collected rain?' So Ivan, will you give us a quick reminder of our lotions available for our volunteer today."

Ivan held up a sheet of paper from which he read, "Well Mr E, will our guest choose bottle 'A' Piggiest; Porkiest, Dungiest for the girl who likes to waft the smell of the outdoors wherever she goes? Or will it be bottle 'B' Stinkus de la Toilet for that bathroom memory of Uncle Jack? Or finally will it be bottle 'C' Drego los Pipo los Drainos, for that washed out smell of a nearby drain?"

"You know," said Lady Georgiana, quietly to Basil and the Professor, "I think that they actually rehearse this beforehand."

"I know," whispered the Professor back, "sad, isn't it."

Basil just rolled his eyes. He wasn't looking forward to these new lotions that Mr E had created, whichever one was chosen.

"Well, guest" continued Mr Ritant, "It's a wonderful job for you, sniffing a smell or two. So what will it be?"

The volunteer briefly smelt each bottle and then, after retching and catching her breath, chose the farmyard lotion. Several crates of it were handed to the crowd, who all paid for them and reluctantly began to put the lotion on.

"Thank you, thank you, a round of applause for our volunteer," said Mr E. "Would you like to return to the audience now please? Go on, get off. Thank you, thank you," and with that he gave the volunteer a helpful push on her way towards the stairs at the end of the stage.

The bottles were passed across the crowd and eventually they reached Lady Georgiana and her friends. She looked at the little container in her hand and, after some mental preparation, unscrewed the top. The immediate waft of the lotion caused her to screw up her nose and she looked at the Professor and Basil who themselves were holding and opening theirs. Slowly they put a small amount of lotion on their necks and wrists.

"Can I have some?" said Scrub, briefly removing his helmet.

Lady Georgiana turned to face Scrub and emptied the rest of her bottle onto Scrub's head so that it ran down the back of his hair.

"Thank you, M'lady," he said. "You're so very kind. You do this for me every day."

"Don't mention it," she replied, abruptly turning back to face the stage.

Mr E had been pacing up and down to see that everyone was putting the lotion on and, once he was satisfied with what he had seen, walked back to the microphone.

"Obviously," he said, "I will be sending out my sniffer squads into the city later on today who will be using their sniffing devices on random passers-by, to make sure that they are wearing the correct lotion. If they find anyone without an official smell of the state on them, they will automatically apply a double dose to the offending party. And," he added, pausing for a moment to make sure that everyone was listening, "I am pleased to also announce, that we have had an astonishing breakthrough in our science labs last night. I am delighted to reveal that we've just managed to produce a gravy version of these lotions so that, anyone found not smelling correctly today, will not only be given their extra dose from a sniffer squad but will also be able to eat some with their evening meal. We will obviously have representatives of the palace present at the offending person's evening meal time to make sure that it is all eaten up."

The crowd stood frozen, mouths dropped open, gawping in disbelief at Mr E's last comments. How could someone come up with something quite so disgusting?

- -

Back near the top of the palace stairs, Lady Georgiana returned from her thoughts and composed herself. What a day so far! Could it get any worse? She climbed up the remaining few steps and entered the palace public library. Walking across its bare timbered floor, passing through several rooms, she turned right into the languages area. At the far side of the room was a section of books called 'Discerning the Dialects of the Ancient World'. Not surprisingly, it was empty of people.

Glancing over her shoulder, to make sure no-one was looking, she approached the bookcase and pulled a brown book half out from a top shelf whilst at the same time pushing a large book on the bottom shelf with her toe. The whole wall of books swung forward, like a door, and through the gap Lady Georgiana stepped. The book panel closed behind her and the brown book that she had pulled fell back into place - and she was gone.

Chapter 10 – The Resistance In Your Hands

Lady Georgiana walked along a short corridor and descended some steps to enter a windowless chamber. Lit by several gas lamps, it had a large oval table which filled the room's centre. Around it sat a variety of people, some of whom looked quite important (or thought of themselves in that way). Fidgeting impatiently and checking their pocket watches, several of them gave each other a murmur of relief as Lady Georgiana seated herself at the table's far end next to Basil.

"Why do you always have to sit so far away from everyone else?" she whispered.

Basil shrugged his shoulders. He wasn't in a good mood and the smell of the latest lotion was irritating his nose and throat.

"Right!" said a gentleman at the other end of the table. "Now that we're all here, as clerk to the council, I'm going to officially open this meeting of the resistance. We have a couple of important issues to look at today, which must be dealt with before we close, so let's start. Items for discussion are the loss of our leader Sir Frederick James, who was flushed away yesterday and our latest plans to bring either water or some alternative means of washing into the city again. So first, our thoughts about Sir Frederick. Comments anyone?"

"Had it coming to him, I thought," said Basil. "Especially after his last so called 'master plan' to get us all fresh water. Quite ridiculous really."

"Basil!" said Lady Georgiana sharply. "Now that's not called for. Sir Frederick put his life on the line for all of us several times and now he's finally paid the price. We shouldn't say such things about him."

"Why not?" said another voice from the other end of the table. "Basil is right. He was quite a nincompoop!"

"Hear! Hear!" cried more voices with, "I agree, better off without him!"

Lady Georgiana's mouth dropped open with surprise. "Well," she said finally, a little lost for words. "Ladies and gentlemen, I still think that despite all of Sir Frederick's shortcomings we should be a little more generous to him and the memory of him than that. He was, after all, on our side and wanted to see the city freed. Come now everyone, let's at least remember that."

Her comments were met by a morally subdued silence.

"Err, yes," said the clerk. "I think we can all agree with Lady Georgiana. I'll enter in the minutes that we miss Sir Frederick's unique ideas and talents and we're very aware of our great loss; losing, that is, such a good and well-meaning friend."

This seemed to satisfy everyone. The meeting went on for a while with general talk about the way forward, now that Sir Frederick was gone, until a younger, female member of the group popped the question, "So, Lady Georgiana, as the next highest ranking member of the nobility in the city and with the success that you've brought us over the years, we take it that this part of the resistance movement is now in your hands?"

Silence again descended on the room as every eye looked in her direction. Lady Georgiana paused, she had not thought about the question. She'd been so busy recently and the arrest and flushing of Sir Frederick had happened so quickly, that she'd not stopped to think about who was to be in charge now that he was gone. Basil shuffled in his seat, leaned back to scratch his growing, protruding stomach and raised an eyebrow with a "Well what are you going to do now?" look on his face.

"I hadn't really given the idea much thought," Lady Georgiana replied with great honesty. "But, now that you come to mention it, I think that the answer must be... of course, well of course, the answer is, well I suppose, err, it is yes."

"Quite rightly so," said a voice from the group and this was met with other compliments from around the room. Basil just sat there, wearing a frown on his forehead and chewing on his teeth. Lady Georgiana smiled politely at the compliments that she was receiving from everyone but knew their expectations were high and that she would have to deliver some results pretty quickly.

"So, what's your first big idea?" was the next question. "How are we going to get water back into the city without Mr E finding out?"

Lady Georgiana straightened her posture and folded her arms. She really had not been expecting this and felt quite put on the spot. She breathed in slowly for a few seconds and put on a firm but friendly face making sure that she looked both intelligent and calm, though she felt neither.

"Well," she began, "keeping in mind some of our more recent failures that we've all experienced, I think we now need to draw some useful lessons from them and make sure all our future tactics do not make the same false assumptions and errors of judgement. So let me first outline where we have come from in this last year, why some of the different plans failed and, in my opinion, what options we therefore have for the future."

Lady Georgiana didn't quite know where her little talk would lead as she didn't have any immediate large scale plan in mind, but she reasoned that if she talked for long enough, then some new idea might pop into her head as she went along. She began by outlining the very seasonal master plan of
Sir Frederick which took place half a year ago at Christmas time, when they had all agreed to dress up as Santa. The idea was to make everyone in the city look plump and fat in their Santa suits by stuffing several hot water bottles down their shirts and to use these to carry and distribute illegally gathered rainwater. A Santa would walk up to another Santa during rush hour and give them a big, long hug. Whilst they were in the embrace one Santa would wobble his belly in order to loosen the hot water bottle from his stomach area. The other Santa would then drop his hands to catch it as it fell out of his friend's costume and stuff the hot water bottle up his

own shirt. That way the water could be passed from person to person on the streets of Clearwash City without the authorities knowing about it.

However, the main problem with this was knowing which Santa was carrying water bottles and which was not. To add to the confusion some of the city folk were incredibly fat and, even though they didn't have any water bottles on them, would find other Santas coming to cuddle them. This resulted in some Santas being held onto for long periods of time without any water bottles coming out. (During rush hour it's quite hard to hear what someone else is saying in the streets of the city; let alone when someone is speaking from behind a big, white bushy Santa beard with cotton wool stuffed in their ears. So, it wasn't surprising that one could not hear the other person say that they didn't have any water).

This was highly embarrassing and had caused several Santas to have fights and wrestling matches in the street, trying to get free from each other. There was also the problem that seeing lots of Santas all hugging every two minutes in the streets looked very strange, plus the problem of dropping the water bottles every now and again, which eventually led to a couple of people being arrested, tried and then flushed out of the city.

"Therefore I must conclude," said Lady Georgiana, "that using costumes to transport water across the city has turned out to be more than a little faux-pas."

She then talked about the plan to introduce fake molehills onto the city's central park to give the impression that it had been invaded by an army of the little rodents. However, instead of real moles, they were to use plastic ones which would contain water. The idea was to send out a party of mole trappers who would somehow "catch" one or two after some heavy rain and pretend to take them home as pets, only to empty the water out of them once they were in their homes. The plastic moles would then be put back at night-time, deep in the ground, with a rubber tube that ran up from their mouths to just above the ground's surface, ready to gather any fresh rainwater that fell.

"And this," said Lady Georgiana, "seemed to work well until we realised that the dogs that belonged to the palace used that grassy area where the mole hills were located as a latrine making the water unusable. It is also a great pity that this problem was not detected straight away - causing a lot of distress to quite a large proportion of the city population. That night when they had all secretly washed their hair with the contaminated water stays in my mind, terrible thing really. I've never seen any group of people so readily rush to use the lotions of Mr E on the following morning to cover up the smell. Eventually, of course, a dog dug up a mole, thought it made a very nice toy, dug up another and another and the game was up. So I conclude that we don't in any way want to try and collect rain water inside imitation animals."

Lady Georgiana went on and on listing all the different plans that had either nearly succeeded or completely failed. She recalled stories that ranged from water stored in hollowed out carrots to books with built in water pistols. From babies' nappies that contained pre-filled water sachets in their linings to pet gerbils who had an extra layer of material glued onto their underside, which had some of the Professor's dirt removal chemicals on it. "Just pick up a pet gerbil every now and then and rub its tummy over your face to release the cleansing cream," he had said, when announcing it to the resistance council. "Put your germs on the gerbil" was his advertising motto, though this later had to stop due to members of the public being bitten on their noses by the annoyed rodents.

"And finally," she concluded, "we had the failed attempt of the Professor to create a bubble gum soap that we could wash with, though personally I'm not displeased that particular experiment didn't succeed."

"Yes, yes, this is all very well," said the Clerk, "but we want to know what your new plan is. What is it that we need to do next to secure some kind of secret water supply to the citizens of our great city?"

"Well," replied Lady Georgiana. She paused for a moment, still waiting for inspiration. The listing of all their past failures had made her feel quite depressed and low. It was hard to see how anyone could succeed in these circumstances.

"I feel," she continued, "that our first point of contact should be... I mean that our main focus of attention now needs to be... Well it needs to be..."

"It needs to be the waterworks," piped up Basil.

"The waterworks?" repeated Lady Georgiana glancing at Basil in disbelief. "Err, yes," she said trying to sound unsurprised by the idea, "Our next focus of attention is, of course, the waterworks."

Lady Georgiana glanced at Basil again who shrugged his shoulders and gave a half smile back. A stunned silence followed that seemed to linger in the air for ages. Finally, the clerk to the meeting spoke up. "The waterworks building has been closed and condemned as unsafe for the last sixteen years," he said. "Every leader of this council has completely rejected the idea of going in there. It is well known that two teams of people have entered there in the past and have completely disappeared. No one in their right mind will even consider re-entering. On top of that none of us knows how it used to work, when it did all those years ago. Even if we did get in there, we wouldn't know what to do. Is this idea just a notion that you've plucked out of the sky or is it something that, for some strange reason, you've been considering?

"Lady Georgiana, the Professor and I have been working on this for some time now," said Basil. "You can see from Lady Georgiana's report that all the ideas of this committee, and indeed of the other rebel committees, have done nothing but fall short of a viable solution. So, it is to the waterworks that we again need to look and we think we finally have the solution to getting it working again."

"But that's madness," said the Clerk. "You'd be going into the most dangerous building in the city."

"So Mr E tells you," replied Basil. "But that's not necessarily true. I don't believe half the stories we've been told about the place and now a small group of us think that we can make it through to get the place working again. Once that happens there's nothing to stop us. There'll be so much good clean water for everyone that even the guards won't support Mr E any more. They're getting as fed up with him as we are."

"But how will you get in there?" said the clerk. "You can't just walk up to the front door. It's bolted, locked, barred and covered in scaffolding."

"We'll descend into the city drains during rush hour. It's quite simple when there are so many people about. The guards will never see us. Then we'll make our way underground. We believe that we can enter the waterworks from beneath, which should be much safer than going from the top."

"Unless the whole thing falls on top of you!" replied the clerk.

After the meeting had finally finished and the resistance council had begun to disperse, Lady Georgiana and Basil left the palace together and made their way over to his house on the edge of the great square. Scrub met them at the palace gates and tagged on behind.

"Basil, what are you trying to do to me?" said Lady Georgiana, now that they were out in the open air and away from anyone else. "Where on earth did this ridiculous waterworks plan come from or is it just another one of your 'spur of the moment,' impulsive and thoughtless ideas that just popped into your head?"

"No, it isn't another one of my ideas," said Basil, looking a little affronted by Lady Georgiana's abrupt comments.

"Well whose was it?" she demanded. "Was it the Professor's?"

"No", he replied. "It was actually from someone closer to you than you think."

Lady Georgiana, taking Basil's words literally, saw Scrub and stared back at Basil in disbelief.

"No Georgie, it was in fact your father's idea originally," said Basil, correcting her. "And developed by you, I believe, several years ago when you commissioned the Professor to look into the wheel combinations that drove the waterworks. He and his team have had several breakthroughs in the last few months in discovering how it used to work and I think we should look into it. I believe they now know where the wheels controlling the water supply are, how to get to them and how to start them working again."

"Why wasn't I told?" said Lady Georgiana. "A piece of news such as this should have been relayed to me straight away."

"Ah," said Basil, looking a little sheepish. "That's what I said to the good Professor, but he was rather hoping that his bubble gum experiment would come off first, as he'd spent so much time and effort in trying to make it work."

Lady Georgiana just scowled at Basil. "We don't put personal ambition above the good of the city," she said.

With those comments each went their separate ways. At the very same moment of their departure, one of the less prominent resistance council members (who had briefly visited the palace's private family library to deposit a book) also left the palace grounds. Slipping out of its front gates and this young and newish member of the resistance chose to discretely tail Lady Georgiana. Wearing a dark cloak with a hood, she was able to keep her appearance characterless and her following undetected.

Using the shadows and alleyways as cover from which to keep her target in sight, she kept track of Lady Georgiana across several city blocks until eventually she left the central part of the city behind and entered a more rural area; a place where there were more wide open spaces and the metropolis almost turned into countryside. Her tracker watched from a distance as Lady Georgiana passed through the front gates of her mansion's courtyard and approached her stately home. The young, hooded woman then broke off her pursuit. Travelling a little further away from the urban streets towards what was once an industrial part of the city, she entered a small disused mill. Climbing the stair, she entered the building's top chamber where there was a table and a large bird cage, housing a handful of homing pigeons. She sat at the desk and penned the following message.

"In the reign of the King... The Lady is now in charge of the resistance committee. The blueprint plant has finally worked. Her focus is now on the waterworks. Anticipate a team excursion within days. Anna.
P.S. Tell my Dad to save me some pie!"

She then took out from her pocket a translation booklet and used it to rewrite the same message, but this time in a coded form on a much smaller piece of paper. Then, rolling up the little scroll, she placed it into a miniature tube and attached it to the leg of one of the homing pigeons. Off it flew, out across the city and into the desert to deliver the message.

Chapter 11 - What A Dingy Place!

It was a few days later that Lady Georgiana, the Professor, Basil and Scrub made their way through the bustling streets of Clearwash City, knowing that they were on a mission to save everyone from the power of Mr E. Operation drainpipe, it had been called and so the 'Drainpipe Gang' as they had been nicknamed by the resistance movement (not to the liking of Lady Georgiana) had begun their quest. It was rush hour and every street and cobbled alley was full of people running, rushing, scurrying, dashing, darting, shouting and yelling; just the cover they needed to disappear for a few hours. The band of four split up. Lady Georgiana guided Scrub along the main road running through the heart of the city whilst Basil and the Professor deliberately lost themselves amongst the crowds, ducking and diving through the raucous sea of swarming people.

Going their separate ways they walked on and on, through avenues, alleyways, highways and narrow byways, through dirty backstreets and broad boulevards, entering goods shops, workshops, factory sweatshops, picking and finding their separate routes across the manic city, all this trouble to ensure they weren't being tailed by the authorities. Dotted across their paths were many small market squares, filled with stall upon stall of unwanted junk - all dressed up to look upmarket and respectable, open-air cafés selling state authorised food (no drinks) and city parks filled with browned grassy banks and thistle-ridden landscaped borders.

Basil wandered along the edge of one of the city's dried-up canals to finally visit a gentleman's reading house, where he joined several like-minded and like-bellied friends. They all stood or sat together in a wall-to-wall mahogany panelled den, books opened but talking about anything except the contents of the manuscripts in their hands. Whilst his friends were engrossed in a vibrant conversation, Basil purposefully leaned back onto the wall behind him. To no-one's surprise a narrow gap briefly appeared and he disappeared through it, into a tunnel that wound downwards. In the meantime the Professor had made his way towards the city outer circle and into an old theatre. Having watched the first five minutes of an appalling play, he sought out the men's toilets and locked himself into one of its cubicles. Moments later he swivelled the toilet sideways to reveal a small, narrow stairway. Down he went into the ground with the lavatory closing over the hole in the floor behind him.

Lady Georgiana took Scrub for a good walk. After navigating the crowd on Main Street, the largest shopping mall in the city, they went off through many side alleys into a series of small craft shops; stopping briefly in each one for a quick browse before leaving through the tradesman's entrance at the back. Finally, they arrived at a street corner, outside a popular café, where plenty of people congregated. As soon as Lady Georgiana and Scrub appeared, a good number of the townsfolk left their café tables and gathered into a large huddle around them to engage in a raving dialogue about the weather. Whilst this was going on a sewer service-hole cover was lifted by some members of the group, whereupon Lady Georgiana and Scrub promptly descended into the drain. Above them the pack of people continued their boisterous discussion until the two travellers were underground, out of sight and the man-hole cover replaced.

The twosome found themselves in a dingy, grimy tunnel smelling of damp with several passages running off in different directions. The walls were covered in bright yellow-brown clay that ran wet, causing the mud to ooze down each brick, making them sticky to touch. Bending down to avoid bumping their heads on the low ceiling, they slowly edged their way forward taking care not to touch the tunnel's sides.

"Never quite figured out why there is so much dampness down here," said the Professor, joining them from one of the side passages.

He took out a compass and pointed the party in a northerly direction. They followed the winding passage for several minutes until it ran into the principal drainage channel that passed underneath the city's high street. There they met Basil and continued their journey together. Looking up, they could see through the large iron grids to the street above where the people were still busy with their rush hour hustle and bustle goings-on. They followed the now very large tunnel for a few miles, picking their way between the puddles, mud and the odd rat that scampered across their path. After a brief rest they eventually took another side tunnel that led them back out into the open air.

Now at the city's edge, the four friends could see directly ahead to the great city wall; that awesome historical boundary that kept them locked inside their day-to-day prison. Behind the wall, towering into the sky, were the immense mountains and hills that ran along the northern boundary of Clearwash City. Years ago they had formed a natural protective barrier against outsiders when the city was originally built, but today these ancient watchmen made up a huge part of what the city inhabitants called, "the confinement blockade."

Still keeping to a northerly course, they hurried on in single file past a series of red-bricked buildings, badly in need of repair and onto a narrow pathway across a wild meadow. Everyone's hearts raced now that they were exposed in the open air, so they moved at a quick pace, glancing up nervously into the sky to look for signs of police patrol balloons. When the small winding path led them in-between some dense bushes and overgrown brambles, they slowed a little - the thorny shrubbery giving the travellers a little more cover. Ignoring the scratches and scrapes received from the undergrowth, the foursome walked until the line of bushes disappeared and an open cobbled courtyard came into view. The courtyard was not only broad, stretching out left and right for a good distance, it also ran right up to the foot of the mountains. There wasn't any city wall here, but then again, there wasn't a need for one; the mountain's rock face was sheer and high and only a fool would try to scale it.

Next to the mountain, in fact built into the side of it, was what looked like a very large, run-down warehouse – one that had seen better days. It was the waterworks. Pinned along the top edge of the building's western wall was a series of white letters that together read, "The Waterworks of Clearwash City", but the letters were now quite spoilt and discoloured. Underneath this lettering sat a row of long, narrow windows. Together they gave this ageing, eerie structure a look similar to that of an ancient church; one that perhaps wanted to catch as many shafts of available sunlight as possible within its cold, thick walls. On the roof, in fact protruding out from its very centre, was a large metal dome. A broad rim ran around the dome's base, making the building look as if it was wearing a gentleman's bowler hat, ready to go out for a social event or business appointment.

At the building's southern end, fifty or more steps ran up to two very large front doors, set under a grand archway.

Above this archway, stretching across the face of the building, was a vast stained-glass window. It was covered in scaffolding but, despite this, the painted figures of a great lion and a prowling bear, standing opposite each other underneath the flight of a soaring eagle, could still be made out on the glass as each section peeped out between the scaffold gaps. Together they formed the representation of a majestic crest. It gave this part of the waterworks a regal look, quite contrasting with the rest of the dirty construction. Despite its slightly odd exterior, however, it must have at one time been a very splendid building.

Next to the waterworks stood a very large, yellow industrial crane. Rust had feasted on its metal frame and from its long mechanical arm a wooden box dangled on a chain - where the last window cleaners had been working just before the waterworks had been shut down.

"I thought we were going to enter the waterworks from beneath it, through the drainage system?" said Lady Georgiana, as they hastily entered the cobbled courtyard.

"Well, actually, we're not quite going in that way," replied the Professor, glancing over his shoulder.

"But," added Basil rather quickly, "as I said at the meeting, we're not going in through the front doors either."

"We are sort of making our entrance from below ground," continued the Professor, "but it isn't that deep and we're not quite sure from the few sheets of blueprint plans we have, just how deep it does go. However, Basil couldn't tell the council that for fear they might not let us try this at all."

"Perhaps I wouldn't have come with you," said Lady Georgiana, "if I had known that."

"That's not a very comforting thing to say," said Basil, trying to sound a little put-out by her comments, but Lady Georgiana's silence was louder than Basil's objection.

They crossed the courtyard and walked along the western side of the waterworks, sometimes touching its large bricks with the tips of their fingers to make a personal connection with the great historical structure. There was something about the old building that was almost 'other-worldly' or perhaps spoke of a time past when the city was free and that freedom hadn't quite completely leaked out of the brickwork yet. To touch the building was to somehow touch and engage with the freedom it once enjoyed.

Arriving at the far northern side of the waterworks, they saw that it merged straight into the lofty, grand mountain; a great wall of stone that stood on watch, day and night, keeping a constant guard. Here they also noticed four very large pipes that protruded out of the waterworks' roof. These ran up the side of the mountain's rock face for some distance and eventually disappeared into it. About a stone's throw away to their left was a small shed, towards which the Professor led them. Circling around behind it, they found a cellar trap door amongst the long grass and weeds.

"Our newest discovery to gain entrance into the waterworks," said the Professor, a glint of excitement in his eyes.

The trap door opened up to reveal ten steps, giving them entry to a small passageway. This they followed in almost pitch darkness. The Professor took the lead, moving slowly, feeling the way with his hands, whilst everyone else walked behind, holding onto the shoulders of the one in front.

As they walked Scrub whispered, "Will this make everything work?"

"It has to work Scrub," replied Lady Georgiana, "or we'll be needing a wash forever, which in your case won't make any difference I'm sure. But for the rest of us… we need to take a bath every now and again."

They followed the dark tunnel for a few more minutes, continuing to feel their way with their hands as it twisted this way and that. Finally, reaching yet another flight of stairs, they found at the bottom a door that seemed quite stuck when they first tried to open it. After much pushing it gave way and they stepped onto what looked like a long metal walkway. Dimly illuminated by what looked like thin strips of fluorescent paint that ran along its edges and down its middle, the walkway itself slanted in a downwards direction, running a long, long way towards a hazy light at the bottom.

"How far down does this go?" asked Lady Georgiana. She now had the feeling that when she'd agreed to this venture she'd been woefully ill informed and that they'd bitten off far more than they could chew.

"Don't let the large building that we saw above ground deceive you," said the Professor. "Most of the waterworks is actually underground. It's much grander and loftier in both size and stature than we first imagined. Even the blueprint building plans that we were working from when we started this project didn't really show us the true size and extent of the build. They only displayed the top four floors, which we initially assumed was the building's complete construction but, recent finds of more diagrams and calculations based on how we think the building worked, show us that there has to be much more of it. In fact, we now think that it is built deep into the mountain, but how far back it goes we don't know and from somewhere in there, we believe, is where the water supply actually originates. Just imagine that! Perhaps there's an enormous cavern in the heart of that great rock filled with wonderful fresh, clean water? The waterworks does something amazing with it. It uses very little power of its own. It's the water pressure from the mountain supply that's used to drive most of the building's energy needs. From what we can make out the water pours in through those four large pipes that we saw at the back of the building and this then turns cogs and turbines to make everything work. It's quite amazing when you think about it."

Very cautiously they made their way down the walkway, deeper and deeper underground. When they finally stepped off at the bottom they found themselves walking into what seemed like a very large hall. The floor was wooden but the walls were made of panelled iron that was moist and dank. The air smelt stale and clung to the travellers as they walked through its clammy atmosphere. All over the walls and high above were rusty water pipes twisting and turning like tangled spaghetti. Far, far above them, they could see gaps in the roof where small parts had fallen in, allowing thin shafts of light to fall down to the floor where the party of four stood. An eerie feeling swept over the quartet. They suddenly felt very small and out of place. The room was so large and the equipment and machinery that they could make out in the dim light was much more advanced than they had expected. It was like stepping onto an alien spaceship where you don't quite know what anything around you does and you dare not touch anything in case you make a terrible mistake.

"What a vastly peculiar and very dingy place," said Lady Georgiana, stepping over some rusty piping and then picking up her skirt to walk through a shallow puddle. Her voice echoed off the walls as she spoke.

"Yes," said the Professor, "I do believe that Mr E has deliberately let all this become as run down as possible over the years. I don't believe his story for one moment about the waterworks becoming unsafe for use."

"Neither do I," said Basil, "but it must be perilous in some way now that it's been left standing for all this time and so many people have disappeared trying to get in."

"Whereabouts in the building are we?" asked Lady Georgiana. "I mean, what does this room do?"

"This, I believe, is the main water pipe chamber," said the Professor. "There are thousands of pipes in this room which guide the water into the different cleansing chambers on the eastern side of the building. Now," he said, waving his hand to stop everyone from walking any further. "In theory this part of the waterworks should be quite safe for us to walk through but we still can't take any chances. So keep to the edge of the room. There is a large basement underneath this wooden floor, which would mean quite a fall if the floorboards collapsed beneath us. The floor around the perimeter of the room, however, should be strong enough to hold us up if we keep close to the wall. At least, that's what we believe."

"Great, thank you very much for telling us beforehand" said Basil sarcastically.

They gingerly skirted the room's perimeter. As their eyes adjusted to the darkness, they could see so much rubble strewn across the floor it would have been impossible to cross without tripping over something.

"Keep going," said the Professor, "but very slowly. Our eyes will get used to the dark as time goes by but we must not be hasty. I don't want to be carrying someone out of here because they've had a fall."

Everyone moved forward cautiously, one behind the other, going step by step and little by little.

"Goodness, gracious me," remarked the Professor a minute or so later, more to himself than anyone else. For to his immediate embarrassment and obvious shame, he suddenly remembered his small portable gas lantern and pulled it out of his jacket pocket. A couple of match strokes later, he held it up to light the way. Its small light streamed out into the darkness, bouncing from one metal object to another. They could now see more clearly the twisting shapes of countless pipes and tubes that ran throughout the great chamber.

From the ceiling many of these pipes ran down to the floor in the middle of the room where they entered a large, square storage container. From this container's base multiple tubes protruded like the tentacles of a giant octopus. These ran along the floor and then down into the basement. The four especially large pipes, which they had seen on the outside of the waterworks running into the side of the mountain, dropped into the room from the centre of the ceiling. Twisting around each other, they went down to the ground, straight through the floor into the basement below. These same pipes returned through another part of the floor and separated from each other, going back up through different parts of the ceiling again to who knows where? It was a most complicated room but, in a way, quite elegant and beautiful to look at.

After gingerly navigating the room's edge they finally came to an archway set into the southern wall. Through this they went and then down a long corridor. Passing through yet another archway they entered a square room which contained many large cylinder-shaped metal containers, taller than buses. The four of them rather timidly passed in-between these strange objects that lay dotted across their path; feeling somewhat small and overshadowed by their imposing presence.

The Professor led them to a door on the far wall. Through it they went, stepping onto a metal-railed balcony that ran along the edge of a long chamber and ended at another door on the opposite side of the room. As they walked, something shimmered beneath them in the half-light cast by the Professor's lantern. Lady Georgiana took hold of the Professor's arm and pulled it down to shine the lantern's light across the floor. There, down below in a central sunken area of the room, was something that made their mouths drop open and their hearts soar, something that they had not expected to see and had not seen for many a year; a square pool, filled almost to the brim with what seemed to be clean, crystal-clear water.

Chapter 12 – A Quick Dip

The four friends just stood looking at the pool below them. It had been a long time since they had seen such a body of water all in one place. Their only sight of it for years had been in small bottles handed out by the city authorities - and that for drinking purposes only.

"So, there is still water here," whispered Lady Georgiana.

"I knew it!" added Basil, shaking his head with disbelief.

Each looked at the other with amazement and delight and, as the Professor continued to move his lantern, they saw to their left a broad flight of steps going down to the water's edge. Without thinking they instinctively found themselves descending them. Once at the bottom they peered over a small gate; before them was the most delightful invitation to be clean they had seen in years.

The Professor hung his lantern on the balcony railings above and a few moments later had the gate's latch lifted. It swung back to reveal more steps going down into the beautiful, clear water. He knelt down to touch it with his little finger, lifted a droplet to his nose, smelt it and then licked it. After tasting, he placed his fingers in the pool and splashed them, sending ripples running across the smooth surface to the other side. Cupping both hands in the water, he brought them back to his mouth and drank, slurping up each gulp. Then, wiping his mouth and newly growing moustache, the Professor smiled and beamed with delight his pleasure at having such a wonderful drink.

"It's beautiful, clean water," he said, sitting back with almost delirious pleasure. "Delicious," he added.

Lady Georgiana, Basil and Scrub quickly bent down to taste it too. Cupping their hands, they took in mouthful after mouthful; water had never tasted so good. Basil couldn't contain himself. He splashed it over his face and beard with great delight. Pulling out a handkerchief, he soaked it in the water and thrust it down the back of his neck.

"Oh, I'm having a wash," he said with elation. "Look everyone! I'm actually having a wash."

Throwing off his jacket and quickly rolling up his sleeves to his elbows, he began rubbing the water up and down his arms, onto his neck, then in and out of all parts of his bushy beard. Scrub too had quickly moved from sipping the new water to putting his face right in to drink. Once his thirst was quenched, he happily kept his face in the water, blowing big bubbles through his mouth and nose, just having fun. He then splashed it over the top of his head whilst Lady Georgiana sat back on the steps and laughed at them both, still dipping her cupped hands into the water and relishing each sip. The Professor leaned forward again to get some more water but, as he did so, his foot slipped on the stair. He stumbled and slightly knocked into Basil from behind who, as a result, was forced to take a few steps down into the water to steady himself.

"Hey," he shouted back at the Professor, with a smile and pointing to his now very wet feet.

"Sorry," replied the Professor, with a grin.

Basil picked some water up in his hands and splashed it at him and the Professor carried on the game by sending some back. Scrub thought this was fun too and began splashing anyone who was in reach. The event quickly turned into a friendly water fight till the Professor quickly grabbed Scrub around the waist in order to throw him in - but slipped again in the process and sent them both tumbling into the pool.

"Oh my," laughed Lady Georgiana, at the sight of the two of them when they resurfaced.

After watching them splash each other till they were soaking wet, Basil waded down a few more steps to help pull them out. Lady Georgiana reached out her hands to help too, but as soon as her hands were in theirs, the three men, with a twinkle in their eyes, jumped back together into the pool taking Lady Georgiana with them.

"Oh no you can't," she cried, but anything else that she was about to say was muffled as she went under the water.

About ten minutes later they were all sat on the stairs again, resting and relieved from the fun that had briefly transcended their problems. After ringing out their socks and clothes as best as they could, they made their way back up the steps. It was time to face the realities of life and the task in hand. They were still dripping wet but this was of little consequence. The experience had given them a fresh exhilaration and new strength to press on. At last they were clean and right now nothing else mattered.

"If I were to meet my end today then I'd die a happy man," said Basil.

The Professor picked up his lantern and led the dripping merrymakers along the railed balcony and through the door on the opposite side of the room. Stepping into yet another lengthy corridor they halted for a moment, quite taken aback by its length.

"Come on," said Basil, after their brief hesitation, "we may as well just get on with it."

The party of four had mentally prepared themselves for a lengthy walk that day, knowing that their entrance to the waterworks was only the beginning of an extensive journey, but the more they travelled the more amazed they were at the size of the place. As they walked they began to see numerous windows and doors either side of them, leading off into adjacent rooms. More captivating, however, were the various imprinted drawings across the walls that appeared dotted down the walkway. There were illustrations of machines, etches of mechanisms and detailed descriptions of devices, the likes of which even the Professor had never seen before. These strange contraptions and appliances, some of which seemed to be almost magical in their workings, were illustrated and documented in great detail. Written alongside them were technical notes showing how they were assembled and worked. They were fascinating, a working wallpaper of technical instruction.

"Let's not get distracted," Lady Georgiana said to the Professor, when he began trying to write down some of the ideas he was reading. "Let's keep to our plan. We can always explore later when we've done what we came here to do."

The Professor half-heartedly nodded and led them onwards, still staring at the drawings as he went. As they progressed down the long corridor, however, the technical drawings turned into a historical tale. There were pictures of kings and queens who ruled with great grandeur, displaying their wealth and pageantry. Assembled troops, clothed in plated armour with spinning propellor devices on their backs, flew off to make war on their behalf whilst flying metal insects and crab-shaped, robot-like machines worked the fields to bring in the harvest, the abundant produce of the land. Soon it was Lady Georgiana who was slowing down to read and she was the one being reminded about why they were all there and not to linger any more.

"Why are we here again?" asked Scrub, breaking the silence that surrounded them. He had become a little confused with his surroundings and once again sought to make sense of where he was.

Lady Georgiana let out a sigh.

"We're revolting against the establishment," announced the Professor over his shoulder, as he proudly strode in front of them down the corridor.

"Oh," replied Scrub, a little surprised and not quite understanding the phrase the Professor had used.

"Well, that's good," he finally added moments later, trying to sound intelligent and seeking to keep the conversation going. "I've always wanted to be revolting."

"Well Scrub," replied Lady Georgiana. "I am pleased to say that you are already quite revolting just as you are and have been now for many years."

"Thank you M'lady," said Scrub, thinking it was a compliment.

Lady Georgiana's smile soon disappeared, however, when she caught sight of Basil's slight frown.

"Careful Georgie," he said to her, and she knew what he meant.

Eventually their walk brought them to a metal spiral staircase that wound to a great height. The Professor peered up the stairwell, squinting with his eyes to see how high up it travelled. Up and up it went, like a never ending Jacob's ladder that would reach heaven itself if it could.

"This, I believe, is the stairway I was hoping to find," he said eventually. "Up we need to go. The control room to the waterworks is right at the top of the building."

Round and round, up and up they went, taking step upon step upon step. Appearing along the way were various open arched exits that led onto different passageways - but these they ignored. Instead they headed right to the top, following the Professor's persistent and monotonous climb. The clanking of their feet on the steps was a continuous reminder of just how tired their legs were. It seemed as if the stairs lasted forever and would never come to an end. They did, however, finally reach the top. Everyone dropped down onto the corridor floor in relief, with legs that felt full of lead.

"You'd have thought, with their wonderful technology, that they would have invented a better way of travelling through this place," said the Professor, breathing uneasily.

"Which way now?" gasped Basil, leaning his head back on the wall with his legs sprawled out across the floor in front of him.

"I think we're high enough," the Professor replied, still catching his breath. "We just need to move on a little more towards the south side of the building."

After briefly resting, they made their way through several doors and rooms and lastly passed through a door into what seemed at first to be a great, dark open space. It was so large and vast that, when the Professor held his lantern up, its glow wasn't even strong enough to find the ceiling or the sides of the wall opposite; all they could see was an iron grating beneath their feet that was flaky and scratched with age. The room echoed with every step they took, just as if it was all made of metal.

Shining the lantern at their feet and moving the light's beam steadily further away from them, they followed the floor until they could see that they were on a steel platform. The platform seemed to be built over a high open space. From the left and right, running along the very edge of the platform, were a couple of waist high metal railings to keep anyone from falling over and into the abyss below. These railings met on the platform's edge directly in front of them and, protruding out from that section, was a narrow walkway, a bridge, which went straight ahead and across the room and away into the darkness.

"Where are we?" asked Lady Georgiana.

"I assume we are above the main engine room," replied the Professor. We're very high up and I guess that beneath us is a drop right down to the bottom floor where all of the machinery is assembled that runs the waterworks. I think what we're looking for is probably just over that bridge in front of us."

"I don't like the look of it," said Lady Georgiana.

"Nor I," added Basil.

"Well, I suppose I'll have to go first," sighed the Professor, after no-one had spoken or moved for a while. He proceeded cautiously, steadily and gradually. Step by tentative step he edged across the platform and towards the bridge. As he went, he could be heard muttering under his breath something about why on earth had he not thought to bring George along with him. "I'll signal back to you if it's safe," he added over his shoulder.

No-one argued with the Professor. They all stayed put whilst he made his way over to the narrow bridge and shone the light of his lantern along it. The bridge went right out into the darkness beyond. Very gingerly, the Professor put his foot upon it and tapped it several times. The tapping echoed and vibrated across the bridge and out into the open darkness. Then he placed his foot firmly onto the bridge's edge and, gripping tightly with one hand onto the platform's metal railings, very gently lifted his other foot off the floor and placed it onto the bridge next to the other. He wouldn't have told anyone, but he felt quite dizzy with the anticipation that the bridge might possibly give way under his weight at any moment. He inhaled a few deep breaths, seeking to fill his lungs with the courage to move forward and then, with one hand on the railings, he slowly edged on. Every footstep echoed on the metal floor. Clank, clank, clank he went, one step after the other. The three friends breathlessly watched as the Professor's figure, illuminated by the lantern, moved further and further away.

As he reached what was the bridge's centre he felt it sway slightly, or perhaps it was just his nerves making him shake and his balance oscillate. Leaning slightly over the railings, he shone his light down into the darkness to see if he could glimpse anything, but the darkness was bottomless and impenetrable. He moved on a little more and then a little more again. Eventually, after what seemed more than too long teetering over the brink of death, he arrived at the bridge's end and stepped onto another metal platform. Feeling almost elated to have reached it, he called back to the others that he was safe and proceeded to walk on. At the end of this new platform was a tall, broad door. Shining his lantern around its frame, he found the words, "Main Control Room" written above it.

"Yes!" whispered the Professor to himself, he was so tense he could hardly speak.

Turning the handle, the door creaked open to reveal a dusty and musty smelling chamber. The Professor stepped in, holding up his lantern he shone its beam up and down the walls and across the floor. In the middle of the room was a control desk with buttons, dials and other measuring instruments on it. On the opposite wall, at the bottom end of the room, were the pictures of four wheels - one large, two medium and one small.

"Finally found it," he said with a sigh and he almost wept with relief.

Chapter 13 – Spinning Wheels

After each person had cautiously crossed the bridge they all pulled up a chair and gathered around the Professor, who sat like a delighted schoolboy (almost giddy with excitement) at the control centre's main desk; busily running his eyes over the instruments, buttons and dials that surrounded him.

"Will this be loud?" Lady Georgiana asked, a tone of caution in her voice.

"Possibly," replied the Professor, in a matter-of-fact, casual way, "and if you're thinking about the city authorities hearing us, then yes that may be a problem, but the machines in the engine room are well below ground level..."

Taking a scruffy, moth-eaten booklet out from his pocket he fumbled through its dog-eared pages until he found the correct part in his notes.

"...and the waterworks is on the very edge of the city." he continued. "So, even if we are eventually heard, I assume we have a good half hour, even perhaps an hour, to get on with our business and still get out without being caught."

Handing his lantern to Basil he pointed at his book. "Shine it here," he said, pointing to the bottom right corner of the page. Then, running his finger along each line in the book, he carefully followed the instructions and began turning dials, pressing switches and pulling levers up and down. The Professor then pressed a button, causing a small screen from inside the desk to pop up with a keyboard at its front.

"Welcome to the waterworks control system," said a computer voice from the control desk. "Please enter pass code to continue."

The Professor rubbed his hands together and, glancing at the others with a hint of excitement in his eyes, typed in a code and waited.

"Code accepted," said the computer voice. "Enter secondary pass code."

He turned more pages in his book and found amongst the vast number of scrawling letters another code, which he duly typed in. After waiting a few moments, "Secondary pass code accepted," came the computer voice again. "Set up main power and system control."

A few more minutes went by with the Professor typing and turning dials.

"Why is this so complicated?" asked Lady Georgiana.

"Well, the waterworks was never designed to be turned off," replied the Professor. "What we're now doing is something that should have only been done once when it was set-up for the first time. That's why it's taken fifty of my best staff to work at this for more than a year to get it solved."

"Main power generators started," came the computer voice again.

A churning, motorised-mumbling began deep within the belly of the waterworks, as if someone had just turned on an old kettle and the water was beginning to stir. The noise gathered itself, gurgling, burbling and warbling - rising and falling, rising and falling, then rising and falling some more. Finally, it settled to become a sustained rumble - like a long drawn-out yawn. As time went by this rumble-grumble became the backdrop sound to a series of loud, lonesome moans, followed by crotchety, metallic groans.

Somewhere, coming from right back within the mountain, from where the waterworks protruded, metal began grinding upon metal, cog upon cog and components that had lain dormant for years were coming to life. These wakeup sounds echoed down to the building's very foundations; intermittently interrupted by mechanised wheezes, sneezes and coughs that sent convulsive vibrations through the walls, floors, ceilings and doors. This mechanical mansion was now rousing from her slumbers, but this current stir to consciousness showed a bad case of combustive indigestion.

The desk at which the Professor sat shook with each waking tremble. The four travellers felt their journey might be at an end, perhaps the whole trembling building would tumble down on top of them, it wasn't a pleasant experience. Suddenly, the control desk lit up, revealing a shining array of flashing buttons and twirling colours. The room's main lamps, set into and across the walls of the control room, gave a quick glimmer of light and, one by one, burst into a bright flame - emitting a steady orange glow. Everyone shielded their eyes and took a few seconds to get used to the new shiny radiance. The image on the little computer screen flickered and a computer voice said, "Commence waterworks engine start up procedure."

"Here," said the Professor to Basil, passing him the booklet. "Read these numbers out to me and I'll type them in." The Professor, after briefly slapping Scrub's fingers to stop him pressing a flashing button on the desk, began typing in the code as Basil read.

He read number after number for a couple of minutes. Finally a whirring and rumbling sound stirred from deep inside the building's engine room below. Like an overweight giant, with a rumbly upset stomach, the waterworks' engines jerked, jolted and began to move. Wheels, cogs, fan belts and chains screeched and skidded together, juddering into motion. Thud and clunk and thump and clank they went, over and over again it resounded. Thud and clunk, thump and clank, thud and clunk, thump and clank, getting faster and faster with each second that went by. The control room floor vibrated and trembled so much that at times the walls shuddered and shook.

"Are we going to be all right?" called Lady Georgiana to the Professor over the din.

"I should think so," he replied. "I assume this rough start to the engines is because they haven't been used for so many years."

The Professor typed in some more instructions from his book and the eight large main pistons on the engine room floor, which controlled the power supply to the rest of the building, jolted and juddered into action. Slowly they moved up and down, up and down, faster and faster they went, moving in unison with a smooth and graceful motion. The great turbine next to the giant pistons now worked itself into a spin, generating enough electricity for the rest of the building to function.

Now that the lights were on Scrub could see that there was a small window to the left of them on the opposite wall. He got up from the desk, walked over to it and, wiping the dirt off it with his sleeve, peered through.

"Look, Lady Pluggat," he said. "I can see the engine room."

Everyone joined him. Through the murky blur and dirty stains on the windowpane, they could see right down into the vast room below to where the main waterworks' pumps and engines were. In and amongst the numerous, immense machines, giant pistons moved up and down whilst enormous cogs continually turned. They were hard to see, as the window was so dirty, but even their blurred outlines looked impressive.

"Outside," said the Professor. "We can get a better look from the bridge."

They all stepped back onto the metal platform again and onto the iron bridge. Directly above them, three clusters of suspended spotlights shone out a dazzling and illuminating radiance, flooding the area with a brilliance so intense it was close to daylight. Shielding their eyes from the glare, they could see these lights were hung from a vast and high domed, metal ceiling, but they couldn't make out much beyond that due to the astonishing brightness. On the wall around the great circular chamber, smaller lights shone giving illumination right down to the engine room basement.

Peering over the side of the railings, they gazed down to where the colossal machines (driven by pistons, pumps and running wheels) were dotted across the great floor's expanse. It was astonishing to look at, a marvel of mechanical engineering. Their fluid, motorised movements cast an almost hypnotic spell over the group who stood absolutely still, mesmerised by what they could see. After a few more moments the sound quietened, the shuddering stopped and all that could be heard was the humming of the main engines and the clunking of the pistons and wheels. To their delighted ears it was a musical song; the chimes, clicks, clanks and clunks of a vibrant tune called 'Freedom'.

"It's amazing," said Basil. "How ever did they do it?"

"I do believe," replied the Professor, "that today we are living in the dark ages compared to our ancestors who built this. It's a technology way beyond our own, created by a people who I suspect were very much our superiors in every way; I just hope that none of it ever needs fixing."

He was just finishing his words when the domed roof above them clunked very loudly. It was so loud, they all jumped with surprise. It clunked again and slowly the round domed part of the roof began to revolve. As it moved, the clusters of suspended lights dimmed and sections of the roof opened up to reveal the blue sky above. Through these opened vents, gusts of air blustered in like wafts of rushing wind. Then, as the roof continued to rotate, the sizeable room around them was also suddenly enlarged by the wall opposite sliding open, like a giant door. Through it they saw a great archway and beyond that a long aisle; so large you could have been looking down the centre of a vast cathedral.

Along the sides of this great aisle were open doorways to more tall rooms and chambers. At the very bottom of the aisle, set high into the wall, was the great stained glass window they had seen when first viewing the waterworks from outside. The great picture of the lion, the bear and eagle brought streaming light down to the floor. With the fresh air gushing about them from above, the walls moving and the roof rotating, it was as if the waterworks were alive and could breathe at last.

"What are those down there?" said Lady Georgiana, pointing a little way down the great corridor.

Everyone looked down in the direction she was pointing. On a wall, just beyond the third great arch in that long and wide corridor, were four large wheels. The largest one was huge, almost as big as a house, the second and third half the size and the fourth much smaller. The three larger wheels were suspended just above the ground; hung and fastened to the wall on a large single pin that ran through each wheel's centre. The fourth, much smaller wheel, was hung several feet off the ground and had a small stairway built into the wall next to it for access. All four were a deep, dark crimson (red as blood) and stood out against the background of white, marbled stone that lay behind them.

"Those are the wheels that control the water supply to the waterworks," said the Professor. "Well, well, well. I never thought I would see such an incredible sight. They, my good friends, are our keys to freedom."

"Waterworks engines started and running," said the computer control system.

"We're in business," said the Professor. "Come on, time is going by."

Going back inside the control room they noticed a large hole had opened up in the ceiling at the room's centre and from it around twenty metal pipes had descended; each pipe having a monitor attached to its base. These monitors were suspended just above head height and displayed images of rooms within the waterworks. They could see luxurious offices, hallways, different parts of the engine room below, the great pipe chamber through which they had come earlier (though this was still dimly lit), storerooms, other rooms that looked like water purification chambers and many stairways and corridors. All of the rooms looked stylish and grand with leather bound chairs, silver framed windows and doorframes made of gold, like that which would be made for the residence of a wealthy king or queen. After briefly looking over them, the Professor called the team back to the control desk where he continued to work. He pointed to the desk monitor, which was now showing a picture of the four great wheels on it, one large, two medium and one small.

"Now for the wheels," said the Professor.

He touched the screen where the wheels were displayed and the images of the wheels zoomed in, giving a closer view of each one. Next to each wheel was a set of numbers which the Professor typed into the keyboard.

"Wheel one unlocked," said the computer.

"Wheel two and three unlocked," it said again, as the Professor continued to type.

He pulled up wheel four on the computer screen and typed again on his keyboard inputting number after number.

"Wheel four unlocked," came the computer's voice.

"Yes!" said the Professor, sitting back into his seat and flinging his arms up into the air. He looked briefly at each person with a genuine smile of relief on his face. "That's the mountain climbed," he continued. "Now all we have to do is sensibly descend down to the other side and we're done."

"What's next?" asked Lady Georgiana, looking on with great anticipation, but before she had finished speaking, part of the wall to their right opened up to reveal a lift shaft and within moments a lift appeared, filling the gap.

"Wheels ready for manual start," said the computer.

"And descend is just what some of you are about to do," continued the Professor, pointing at the lift.

"Descend?" said Lady Georgiana. "To where and what for?"

"Well," replied the Professor, turning over the page of the booklet that Basil was holding and pointing to four pictures of wheels on it with numbers next to them. "We just have to physically turn those wheels on the walls to let the water back in."

The other three looked at the Professor in astonishment.

"Have you seen how big they are?" said Lady Georgiana. "It would take an army to move them even an inch."

"Physics, M'lady," said the Professor, in an excited tone. "Physics and the beautiful laws thereof. Those wheels are brilliantly suspended and it won't take much to move them now they're unlocked. You'll see."

Lady Georgiana looked at Basil who simply returned her gaze with a "Don't look at me, I know nothing about this," expression.

"All I need you to do is to go down to the engine room floor and then follow my instructions as I call them out to you," said the Professor.

"You're not coming down with us?" enquired Basil.

"As much as I would love to come down with you, right now time is passing and we need to get this thing finished. I shall resist my urges and stay put. Each wheel has to be re-locked once it's in the right place," replied the Professor, "and that can only be done from this control desk. There will be plenty of time for me to walk amongst and gaze at those wonders below once the city has its water supply again."

"But how will we hear you?" said Lady Georgiana. "It's such a long way down."

"Through the phone tube system," said the Professor, pointing to a small piece of piping that stuck out from the side of the control desk. "Phone tubes were the main points of communications when the waterworks was first built. You'll find plenty of them sticking out of the walls down on the engine room floor and all along that great passageway. Just blow some air through one near the wheels and then I'll blow back through mine and we can talk."

Lady Georgiana looked very doubtful and hesitated, looking dubiously at the Professor. The Professor, however, just returned her stare with a gentle smile and glanced in the direction of the lift.

"Our freedom is awaiting us," he said.

"All right, I'll do it," said Basil, walking over to the lift.

"I'll come with you," said Lady Georgiana and followed him in.

"Can I come too?" said Scrub.

"No," replied Lady Georgiana. "You stay with the Professor. I don't want you touching anything. I'm feeling nervous enough as it is."

"Oh please can I come?" replied Scrub, walking up to her with big yearning eyes. "I won't touch anything I promise."

"Oh, very well," sighed Lady Georgiana, not in a mood to argue. "But don't touch a single thing! Do you hear?"

The lift shot down to the ground floor at a surprising speed but slowed enough at the end for a gentle stop. Lady Georgiana, Scrub and Basil got out feeling more than a little unsettled from the experience, but this was soon forgotten when they found themselves standing on a raised stage which looked across and down onto the waterworks engine room floor; it was an incredible sight. The size of the wheels, levers and pistons were much larger than they had imagined from their last vantage point on the bridge at the top of the chamber.

89

They stood quite awestruck by the room's strange dusty, rusty, metal beauty. Each set of machinery was as large as a double decker bus and had numerous wheels and cogs intertwined through it, so complex that sometimes it seemed that there were wheels within wheels and you couldn't quite tell where one began and the other ended. Turning, cranking, clinking, clanging and clanking, one cog moved another which in turn moved another and another - a giant jigsaw of chains, belts, cables, gears and mechanised components all doing their own work, but each also affecting the work of everything else around them. Their automated, rhythmic workings, like an orchestral throng, sang a symphonic anthem to the wonders of mechanisation.

Lady Georgiana found a phone tube sticking out of the wall. She blew down it and eventually the Professor's voice came through.

"I'm here," he said, in a muffled, squeaky tone.

"We're almost on the engine room floor," she replied.

"Wonderful," came the reply. "Just let me know when you reach the wheels and remind Scrub not to touch anything on the way."

A series of around thirty lamps, on long stands, stood on both edges of the stairway that ran down from the platform to the engine room floor. Every other step down had its own lamp, shining its bright light to point the way along this glitzy stair - as if you were a lone singer in a theatrical production making a grand entrance to the audience below. It was like saying a big "Welcome to the show!" and "Here's where you enter!" Scrub wanted a closer look at the lamps; he found their pathway of light going down each step fascinating, but soon Lady Georgiana's iron grip was felt on his elbow guiding him past them and on they all went.

After descending this broad stairway, they cautiously made their way towards the many humming and hissing engines and appliances. Moving amid the machines, they found themselves instinctively keeping a little distance from them. The fluid movements of the strange mechanical creature-like contraptions were accompanied by bizarre inhaling and exhaling noises – it confirmed Scrub's suspicion that these machines were actually alive and each had its own set of metal lungs and was just getting used to breathing again. The three companions, quite unnerved by these sounds, smells and movements, passed on as quickly as they could.

As they went, the floor echoed everyone's footsteps. It was made from long, thick wooden beams of polished dark brown oak and, even though a thick layer of dust had settled on the great timbers over the years, it looked very expensive. The echoes of their steps made their quality shine through and this 'footstep accompaniment' made it impossible to pretend that you were quietly passing through, hoping not to be noticed.

Under the immense archway they went, entering the great central aisle. It ran deep underground for much of the length of the building. After giving a passing glance to open plan rooms on their left and right, their attention was arrested by the grandeur of the long, majestic corridor upon which they now trod. Two lines of pure white marble pillars stood to attention along the walls on either side of the aisle, like ever watching, aged sentries. From the ground, these ancient stone custodians towered up to the roof where they became soaring arches that met each other on the high ceiling in remarkable swirling patterns, like the tangled mass of a glorious tree canopy. Their heavy beauty made the central walkway feel airy and spacious. The three companions thought themselves as small as insects as they walked beneath them. They felt that they had entered into some kind of religious, sacred space.

After a short time of walking they came upon the four wheels. A deep crimson red, they hung on the wall to the right of the aisle, each suspended on a single projecting pin through its centre. Lady Georgiana looked at Basil who blew out a long breath of air, shaking his head in disbelief at the job ahead of them. They were enormous – the largest wheel opposite them, as tall as a house. Standing with their backs to the wall, the three very small people gazed up at its grand, circular frame. The solid iron circle loomed high above them, looking very heavy and completely immovable.

Chapter 14 – Oops!

It wasn't the wheels, however, that kept their attention. They had already noticed on their short walk down the great passage that their presence was somehow being monitored, for smaller lights, embedded into the corridor walls, began to glow when they appeared next to them. These lights kept pace with their progress as they travelled along, giving that extra fine-tuned illumination to their immediate path. Behind them, once they had walked on, they turned off again. It was as if the waterworks knew where they were and was gratefully helping them along, or perhaps it was disinterested, coldly watching to keep an eye on what they were doing, you couldn't quite tell. Either way Basil, Scrub and Lady Georgiana felt a little unnerved, turning what would have been a fascinating walk into an eerie and uncanny experience.

Their attention on the wall lights and crimson wheels didn't last for long. It was abruptly interrupted by a sharp sparking noise, coming from somewhere behind them. Twirling on their heels they saw in the wall a narrow archway, an alcove, which led through to a very small chamber. From deep within this chamber, little multi-coloured lights were igniting and glowing – materialising from what seemed to be out of nowhere. Sparking on and off, these small, bright luminosities appeared and disappeared in mid-air; at the same time generating a strong electrical charge and creating an almost piercing fizzing sound. All by themselves they flickered and shimmered in the little room, hanging in a narrow space of nothingness. As their brilliance grew in intensity, they briefly lit up their immediate surroundings to reveal the floor space and four walls of the small bay. Lady Georgiana, Basil and Scrub stood motionless, watching as the tiny room came to life with glowing and shimmering colours. Perhaps it was an invitation to them to come in? Without him realising what he was doing, Scrub's legs and feet began to move him forward towards the chamber. His sudden movement was in response to a swelling urge that fountained within him to seek out and inspect the dazzling radiances. Lady Georgiana, however, put her hand out to halt his progress.

"The waterworks wants us to go in," he protested, but she shook her head.

Gradually the lights increased their brightness and intensity. Their strong static charge saturated the air, sending a tingling through the atmosphere that ran through the onlooker's fingers, clothes and bones. Within moments a sharper brilliance, representing what looked like a picture of some kind, briefly appeared amongst the fizzing lights. Then it vanished. A few seconds later it appeared again, stronger still, flashing and trying to establish itself as an image, before quickly diminishing. Reds, greens, blues, oranges, browns and yellows now materialised in and amongst the glowing aura, moving between each other, seeking to come together, trying to form a jigsaw impression of reality. Finally, as the lights stabilised and settled into place, the blurry image came into focus revealing a graphical impression of a stunning, perfect and magnificent city - a most beautiful place.

Taking a few steps closer, the three of them stood with mouths opened wide as they observed the image in amazement. They watched as the hologram began to move and change, just like a virtual guide walking them through a three dimensional image. The hologram zoomed in on the city to show one of its streets, then zoomed along that street and continued travelling down into another street and then another. The view changed from place to place, building to building and scene to scene. It quickly travelled throughout the vast metropolis running along the veins of each main road and highway. Parts of it they clearly recognised and others were difficult to make out or discern. It stopped briefly, focusing on the palace at the centre of the city. Then on it went through gardens, orchards, lawns, alongside grand buildings and mansions, gardeners' allotments, children's play areas and then away towards the outskirts of the city; passing through and amongst factories, workshops, barns and great industrial towers. They all seemed to somehow fit in with each other, making a perfectly balanced environment. The holographic film went on for just short of thirty seconds until the picture focused on the waterworks building, where it stayed for a few moments.

Whilst all of this was happening Lady Georgiana reached out to take hold of a phone tube that was sticking out of the wall. From the corner of her mouth she blew down it, her attention still very much fixed on the hologram. She wanted to say down the tube, "Professor, you need to see this," but instead the Professor's voice came back before she could speak.

"I know," he said. "One of the monitors up here has latched onto you. I've been watching you since you walked onto the engine room floor. Isn't it amazing!"

"Can you see the hologram?" Lady Georgiana asked.

"Yes," came the reply.

The image before them zoomed in on the waterworks building and went inside. Up, down and around the rooms and stairways it rocketed, flashing by the different spaces and places. It must have covered over a hundred rooms in a matter of seconds, too much to take in, only leaving the viewers hazy impressions of the contents of the grand building. To end the movie, it displayed the engine room in all its shiny finery, with the machines polished and shining bright. From there it travelled down the corridor of the great aisle to where they stood. Then it stopped, fizzed a bit again and vanished.

"What was all that about Georgie?" asked Basil, in the almost creepy stillness that followed.

"Not sure," replied Lady Georgiana, shaking her head and still looking slightly stunned. "But it was..."

"Amazing," added the Professor down the telephone tube.

"Why did it happen?" asked Basil again. "Did we do something to set it off, whatever it was?"

94

No one was quite sure about this but in a flash the little room lit up again, this time with normal lighting from within its ceiling and walls.

"Terminal one is now operational," came a computerised voice from somewhere in the room." The back wall to the little room opened up to reveal steps going up to a platform but they couldn't quite see what was on it or how big it was.

"I think you've just opened up some kind of travelling facility," came the Professor's voice. "Just by standing next to it."

"Professor, how can you see us?" Lady Georgiana finally asked, once she'd taken in a little more of what was happening around her.

"I think the monitors here feed from cameras that appear in the lights on the walls," he replied. "I seem to be able to see you wherever you go."

"No!" said Lady Georgiana to Scrub, who was just about to walk off into the room where the hologram had been. "I'm not interested in travelling any more than we have to."

Scrub frowned but knew his desire to explore wouldn't be fulfilled.

"Right," said Lady Georgiana. "Let's keep focused and get these wheels turned. Professor, what do we do?"

"Now everyone," came back the Professor's voice, spluttering out and sounding like he was speaking whilst holding his nose. "I need you to turn the largest wheel first. You should be able to see that the rim of the wheel is broad enough for a person or persons to climb into. So all I need you to do is to step inside the wheel and walk in an anti-clockwise direction, as you walk the wheel will turn. I will stop the wheel from up here by locking it in place when it has turned far enough."

After Basil and Lady Pluggat had exchanged brief nervous glances, they climbed into the rim of the wheel whilst Scrub looked on. The inside rim wasn't smooth at all but had steps cut into it like a continual stairway. Very gingerly, step upon step, they began to walk together and, as they ascended up the inner side of the wheel, it began to turn. At first they were quite hesitant of the wheel's rotation and stopped walking when it began to move, but eventually they got the hang of it and walked at a good pace so that the wheel revolved steadily. Then "clunk" it stopped.

"Right, now for the middle sized wheels," came the Professor's squeaky, muffled voice from the phone tube again.

They stepped out of the first wheel and climbed into the second. In the same way they quickly got it moving until, "clunk", it stopped.

"Excellent," came the Professor's voice again, sounding very happy, "Now for wheel three."

This, again, was done quite quickly and the confidence of the group was rising all the time.

"One of you will have to go up the small stairway that's next to wheel four and turn this one by hand", said the Professor. "Once this wheel is turned, water will be restored to the waterworks and we'll all be free!"

Basil walked over to the narrow stairway built into the wall next to wheel four and ascended the steps. With great anticipation rising within him, he took hold of the wheel and was about to turn it.

"Wait!" said Lady Georgiana, cutting in. "This is quite safe, Professor, isn't it? I mean, you have looked at all of the possible things that could happen from turning these wheels?"

The Professor took a few moments before answering her.

"I'm quite confident that all will be well M'lady," he eventually replied. "My team have worked really hard on this for over a year now in order to get this right. It's true that we've never tried this before and flooding, I suppose, is a possibility but I think that it's worth the risk don't you? Otherwise we'll be stuck in this mess with Mr E ruling over us forever."

"Well," said Lady Georgiana, still unsure of what they were about to do. She paused, thinking things through. "Oh very well," she said, still not convinced that their actions were either sensible or correct. "Basil, go on."

Basil took hold of the last and smallest wheel to turn it, but to his surprise, it seemed quite stuck. He tugged at its outer rim several times to get it to budge, but it still wouldn't move.

"I can't seem to shift it," he said.

"Professor, the wheel is stuck," called Lady Georgiana down the phone pipe.

Basil continued to try and try again, but to no avail.

"Put all your weight onto it," said the Professor. From viewing Basil's efforts on the monitors up in the control room, he thought Basil wasn't doing such a good job.

"I've been doing just that," came Basil's frustrated and exhausted reply.

"I'm sorry Professor," said Lady Georgiana, once Basil had given in. "It just won't budge."

After a few moments of silence the Professor's voice came out of the pipe again.

"All right, I think I have a solution. I'm going to take off the secondary brake system. It may be that the wheel has frozen onto it over the years and this is causing it to stick. I will not be able to stop the wheel turning from up here as I did the first three wheels though, so just listen out for my voice to tell you when to stop turning. The wheel has to complete five full rotations. Ok?"

Lady Georgiana looked at Basil who nodded his head in agreement.

"Ok, that sounds fine," said Lady Georgiana. "We'll count the number of turns and I'll pass on your message to stop."

Basil and Lady Georgiana heard a clunk from somewhere behind the wall and the Professor's voice boomed out from the pipe, "You're clear to turn the wheel."

Basil took hold of the wheel again, but after trying and trying, it still wouldn't turn. He pulled on it, rattled it, tugged it from left to right, but still to no avail. In the end, out of sheer frustration and quite out of breath, he put his foot onto the bottom rim, heaved himself up onto the wheel, put his knees between its spokes and hung his fat belly onto its left edge with all his weight, trying to rock it into an anti-clockwise motion.

"I'm not sure that's a good idea," commented Lady Georgiana.

"It's very tight," said Basil, "and I don't think that it is going to..." but before he could say any more the wheel suddenly gave way and spun. Not expecting this sudden jerk and quick rotation, Basil fell off the wheel's edge and went tumbling back down the stairs. Behind him, energised by the pressure from the weight of Basil's fat tummy, the wheel spun round and round and round and round.

"No!" called the Professor down the phone tube. "Stop it spinning!" but it was too late.

Chapter 15 – The Big Red Button

Lady Georgiana wanted to run up the stairs, catch hold of the wheel and stop it but Basil's sprawling body blocked the way. It took her more than a few seconds to navigate the gaps between his flapping arms and legs so she could step onto the stairs. Then up she quickly ascended to stop the wheel's motion. She grabbed the edge of the wheel's rim to pull it to a halt but was surprised by the strength of its rotation, which immediately took her arm with it. Briefly, for a terrible moment, it lifted her right off her feet and into the air. Moments later, however, it stopped. Dropping to the ground, Lady Georgiana walked to the edge of the stairs and stared down at Basil, not quite knowing what to say. Basil, still a crumpled mess of jumbled arms and legs, rolled himself over onto his back. Still dazed from his tumble, he lifted his head slightly and helplessly returned her stare.

"Oh well done!" came the Professor's voice, sounding very annoyed. "How many times did that go around?"

"I don't know," said Basil gathering himself, looking both flustered and embarrassed. "It all happened so fast."

"Now what are we to do?" asked Lady Georgiana.

"Well, we have to be correct with the number of turns," said the Professor. "Who knows what could happen if we get it wrong."

"Well I don't know how many times it turned," said Basil, a little humiliated. "It just suddenly gave way and spun without any warning. How was I to know that it would do that?"

"Now Basil," said Lady Georgiana, walking down the steps and helping him to his feet. "Don't get upset. It wasn't your fault."

"But what are we to do now?" said the Professor. "We can't just leave it as it is."

"No, I don't think that we can," said Lady Georgiana. "But how many times the wheel turned, I don't know."

"It has turned fourteen times," said Scrub, confidently.

"Fourteen times?" said the Professor. "How do you know?"

"I was counting," said Scrub.

"Yes I'm sure you were Scrub," said Lady Georgiana, glancing in Scrub's direction. "Now please be quiet, this is important."

"But it did M'lady," said Scrub. "It went round fourteen times it did. I was counting."

"Scrub, no one was counting because the wheel moved too fast for any of us to see," said Lady Georgiana. "Now please be quiet."

"Well, how many times shall I turn it back?" said Basil.

"How would I know that?" said the Professor. "You were the one who was spinning it round and round".

"I wasn't spinning it round and round," said Basil defensively. "I was simply trying to turn it."

"The wheel went round fourteen times," said Scrub again.

"I haven't got a clue," said the Professor sharply. "It's only months of hard work completely wasted now, isn't it it!"

"It wasn't my fault," said Basil.

"The wheel went around fourteen times," said Scrub again, talking to himself.

"Well, I don't know whose fault it is if it's not yours," said the Professor. "You were the only one spinning it."

"I was not spinning it!" said Basil, getting very annoyed. "It was stuck, I took your advice to put my weight onto it, it suddenly moved; it was all an accident!"

"Yes, I'm sure it was," replied the Professor, sarcastically.

"Now that's enough!" said Lady Georgiana, calling down the phone tube. "Professor you are not being very helpful and I cannot see how this problem could have been avoided. Now, we must decide sensibly, with clear heads, what to do next."

"Well it definitely hasn't turned five times," said Basil, "but how many more times it turned and which way to turn it now I don't know."

"Me neither," said the Professor.

"Nor I," said Lady Georgiana.

"The wheel went round fourteen times," said Scrub again, sounding more and more sure of himself. "I was counting".

"Oh Scrub," said Lady Georgiana in an exasperated tone, "do shut up!"

"Well we haven't got anything else to go on M'lady," said Basil. "Scrub seems to be the only one of us who has an opinion on it."

"That doesn't bring me any comfort at all," said Lady Georgiana. "Knowing Scrub's basic grasp of maths I'd rather trust a monkey."

"Thank you, M'lady," said Scrub.

"That wasn't a compliment!" she replied.

"I still say that we haven't got anything else to go on," said Basil. "Who knows, he may be right. It may have turned fourteen times."

"It may have turned forty times for all we know," the Professor added cynically.

"Oh do be serious Professor!" said Lady Georgiana sharply.

"Well you might as well listen to Scrub as listen to anyone in this case," came the Professor's tired voice again. "I haven't a clue what to make of it. Turn it back nine times if you like. As far as I'm concerned we'll never get it right now."

Everyone was quiet as they thought about the matter.

"It definitely went round fourteen times," said Scrub. "I was counting."

"Oh, do as he says," said the Professor. "Turn the wheel back nine times and have done with it."

"What do you think Basil?" asked Lady Georgiana.

"I don't think that we have any option but to listen to Scrub," said Basil. "I'm for turning it back too."

"Very well," said Lady Georgiana, in a dispirited tone. "I haven't a clue either so turning it back it will have to be."

Scrub looked very pleased that they had taken his advice.

Basil took hold of the wheel and turned it back nine full rotations so that, as far as they could tell, the wheel had now turned five times.

"And what now?" said Scrub.

Back in the control room the Professor leaned across the main desk and turned a dial. All four wheels on the monitor screen lit up. Then a large red button on the edge of the desk suddenly glowed and flickered brightly.

"All I do is press this button," said the Professor down the phone tube, "and the water valves will open to flood the pipes in the main chamber and everything will start working again."

Scrub crossed his fingers whilst an agitated Lady Georgiana cast an unsure glance at Basil. In response he walked over to stand by her side. Their moment of truth seemed to be coming to a crescendo of fulfilment.

"In the fullness of time Georgie," Basil whispered from the corner of his mouth. Lady Georgiana gave him a brief, weak smile in return.

The Professor looked at the button he was about to press and hesitated, surprised by his indecision and delay. Gently resting his finger on the bright, shining circle, he swallowed and felt the responsibility of what he was about to do. One press and that would be it, no going back. What would happen, he didn't quite know. Freedom or disaster? Would it work or would they all die? He glanced across the room, scanning up and down the monitor screens that displayed the different rooms in the waterworks. Despite all his scientific training and years of experience, he knew that he was completely out of his depth. This living machine that he was about to stir into action was beyond him. Was he about to set free a tamed beast or unleash a monster?

"You're a fool," he said to himself. But, despite his reservations, he moved his finger into an upright position so that it pointed straight down onto the illuminated button. He had been so careful for so many years and nothing had come from it. Perhaps taking a risk, throwing caution to the wind, giving it a go no matter what the cost, was the only answer to their problems now – but no matter how many times he tried to tell himself this, he still couldn't quite detach himself from the enormity of the situation. So, gritting his teeth, breathing in and closing his eyes (as if this somehow meant he wouldn't be a witness to his own actions) he leant forward so that his chest almost rested on the desk.

"In the fullness of time..." he said to himself, trying to provide an excuse for his recklessness.

Then, with a very dry mouth, he forced his finger downwards. The button flattened and the Professor quickly took his finger away; jumping back into his seat as if he'd received an electric shock.

"Valves opening," the computer voice said.

A low groan, almost a growl, came from somewhere behind where the wheels were. Clunk, ker-clank it finally went. The reverberating sound travelled down the walls of the waterworks and echoed on through the corridors nearby. It repeated and repeated off into the distance and back up into the mountain itself. Lady Georgiana thought it was like the final kiss to awaken their sleeping beauty, their stunning and charming princess who was the life and soul of the party; the one to whom everyone looked for guidance, comfort and stability. Like any fairy-tale princess, she would make everything right in the end, but this old girl had slept for a long time. Had they awoken the maiden of their dreams or, as Lady Georgiana actually felt in her gut, had they unleashed a damsel, so distressed, that in turn she would unleash a nightmare? Time would tell and until then there was just a deafening quietness in the heavy air.

"And now we wait," called the Professor's voice down the phone tube.

"Wait for what?" said Scrub.

"The water," said Lady Georgiana, taking in a deep breath.

"Oh," said Scrub.

Chapter 16 – Juddering Pipes!

The three of them stood in the long corridor for nearly ten minutes whilst in the control room the Professor twiddled his thumbs and tapped his feet together as he sat back in his chair. Time slowly ticked by but not a trickle or splash of water was to be heard. Basil looked at Lady Georgiana who in turn returned his stare. More time went by and still nothing happened. Basil began to pace up and down the great aisle, trying to hide his impatience and the Professor folded his arms again and took to walking in between the furniture in the control room. Lady Georgiana continually glanced back at the wheels on the wall, listening for signs of something happening, whilst Scrub picked at something in his ear.

Eventually the Professor typed again on the keyboard to check the codes he had entered but after about ten more minutes of checking he said, "I've checked all my codes again and they're all correct."

They waited for another ten minutes but time was passing by and the Professor's window of 'half an hour to an hour' before the city authorities could possibly turn up was already nearly gone. More time went by with the Professor checking his pocket watch and going over his calculations and numbers. He fumbled through his booklet, looking over every procedure that his team had written down and finally sat back in his chair. With a look of exasperation he spoke into the phone tube, "We must be missing something, but to be honest, I don't know what."

Silence settled in the hearts of the company of four, who felt helpless to do any more when surrounded by such great engineering. Lady Georgiana had, for a few moments, allowed herself to feel that they were finally on the very edge of success and it was the height of frustration not knowing what now eluded them.

"I'm sorry Georgie," said Basil turning to Lady Georgiana. "Time seems to be up and it looks like nothing is going to happen today. I don't think we can risk being here for much longer. Perhaps the water just simply isn't around anymore or we need to do more work and come back again another time. At least we know that the waterworks is working."

"Back to the drawing board," came the Professor's voice down the tube with a sigh, "and my fifty brain box helpers sweated it out for over a year to get us this far. Perhaps, as Basil says, we can come back and try this all again in a few weeks or months. Anyway without knowing exactly where the last wheel has been turned to, we can't guarantee any success at all!"

Lady Georgiana looked down at her feet, soberly accepting the fact that they had, for the present, failed. They had come so far and seen so much. It seemed to go against every inclination of her heart to just give up. She also hated the long list of failures and mistakes that the resistance had made over the last few years and hadn't wanted to add another blunder to it.

"Wait," she said, feeling a flash of inspiration surging through her, "couldn't we just turn the fourth wheel back to where it was before we started and then turn it from the beginning again?"

"Good idea," said the Professor, a little startled at their corporate stupidity in not thinking of this earlier. "Basil, do something useful and turn that wheel back."

"How far back?" said Basil.

"Just back to the start," said the Professor.

"And how do we know where the beginning bit is?" said Basil. "How do we know if any of these wheels were at the correct starting point when we first turned them?"

At these words everyone was taken by surprise, even Basil himself, who hadn't quite realised what he had said until the words came out of his mouth. All stood still, suddenly realising the magnitude of Basil's statement.

"Oh dear," said the Professor. "I don't think that we took that into account when we started this project."

"Right!" said Lady Georgiana angrily, "let's get back outside before we are missed and get into trouble for being here in the first place. What a waste of time this has been! Professor, get ready to turn all of this off, we're coming back up in the lift."

"We don't need to turn it off," he replied. "It all goes into one of those low power modes after an hour anyway; one of those energy saving things invented years ago."

Lady Georgiana turned, walked back up the aisle and across the main engine room floor with Basil and Scrub finding it difficult to keep up with her quick pace. They entered the lift again and soon found themselves in the main control chamber. Then she led them through the door they'd come in, across the bridge and walked through the different rooms and corridors until they eventually came to the long stairs.

Down to the bottom they went with their feet clanking on every metal step. Through the long corridor, the pool chamber, the square room with the cylindrical containers and along the last corridor until they reached the main pipe chamber again - from which they had first entered the waterworks. The Professor followed at the back, feeling particularly bad about the whole episode. This was the second time in one week that he had failed and it was difficult for him to swallow.

"Walk in single file," said Lady Georgiana, when they began to edge slowly around the perimeter of the main waterworks pipe chamber. For some reason, the lighting was still not working too well in this last part of the waterworks, despite the engine room coming to life. On they went, one behind the other, going cautiously and making sure each step taken was safe. They stopped when they reached a darker area of the room, passing the Professor's miniature lantern up the line to Lady Georgiana. She held it aloft and started moving again but suddenly she stopped and stood motionless.

"What's the matter?" asked the Professor.

"Shh," she replied.

One of the pipes on the wall nearby trembled and shook. Then, just as quickly, it became still again.

"What was that?" she said.

"Not sure," said Basil.

They listened intently in the silence.

Then judder, judder, judder, the pipe rattled again.

Lady Pluggat reached out and tentatively touched the pipe with the tip of her finger. She then tried to shake it, but it was difficult to move.

"What's happening?" she said. "What made it do that?"

She shone the light of the lantern above their heads over the piping, but they were all still and nothing was moving. Everyone stood holding their breath, listening intently and casting their eyes over the spaghetti tangle of tubing that surrounded them. Moments more went by and then, judder, judder, judder, went another pipe somewhere high up above them.

Splosh! A jet of muddy water shot out of a pipe on the far wall and spilled onto the floor, dripping its muddy brown liquid into the fresh puddle beneath it. The party of four glanced at each other, a little lost as to what to say. More silence followed for a few seconds and then, "I can hear something," said Lady Georgiana.

"You can?" asked Basil.

"Yes. Can't you?" she replied. "It's a kind of dull, clunking sound."

They all stood listening and then - yes, there was a faint repeated clunking noise that was getting louder and louder. On and on it went like a ticking clock.

"Yes I believe I can hear it too Georgie. I believe I can," said Basil.

"I wonder what it is?" said Lady Georgiana. "Professor, do you think that..."

"It's getting louder," interrupted Scrub "And I don't like it."

There was a pause for an instant as they stood there listening. Clunk, clunk, clunk, clunkety clunk, it went. Then judder, judder, judder, as one of the main pipes at the top of the room shook and vibrated, scattering bits of rust and dust down onto the floor beneath. Covering their eyes from the dust cloud and dirt that fell, they hastily held handkerchiefs to their noses to breathe. Then silence. Nothing moved. All was quiet. Not a sound but the drip, drip, dripping from a pipe somewhere in the room. Silence was followed by more silence as Lady Georgiana shone the lamp up and down and across the chamber. Everyone stood motionless, listening and waiting, but for what, nobody was quite sure.

As the dust finally settled the sound returned again. Clunk, clunk, clunk, clunk, it continued until judder, judder, judder went the pipe again. Whoosh went the sound of water rushing through another pipe on the far wall. Then, one by one, pipes began to rattle and shake together with more sounds of whoosh, whoosh as water sped from pipe to pipe. Then another whoosh and a swish, as water filled the pipes throughout the room.

"Yes," said the Professor eventually, with a smile slowly appearing on his face, looking both excited and relieved.

"Yes?" enquired Lady Georgiana, in a questioning tone. "Yes, what?"

"Well, it could be that the wheels we turned are having a delayed reaction," he replied. "Maybe the water is coming in after all."

Scrub still wasn't happy so he edged his way out of the chamber, back under the archway they had just come through and stood listening from the safety of the corridor.

"Do you really think so?" said Lady Georgiana, glancing hopefully at the Professor and shining the lantern this way and that, across and around the four walls.

"Yes," said the Professor, as he listened some more. "In fact, I'm quite sure of it. That is definitely the sound of water moving in the system."

"Then why are the pipes rattling?" called Scrub, from the corridor.

"Oh that's just the air moving out of the way for the water to come down," replied the Professor.

To everyone's relief the lights in the room suddenly flickered and came on, first one cluster on their right, then another in the middle and then the rest, illuminating everything. Now they could see clearly, the magnificence of the room, its complicated piping structure, took their breath away.

"Oh," said Basil with great delight, "simply wonderful! This means we've done it, doesn't it?"

"I think it does," replied Lady Georgiana, in an 'I can't quite believe this,' faded voice.

Now pipe after pipe seemed to move slightly as water ran through them. They could hear its sound rushing, gushing and following its course. Up and down and around the sound went. Relief poured its healing balm into the hearts of the three onlookers who felt they were in the very best place in the world.

"No more Mr E. No more lotions! We've done it!" cried Basil when he couldn't contain himself any more.

"Yes, I believe we have," said the Professor laughing as he spoke. "Isn't that rattling of pipes the most beautiful sound you've ever heard? Water, water is coming back into our city."

"I can have a bath," said Lady Georgiana, relishing the thought.

"I can have a proper shave," said Basil, scratching at his beard.

"This is it," said the Professor, "the turning point in our city's history. What we can now hear is the sound of freedom. Freedom to the city!" he shouted at the top of his voice.

The three of them stood in the room staring at the pipes as they continued rattling away. Cheers went up from the small band of triumphal singers. "Freedom," they all began to sing out. "Freedom!"

"Yes, I think you're right Professor," said Lady Georgiana, breathing out a sigh of relief once they'd run out of breath from yelling. She passed the lantern back to the Professor and gave him a big smile.

"I know I'm right," replied the Professor, putting the little lantern back into his jacket pocket. "All we need do now is turn on the pipes that run through and under the city and there will be water restored to everyone's homes.

"How wonderful," said Lady Georgiana, a little stunned by the quick turnaround of their fortunes. "And to think that just the four of us here, I mean that just by ourselves in such a short time, well it's amazing that we've been able to, we've been able to..." but just then she stopped. "It's gone all quiet," she said.

Everything had stopped. No rattling, no whooshing, all was quiet and still. Not a sound but the drip, drip, dripping of water from some of the more rusted pipes.

"Is that it?" said Basil. "Is the water back in the system now?"

They waited in silence not quite knowing what to expect. Scrub was still standing back in the corridor looking uneasy. Deep down in his gut he had an unshakeable feeling that something was very wrong.

A few more seconds went by and in the distance came the sound of a deep rumble, as if the waterworks itself had eaten a bad meal and was ready to eject something unpleasant from its system. Then there came a long and almost painful whine of a strong surge of air. Bursting through the four large central pipes that ran down the middle of the chamber, it came shrieking and screeching down them; its noise bouncing and echoing off every corner of the room. It was so loud that they all had to put their fingers in their ears, grimacing at the terrible racket.

It whined, yowled and howled from wall to wall and ceiling to floor. Judder, judder, judder the pipes went again. Each and every pipe in the room, both large and small, began to more than just shake, they trembled violently. Then, one after another, some of the larger pipes burst high up across the room spraying and showering the whole area with water. Rattle, rattle, judder, judder, every pipe and tube in the room jittered and jolted. Suddenly it all stopped and once again, there was nothing but stillness and silence.

Lady Georgiana motioned to the other two to move back out of the room and to stand in the corridor with Scrub.

"I don't like the sound of this," she said, glancing at the Professor.

"Me neither," said Basil.

The Professor said nothing.

In the distance, another sound began. It was the sound of a deep rumble which then turned into a grumble that eventually moaned, howled and growled. It rose and fell in crescendos and continued to do this over and over again (like the grumbling bellyaches of a persistent upset tummy). Then it all changed, quietly at first but steadily growing. A whooshing and swishing that turned into a collective sloshing and eventually into the sound of a torrential roar; a roar that can only be accounted for by the presence of lots and lots and lots of gathered, rushing waters.

"Oh no," said the Professor, glancing up, down, not quite knowing what to do or where to put himself.

"Oh no what?" said Lady Georgiana, with alarm written across her face. "What do you mean, oh no?"

"I mean – well just, oh no, that doesn't sound too good," he replied, more to himself than to anyone else. "It sounds," he said. "Oh dear. Sounds like…"

"Like what?" said Lady Georgiana, not really wanting an answer.

"Like we'd better run Georgie," said Basil.

"Run?" said Lady Georgiana.

"Yes M'lady, run," said the Professor. "The water's coming and I think that there is a rather strong possibility that we're in for a little bit of a flood. I think that, in the interests of our own personal safety, the best thing to do in this situation is for us to run. Run!" he shouted, and run they did.

Chapter 17 – The Flood That Engulfed Me

Back down the corridor they sped, but they hadn't taken more than ten steps when, BOOM! the ceiling and part of the back wall of the great pipe chamber behind them collapsed under the weight of the oncoming flood. It burst through carrying a deluge of water along with some very large metal gears, cylinders and piston rods that had been carried by the torrent from somewhere back up in the mountain. Down came the chamber's pipes, clanging and clattering onto the floor. Then crash, the deluge of water, aided by the metal objects that it transported, plummeted straight through the room's wooden floorboards, pouring and spewing itself into the bunker beneath.

Lady Georgiana, the Professor, Basil and Scrub, having been knocked over by the shock waves sent by the crashing flood, scrambled back onto their feet. Looking back they could see the torrent of water still gushing in from deep within the mountain. Within moments the basement beneath the main water pipe chamber had filled and was now spilling over back into the room. The water sploshed and frothed, churning its way across what remained of the chamber's wooden floor. It quickly turned into a guzzling, consuming river that leapt towards them, rushing around their ankles and feet and carrying on down the corridor.

Splashing their way down the icy-cold, watery path they finally reached the door to the next room, but by that time they were already wading ankle deep in the river. The door opened easily and the water spilled in with them. In-between the great metal cylinders they dashed, pelting across the floor at top speed, trying to get ahead of the tide. Opening the door to the pool chamber they expected to find some relief from the flood but, to their horror, saw that the metal balcony on which they were to stand was already an inch under water.

The centre of the pool that they had bathed in earlier had turned into a giant fountain and was bubbling up to fill the chamber. As they had nowhere else to go they stepped onto the balcony, closed the door behind them against the flood, and pulled themselves along by holding onto the balcony's metal railing. It quickly became slow going as the water rose about them, swelling against their legs and dragging them in its general circular flow as it sloshed its route around the room.

When they finally reached the bottom door, the water was almost waist high. Fortunately for them the door to the next corridor opened out from the room they were in, so they could easily step through it and get out of the chamber. Unfortunately for them, wherever they went, the flood water followed. They quickly found themselves swept along the passageway on the crest of a wave. Only when they were a good distance down the corridor, with limbs all a tangle on the floor, did the water finally stop carrying them. From there they shakily picked themselves up and proceeded as best they could towards the spiral stairs. As they ran they caught glimpses of the flood filling the rooms on either side of the corridor. Within what felt like only seconds, the water level rose and sloshed against the tops of the windows.

"If just one of those panes of glass gives way we're done for," reasoned the Professor, but he didn't articulate this thought.

BOOM! A noise from far back in the waterworks shook the building. The sound reverberated through the whole structure. Something big had given way. Seconds later the wall to the pool chamber behind them quaked, impacted by something from the other side. Whatever it was that used to deliver the water from back up in the mountain, it was now broken and bits of it, large bits of it, were tumbling into the waterworks. Within moments a sizeable crack appeared in the floor at the top of the corridor and split the passageway from top to bottom, right under the feet of the running party. Lady Georgiana felt the strength of the tremor as the crack tore open the ground beneath her feet. She glanced back for an instant to make sure that Basil and Scrub were still standing. Stumbling, staggering and slipping, they all did their best to sprint towards the stairway ahead of them; despite being knocked from side to side by the sudden judders brought on by more great thuds, crashes and bangs that shuddered the building.

To their right the corridor windows cracked and splintered as wall after wall of the adjacent rooms on that side of the corridor suddenly collapsed. A tumbling and bouncing metal cog of substantial size bashed and ploughed its way through them and then continued to roll on and on through wall upon wall, followed by other metal objects of various sizes. Jets of spray shot out into the corridor as the windows began to give way. The Professor, Lady Georgiana, Scrub and Basil found their faces sprayed and their feet swamped with the gushing water. Running turned

109

into stumbling and stumbling into tumbling. Behind them the pool chamber wall bulged, buckled and finally fell apart, sending a deluge down the passageway; it burst towards them, a mass of surging water that even a surfer would be terrified to ride out.

The four companions hurled themselves onto the winding stairway and began climbing up as fast as their legs would go. Up and up they went, trying to ignore the jerks and shudders as waves and waves of water hit the bottom of the stairs.

"Keep going," shouted the Professor, when he saw everyone stop to look down. "This stairway may not hold for much longer."

They all began to climb and climb; hearts pounded, feet were tired, legs throbbed and felt like giant weights as they mentally pounded their way up each step. The water below battered and swirled its way down every part of the corridor and, when there wasn't anywhere else for it to go, began to climb higher and higher, chasing up the stairs behind them.

"Faster," shouted the Professor, as everyone began to slow down from tiredness. "Faster I say. It's catching up with us. Keep on going," he said. "Keep on going or we're all done for!"

Bringing up the rear Basil felt his heart would pop. He hadn't exercised like this in years. His breathing was erratic and his mouth felt full of hot liquid, as if he was swallowing thick, heated medicine that no amount of sugar would make palatable. He felt the agony of every step. Between gasps for air he forced his hands, by sheer will power, to grab onto the railings to give a hefty pull each time his legs were required to take him up another step on the never ending stair. Tiredness rippled through his bones, but fear pushed him on.

The water pursued them up every step, their only relief came each time they passed a new level where there would be an open archway, which exited onto other walkways and rooms. These would take a little time to fill before the flood could again begin its chase up the stairwell after them.

Somehow, their pain-filled, aching limbs kept up the pace and eventually they reached the top of the stair. Using the hand railings to pull themselves off the steps, they dropped, out of breath, onto the passage floor; heads down between their legs until their dizziness subsided. The very frothy water, stale and pongy smelling, continued to rush up after them, eating up each step as it went. They eventually struggled to their feet and stumbled down to the next doorway. After opening it, they muddled through, closing the door behind them before collapsing again onto the floor with exhaustion.

"That flimsy woodworm-ridden door won't hold for long," said Basil, holding his chest in pain as he tried to steady his breathing. "We've got to keep on moving."

"I agree," said the Professor.

"There must be an emergency exit somewhere," gasped Lady Georgiana. "Do we know where it is?"

"Not sure," said the Professor. "We need to get back to the control room. Perhaps there we can find some directions or maps of the waterworks that we can pull up on the monitor."

"That doesn't sound very promising," Lady Georgiana replied.

The door that they had just come through was already leaking water from the flood that lay behind it. Stumbling and floundering down the passage, they went through the next door and closed that too. Then they went through to the next door, the next and the next - closing each one as they passed through. A slight sense of relief arose in their hearts when they came to the iron bridge. Onto it they scrambled and crossed as quickly as their tired legs could carry them. The bridge's clanking noise under their feet and its cold railings almost seemed friendly as they walked on. Now, at least there was a huge gap between them and the flood. Their hearts melted, however, when they entered the control room to see that the computer monitor had the words "Error, error, error," flashing on it and the computer's voice rang out, "System failure, system failure."

"Oh that's just great!" said the Professor sarcastically.

"What are we going to do now?" said Lady Georgiana.

Suddenly there was a second and then a third large BOOM! as something, perhaps another wall, gave way towards the back of the building.

"We haven't got much time," said Lady Georgiana. "We need to do something."

The Professor began typing on the keyboard to ask the computer for a map of the waterworks but it simply continued to say, "System failure, system failure." He tried again and finally got the computer back online.

"What are we to do?" asked Lady Georgiana.

"I suppose we could turn back the wheels," replied the Professor, without thinking through the stupidity of what he was saying. "That might help us," he added.

"You suppose!" said Lady Georgiana. "Didn't anyone have a plan of escape if this mission went wrong?"

No one answered her.

The door to the lift opened and Basil stepped in. "Just tell me what to do Professor," he said, and then the door closed.

"No wait!" called Lady Georgiana, but he was gone.

Down went the lift, clunking open as it came to rest at the bottom. Basil wobbled uneasily on his legs as he made his way down the platform stairs and staggered across the engine room floor as fast as he dared without risking a fall. He stopped where the wheels were in the great aisle and, blowing through a nearby phone tube, he called, "Professor. Which wheel do I turn first?"

"It doesn't matter," came the reply. "I've got back into the computer and unlocked them so just turn them all off."

Basil reasoned that the largest and the smallest wheels may possibly be the most important so he spun the small wheel back as quickly as he could to where he thought it was before and then climbed into the largest wheel to walk it back into its original position. As he was doing so, the lift door opened and out stepped Lady Georgiana. She ran down the steps and across the main engine room floor.

"Look Professor!" cried Scrub, back up in the control room. He was peering at one of the monitors above their heads. "Look," he cried out excitedly.

The monitor showed a surging, swirling mass of water rushing through the numerous archways that ran around the engine room's walls. Around the room the flood went, swamping the engines and pistons in its path. Down on the engine room floor Lady Georgiana caught sight of the flood as she ran. It flowed in behind her, completely cutting off her path back to the lift. She sprinted down the great aisle towards the wheels. "Basil!" she screamed, with the flood gathering pace behind her. To avoid being swept away herself, she ducked into the alcove where the hologram had been and up the steep steps at the room's rear, towards the raised platform they had seen earlier.

Basil looked over his shoulder to see the surge of water coming down the aisle. It rushed up towards him, went gushing past him and hit the underside of the suspended wheel that he was standing in. The wheel began to rotate. All Basil could do, to stay on his feet, was to turn to face the oncoming river and scamper inside the wheel's rim, running as fast as he could.

"Look," said Scrub to the Professor again, as he gazed at a monitor that was firmly fixed on Basil and his plight. "Look there! Basil looks just like my fat hamster, Horace," he said with a grin. "Horace does that you know. He goes round on his wheel too. He goes round and round and round just like Basil is doing now. Horace is fat and so is Basil. Funny, don't you think?"

But, for some reason unknown to Scrub, the Professor wasn't amused. He stood back by the control desk, examining the different monitors in front of him. A cold shiver went through him, like a lazy wind, as he watched on the different screens the numerous staircases, corridors, offices, hallways, store rooms and chambers all filling with the flooding water.

"Oh dear," he said to himself.

"Help!" cried Basil, as he stumbled, jumped and ran inside the rim of the great wheel to keep himself from toppling over.

The water continued to pour into the aisle and rose until Basil found his feet wet as he splashed and sploshed his way on his circular treadmill. Then, from down the other end of the great passageway, where the grand stained glass window shone, came the noise of an immense and terrible swell. Out it came; a wall of water powered by many streams all coming together from adjacent walkways. Back up the great aisle it rushed, eating up the tide that was against it and pressing on towards the engine room.

Furniture of various kinds floated in its wake, the legs of tables, chairs and cabinets appeared and then disappeared in the strong current, bobbing and twirling about amongst the swirling, foamy waves. Basil glanced over his shoulder at the mass of water that surged towards him. He could see that very soon he would be swept away. Instinctively, he leapt up and grasped hold of one of the great wheel's spokes that was just above his head. Raising his knees up to his chest as best he could, he let the wheel's rotation take him high up and away from the approaching flood.

This new water surge hit the underside of the wheel, causing it to halt its steady spin. The great iron, circular frame shuddered with the impact and then changed direction, being pushed by the much stronger flow of the current now heading towards the engine room. This sudden change of rotation, however, also bent and buckled the pin on which the wheel was suspended. The bottom edge of the wheel crashed into the side of the waterworks' wall and slowly, with Basil's dangling weight not helping, the wheel began to tip over under the strain.

As the wheel moved away from the wall, Basil found himself swaying in the air over the flood. His hands instinctively clamped their white knuckled grip onto the wheel's spoke whilst his legs kicked from side to side, conveying the panic that was in him. He knew, however, that the great circular frame from which he hung would soon topple over and crush him, if he didn't get off. Having nothing to lose, he took a deep breath and made his escape by just letting go. As he did so, the large pin that ran through the wheel's middle finally gave way. The wheel dropped off its anchor point and swayed, wobbling and wavering in the surging water. Then, after oscillating on its edge for a few seconds like the last few rotations of a spinning penny, it finally flopped onto its face and was seen no more, swallowed up by its new watery grave.

Basil had aimed his sudden fall at a table he'd seen bobbing towards him in the swell and, to his immediate relief, he found that his aim was accurate enough, landing almost squarely upon it. However, his relief was only momentary. His added weight drove the table right under the water and he quickly found that wherever the table went, he followed. Down and out of sight it disappeared - and so did Basil.

Chapter 18 – As Dark As Night

Lady Georgiana found herself stranded near the top of the steps at the back of the room into which she had fled from the oncoming flood. She had initially watched the swell of water nearly engulf her, knocking her over on the stair with a wave that lashed at her legs, causing her to stumble and fall. But with so many open side rooms providing space on the main corridor for the flood to fill, the water level soon temporarily dropped again and she was safe for the moment. Driven by her concern for Basil's safety, she momentarily ventured back into the water and waded out towards the waterworks' main corridor. Initially she went in up to her knees and then deeper still as she crept towards the edge of the room to try and peer out into the flooded aisle. She soon found that she couldn't get very far, however, without being in danger herself. So, after calling his name until her voice was strained, she was forced to retreat back to the stairs once more as the water level began to rise again.

If Lady Georgiana had been able to look into the aisle, she would have seen Basil pop up again, holding onto a table leg as he shot forward in the current. He joined in with the swirling river which swept into the main engine room where the water bounced and sloshed its current into every available space. Basil went with it, pinning his chest against the side of the table and wrapping his arms down the table's sides; this helped cushion the blows when it bumped into something. He clung on for dear life. Together, he and his wooden friend, swirled in, out, and amongst the great machines.

Bump, bash, crash, thump, the table repeatedly found itself crunched as it hit the different objects in its path. Basil felt bruised and numb from the knocks, his situation highly dangerous. He reasoned it would only take one occasion for him to be found between an engine room machine and the table and he would be immediately crushed. So he kicked his legs and tried to guide the table as best he could, though he knew that his efforts would have little effect.

A few minutes later Basil saw his opportunity for freedom when the current briefly brought the table near the partially submerged great platform steps that they had descended when first entering this room. As he swept by, he launched himself towards the stairs, kicking his fat, short legs as fast as they would go and scrambling with his arms. He tried to pull himself free from the current but, to his great distress, found that the strength of the river was more difficult to push through than he'd expected. "Ah," he cried out in panic, feeling his chance of escape slipping away as he zoomed along the edge of the platform's stairs, unable to get onto them. Surely, this was the end of him, swept on and engulfed by the river. Moments later, however, a mighty tug stopped him in his tracks. His coat had snagged on one of the submerged stair lamps that ran down the edge of the stairway. Some of them, still pointing their heads above the flood, stood in a line showing the way up and out of the water. Nodding and bobbing on the current, it took Basil a few seconds to figure out what had happened.

When it eventually dawned on him that his coat was now a lifeline to freedom, he rolled himself over onto his stomach and, hand over hand, pulled his way along his outer garment and back to the lamps. Dropping off his coat, he moved gingerly from lamp to lamp, until he somehow managed to scramble between them and back onto the stairs. Having found his footing, he pulled himself out of the water and back to safety. The sense of relief was overwhelming. Collapsing onto the floor with exhaustion from the cold and in shock from his efforts to stay alive, Basil was briefly sick. Then, after finding his breath amongst his chattering teeth and the shivers that ran through his body, he got to his feet.

"Georgie!" he called out to Lady Georgiana, in an exhausted and subdued voice. He cleared his throat and shouted, "Georgie, are you all right? Are you there?"

Lady Georgiana thought she could hear him and tried to reply but the four walls of the chamber she was in and the sound of the rushing water about her muffled her voice. Another great wall of water came crashing through one of the archways in the engine room. Fearing for his life, Basil ran back to the lift and was soon zooming his way up to the control room again. The doors opened and, in great distress and anguish, he joined the Professor at his desk and told his story about Lady Georgiana.

"She's all right," replied the Professor, comforting Basil and pointing to a monitor screen in front of them. There they could all see Lady Georgiana wading back through the water in the small room where the hologram had appeared earlier and climbing the stairs.

Lady Georgiana had some hope in her heart that Basil was safe. Even though she hadn't seen him get out of the water, she thought his call to her was not one for help but seemed to be seeking after her wellbeing. Dragging her legs through the water she plodded up the steps. Through an open archway she went and onto a raised metal platform. The room she entered was illuminated by the strong glare of lights studded all over the walls and ceiling. They were so bright that, even after shielding her eyes, it took some time for her to adjust to the intensity of the new brightness. When she finally managed to see clearly, she froze in sudden horror, dread and bewilderment. There, on the opposite side of the room, set in a row along the back wall, were five Free Flowing Foamy Flusher machines. Stunned by what she was looking at, she just froze, confused and perplexed by the sight and quite unable to say anything. How could such evil machines be in a place like this?

"I thought these were a moral people?" she said to herself.

She glanced around looking for room exits, but there weren't any. Descending the platform steps and quickly walking across the marble floor to where the flusher machines were, it soon became obvious that these machines were not exactly the same as the one Mr E used. Each machine had a glass room next to it but instead of a huge pipe projecting out of the glass room's top and connecting to the Flusher machine's lid, there was in its place a wide glass tube. This tube ran straight up and through the ceiling. In addition, another wide tube went from underneath the glass room and into the floor.

Inside the glass room was another smaller glass chamber, like a pod of some kind. It stood upright in the middle of the room with a door open in its side for entry. Each of the machines had these pods in them. As Lady Georgiana walked up to the machines they immediately seemed to sense her presence and started to churn up the water that was inside them. Instinctively she stepped back a few paces in revulsion, having seen the Free Flowing Foamy Flusher of Mr E do the same on many occasions.

"Steady yourself," Lady Georgiana reasoned. "Remember, it's hard to know what you're seeing if you don't quite know what you're looking at," she said, thinking of the words of a great sage she had once read about.

A phone tube was nearby so she quickly ran to it, blew down it and was very relieved to hear the Professor's voice along with Basil's too. After exchanging brief questions, asking if Basil was all right, she asked, "What do I do? Have you seen these vile flusher machines?"

"We have," came the reply. "Can you take a closer look?"

"Why?" she replied.

"Because I don't think they're execution machines," the Professor replied.

"Well, what are they?" she asked.

"Just go closer and see," said the Professor. "The closer you get to them the easier it is for us to see what they are. The waterworks is still following you but you need to get close to the machines so that we can have a good look on our monitors too."

Lady Georgiana approached the nearest machine. She thought it odd that hope seemed to rise in her as she did. Running her eyes over every part, her gaze finally rested on the glass pod that stood inside the small glass room. All over it, a semi-transparent writing could be made out, but it was too small to see clearly from where she was standing. Summoning up her courage, she stepped into a place she had once vowed she would never enter, into a flusher machine's glass cubicle. The little room lit up brightly for her and the writing on the pod could now clearly be made out. On it was a list of room names. Lady Georgiana peered at them trying to make sense of what she was looking at. She ran her finger along them and to her surprise the list began to light up. Her finger finally rested on the name, "Main Control Room."

"Destination selected," came a voice from the side of the machine. "Please enter pod to travel."

Lady Georgiana nearly jumped out of her skin at the noise. She shot out of the room and went back to the phone tube.

"They're travel machines," she said down the pipe.

"Yes we can see," came the Professor's reply. "Seems like Mr E didn't invent his Flusher machine after all. He's just found one and corrupted it for his own purposes."

"Do you think it's safe?" asked Lady Georgiana, but before she could say anymore the water outside the room suddenly came over the top of the platform gushing down to where Lady Georgiana stood.

"No time to find out," came the Professor's reply. "Just do it M'lady."

Lady Georgiana rushed back to the machine, jumped into the glass room, stepped into the pod and then closed its door behind her.

"Chamber door still open," came the Flusher machine's voice and Lady Georgiana saw that she had, in her hurry, left the small door to the glass room open behind her. Out of the pod she stepped and closed the glass cubicle door against the oncoming flood. She turned and entered the small pod again, closing that door behind her too. It felt like a tiny space in which she stood; not so small that she couldn't stand, turn or sit down, but small enough to make her feel a little claustrophobic.

"Flushing traveller prepare for new destination. Please confirm your choice."

"Confirm my choice?" said Lady Georgiana. "What's that? What do I do?"

She looked across the pod's surface to see if there was a button she needed to press, there wasn't. For a second time she ran her eyes and then her fingers, quickly all over the inner surface of the pod, up to its top, down its sides and even down by her feet, but there was nothing to press.

"Please confirm your choice," came the Flusher machine's voice again.

"What?" said Lady Georgiana, starting to get into a panic. "How do I do that? What am I to do?"

The flood water that had originally trickled over the platform was now a steady waterfall and the travel chamber in which the flusher devices stood began to fill. It sloshed up the sides of the machines and their small glass cubicles. Higher and higher it steadily climbed.

"Please confirm your choice," came the Flusher machine's voice yet again.

Lady Georgiana banged on the sides of the pod with her fists. She stamped her feet. She jumped up and down, but nothing happened.

"Please confirm your choice," came the Flusher machine's voice again.

"How do I do that? How do I get out of here?!" she screamed.

"Voice command not recognised," came the machine's reply. "Please confirm your choice."

"I want to get out of here!" shouted Lady Georgiana again looking at the flood in the room outside.

"Voice command not recognised," came the machine's reply. "Please confirm your choice."

Lady Georgiana suddenly realised that the machine was actually listening to her voice.

117

"I confirm!" she cried. "I confirm my choice."

"Confirmation accepted," came the machine's voice again. "Destination: Main Controller room. Direction: Upwards and out," said the machine. "Have a nice trip."

It was music to Lady Georgiana's ears. The machine began to churn the water inside it furiously and all of the wheels on the outside of the main water tank turned over and over, just like Mr E's flusher machine. Water spouted up from beneath the pod and began to fill the glass cubicle. Then round and round and round the small room began to spin, but for some reason the pod in which she stood remained stationary. The water swirled and swished in a circle inside the glass room and Lady Georgiana could sense and feel the power of the moving current. Somehow, the machine was going to use the power of the water's movement to send her on her way.

For a moment, the words that Mr E chanted at each of his flushing executions came to her mind, "Round and round and round we go…" but she quickly suppressed them and focused on what was really going to happen. Clenching her fists and closing her eyes, she waited in anticipation for her escape. The room spun faster and faster and the pod shook and trembled, getting ready to be jettisoned up through the pipe above. The large top pipe slowly moved down to the pod and secured itself onto the pod's outer shell. There was a clunk as the two objects met each other. The spinning of the room reached a high-pitched crescendo as the water surged inside it. The flusher machine clunked its last few clunks and the pod juddered ready to blast off up the tube and out of the room. It trembled and rattled and then suddenly… it all slowed down.

The whirring sound of the glass room died as it decelerated its spin. The gushing noise from the Flusher machine seemed sluggish and the spinning wheels on the outside of the machine all came to a halt. Lady Georgiana opened her eyes and to her dismay saw that the terminal room outside had completely flooded and reached the height of the Flusher machine's top. The swamped machine slowed and spluttered to quiet stillness. She banged on the side of the pod, yelling out at the flusher machine.

"Don't stop," she cried. "Don't stop. You can't stop."

Hope drained out of her as the small glass room and the swirling water inside it came to a standstill. Completely lifeless, both glass cubicle and Flusher machine were now still and dead. No sounds, no signs of life and no thought of escape from the flood.

"Don't stop," whispered Lady Georgiana, in disbelief.

The water continued to climb the walls of the travel chamber and, one by one, the lights in the walls across the room spluttered and spat out electric sparks, before dying out. Finally, as the room completely filled, everything became dark, except for a few dim glows on the chamber's ceiling. Now, engulfed by the floodwaters, all Lady Georgiana could hear was the sloshing of the wave breakers still coming down the far corridor from which she had fled earlier. Behind all of the glass, it was a dull noise; a little like the lapping of tiny waves on the seashore.

There she was, inside a glass pod, which was inside a glass cubical (filled with water), which was inside the travel chamber (also filled with water). She was stuck, twice buried alive in a watery grave.

The last few lights in the ceiling went out and complete darkness fell, as dark as night. Lady Georgiana placed her hands against the cold glass pod and felt the chill of her entombment. A surge of panic ran through her. Normally she could suppress her emotions and found great personal pride and honour in being able to process even the most acute pain, but this was different and the outburst took her by surprise.

From the depths of her being, the uncontrollable feeling of desperation welled up and flowed over into her heart and body. She literally quaked with the trauma, acutely feeling the suffocation of her entrapment. After imagining herself suffocating and so gasping for air (and feeling desperately ashamed of herself for being human and weak) she went down onto her knees and rested her head on the side of the pod. She had no strength left and her lips quivered with the trembling fear of dying.

"I don't want to go yet," she said to herself. "I'm not ready! Not ready! Please, I don't want to end like this!" and then she let out a long cry and sobbed with shaking shoulders.

Chapter 19 – On My Knees

"Where did she go?" yelled Basil, looking at a blank monitor screen. "Did she get out?"

"Don't know," replied the Professor abruptly.

Through one of the display monitors they had both watched the flusher machine prepare to jettison Lady Georgiana out of the travel chamber but then, without warning, the image had failed. The monitor screen fizzed a few times and went blank. The Professor repeatedly thumped the monitor to try to get it working. It flickered and simply switched to another image, displaying an alternative room in the waterworks.

"Lost her!" he said.

"Lost her?" echoed Basil. "How could we lose her? Where is she?"

They scanned the other monitors in the room to see if Lady Georgiana had been picked up by one of them. To their dismay she was nowhere to be seen. Several of the rooms on display also filled with water and each monitor also fizzed off. When the image came back again, it displayed a different room, without water in.

"The cameras must be failing when each room gets flooded," said the Professor, a slight tremble in his voice.

"Is she all right?" Basil asked again.

"No idea," replied the Professor, staring Basil in the eye with a look of serious honesty.

Both men looked at each other and exchanged their hopeless dismay.

"Can we find her again?" asked Basil, looking across the many dials, buttons and switches on the control desk.

The Professor ran the tips of his trembling fingers across the different instruments on the desk to see if there was anything that suggested controlling the monitors in front of them, but couldn't find anything to help. He quickly browsed through his notebook feeling baffled and helpless, knowing full well that he'd not written down any notes about controlling monitors.

"I don't know what to do," he replied.

Back inside the glass pod, Lady Georgiana was reasoning through what to do in order to stay alive. Wiping tears from her eyes, she considered the choices before her. To stay inside the glass pod and die from lack of air was her first choice. Her second was to open the pod's door, let in the flood from the water in the flusher machine's glass cubicle and then open the door of the flusher machine's cubicle and try to swim out and through the submerged travel chamber. She would have to swim up over the platform, through the small room where the hologram had appeared and then risk the currents of the flood on the great corridor. She had no idea if she could hold her breath underwater for that long.

"Even if I manage that, how will I get out and back to the control room with the Professor, Basil and Scrub?" she thought. She really didn't know. It all seemed impossible.

"But staying here is certain death anyway," she said to herself out loud. "It's only a matter of time before the air is used up. Do I drown or suffocate? What a choice!"

A few minutes went by as she pondered her options. Neither of them offered any hope and there was no faith in her to try them.

"I shall have to be logical and cold," she thought to herself. "I shall certainly die if I stay here and I'd rather die trying to live than just give up."

With that notion firmly in mind she wrapped her fingers around the pod door handle, knowing that this would probably be the last thing she'd ever do. Even though she had been a very strong swimmer in her youth, she knew that that time was now over and gone. Within moments she'd be submerged in water. How on earth would she be able to open the flusher machine's glass cubicle door and then navigate her way through the dark chamber as well? Her mind, however, was made up; she would die trying to live, for living is more important than dying. Giving up doesn't achieve anything. Whilst you're alive there's hope, but who hopes for anything when they are dead and gone?

"Take your boots and coat off," she reminded herself. "Don't set yourself up to fail even before you've started."

Quickly removing her boots and outer cloak, she took hold of the pod door handle again.

"Here goes," she said.

Filling her lungs, with what would possibly be her last breath, she braced herself and pushed on the door handle to exit into the flooded cubicle and begin her doomed escape. To her surprise the handle wouldn't budge. She pushed again but the pod door was quite stuck. Putting her whole body weight against the pod's glass door she leaned on the handle, but still nothing happened.

"The door must have locked itself when the glass room outside filled with water," she reasoned.

Anger spread through her as she found her last choice had been taken away from her. She pounded and battered on the side of the pod but it wouldn't break or give way. Pummelling the glass with the flat of her hands until they were sore and red, she vented her frustrated anger. Then, in an instant of madness and rage, she kicked and thumped the glass walls until her feet ached, her knuckles were bruised and no strength was left.

"So it's decided for me then," she said, once she'd calmed down; finally resting against the side of the pod and wiping the tears from her eyes. "I cannot get out, so here I stay. This is my end, my coffin, my tomb."

In the stillness that followed she gave up her inward struggle to escape.

"Well Georgiana, it could have been worse I suppose," she matter-of-factly said to herself.

Glancing down at the floor, she bent down and ran her fingers across the expensive coat she had taken off and then the dress that she wore.

"At least I'm well dressed for the occasion," she added, in a trivial tone. Her jest, with a half laugh and smile to make light of the situation (trying to break through her pain and fear) didn't work.

She sat on the floor and ran her fingers through her hair to make a connection with herself for the last time.

"Oh Dad, if you could see me now!" she whispered, closing her eyes tightly and clenching her fists. She tightened her stomach muscles and made her body rigid and taut in order to restrain her emotions. Wanting to be in control again, trying to suppress her overflowing heart, she swallowed hard and shook her head, but it wouldn't last.

"I'm so sorry Dad," she blurted out, in a moment when she finally met herself and the tears began to flow.

Laying her head back against the side of the glass pod, she looked up into the darkness that surrounded her.

"I'm so sorry for the mistakes I've made," she sobbed. "Sorry for losing you, mum, Richard and Emma. I'm sorry for all of the things that I've done that fall short of what you wanted me to be."

No more words came out. In silence she just sat there, her back to the glass wall. Finally she rested her head between her knees.

"I'm just sorry," she whispered, and then cried a little more.

After a few minutes she gained some strength and wiped her eyes and mouth. Looking up at the dark ceiling she continued, "I'm sorry Emma about Scrub, about Stephanus. I've tried to look after him, really I have. I'm sorry that he is unwell. That he has not turned out right. I'm sorry I've not given him more of my time. I just don't think that I was meant to be a mother like you. It's just not in me you know. It's just not in me. Don't know why you left it to me to care for him, but you did and I've done the best I could."

For several minutes more she just sat there in the dark stillness. Then, feeling a stirring inside, she did something she'd not done since childhood, she leaned forward on her knees and prayed. It wasn't that she intended to do so, the prayer just came out of her like an uncontrollable overflow of the heart; a long flood of overflowing and torrential truth (similar to the flood that was trapping her). Strangely enough, however, this flood that came gushing out from her soul didn't diminish her, instead it set her free. She confessed all of her wrongs, her mistakes, opening up the floodgates of her conscience for all to hear, except that (as far as the eye could see) there was only her in the watery tomb to listen, but somehow that seemed to be enough. She acknowledged her shortcomings, her personal shame and made peace with the past, confessing all that there was to say.

After she had finished there was somehow a calmness in the quietness and stillness of her soul. She felt light and more real with herself. Her burial chamber had become a catacomb of holy ground, a solace for a lonely heart. She had passed through the veil of no return, confronted the years of bottled-up pain and anguish, acknowledged her wrongs and was now ready to follow those who had gone on before her. The fear of death gradually slipped away. Her demise was a given fact that she had accepted, swallowed and made a part of herself. She was going to die. Nothing was left in her that she had not, in those few precious moments, overturned. Now she was ready to leave this world, quite free and quite renewed.

Back up in the control room the frustrated Professor had been pulling up different maps and plans of the waterworks on the computer system. Trying to find the correct map amongst the thousands that were on file to view, however, was proving more than a headache. Basil was beside himself with worry whilst Scrub, on the other hand, spent much of his time looking at the flood through the small window. He watched the water steadily climb the sides of the great chamber with a strange fascination, not quite understanding yet that they were to be flooded themselves once it reached them. After a little while his mind wandered again so he decided to join Basil and the Professor at the control desk. Standing behind them, just to their right, he watched their frantic activities and listened to their animated discussions. The two men were beginning to squabble, but this just made the event even more interesting to Scrub. He liked watching people to try to understand them, but often found human behaviour confusing.

Scrub's attention was finally drawn to the right hand side of the control desk where there were a series of shiny buttons. They were small, multi-coloured and bright. Scrub loved colour and was always attracted to anything that was vivid and cheery. He noticed that one of the buttons flashed on and off and, as he looked at it, an urge was kindled deep within him. It was something that he had been warned about many times, but a desire he couldn't control. The urge within transformed itself into a passionate longing and from there it just grew and grew. There it was, that wonderful, beautiful, shining, flashing button. His heart stirred and roused itself with a hankering to just reach out and press it.

"Press me, press me," he felt the button saying to him.

As the yearning arose within him, growing stronger by the second, it was suddenly met by several voices that also rang in his head.

"Don't touch it Scrub," one of them said (sounding like the voice of Lady Georgiana).

"Scrub, don't you touch anything you don't understand," said another (a little like the voice of the Professor).

"Look at what you've done now!" came yet another voice.

He hesitated again, wondering what to do. Then a torrent of voices flooded his mind. They were the voices of many people who had spoken to him over the years.

123

"Did I say you could touch that?"

and

"If it's not yours then keep your fingers off!"

and

"Don't touch a single thing! Do you understand Scrub? I don't want you meddling with anything!"

and

"Leave it alone!"

and

"Why can't you just keep your hands in your pockets!"

and

"Look what you've done now! Never, ever come back here again! Do you hear me?!"

The voices went on and on. He shook his head to clear his mind, it was all too much. He wanted to be good, but Scrub never quite fitted everyone else's pattern of behaviour.

He turned his back to the button and quickly closed one eye, reasoning to himself that, if he only had one eye open, the temptation would only be half as bad. Strangely enough, however, the gaze of his single open eye slowly strayed across the desk to rest on the flashing button again and, once it was fixed, nothing could move it away.

"Press me, press me," the button continued to say.

Scrub struggled and kicked and fought the desires inside.

"Press me, press me," it called again.

His fingers trembled with craving and yearning. He could feel the invisible force within swelling up to a desire that was so strong he was fit to burst and, seeing that Basil and the Professor were distracted, he just couldn't resist himself. Glancing at the Professor and then back at the button, he saw his opportunity. Turning his body sideways, so that his back was now towards the others, he slid his way down to the end of the desk where the button was. Then, gently resting his hand on the table top, he walked the tips of his fingers, one by one, across to where the buttons were. Finally, the tip of his forefinger rested on the flashing button and he felt a surge of elation and importance as he did so.

"Press me, press me," it sang out to him.

(I believe that if Scrub had lived an ordinary life he would have been an inventor; a most extraordinary man who would have changed the world by his creations and discoveries. There was something from that genius still strongly at work within him and it was so strong that he couldn't quite control it.)

"I shouldn't do this," he said to himself, but it was all too much. Down went his finger and then he quickly pulled his hand away.

"Scrub!" the Professor bellowed, seeing what had just been done out of the corner of his eye. "Leave it alone!"

124

Scrub jumped back and just stared at the angry Professor but then he became puzzled by the expression on the Professor's face, for he seemed now to be looking at something on the wall behind Scrub. Scrub turned to see that a part of the wall had rotated, revealing an alcove with a gaping hole in the floor at its base.

"What's that?" asked Basil.

Back down in the travel chamber Lady Georgiana jumped as the flusher machine suddenly came back to life. The outer glass cubicle began to spin again getting faster and faster around her. A muffled voice came from the flusher machine.

"Destination route approved and accepted," it said.

Within moments Lady Georgiana found herself jettisoned up the tube inside the pod and travelling at high speed through the waterworks. She went from tube to tube, zooming through different rooms, some filled with water and others not. Finally, she felt the pod shoot up to a great height and then come to a slow stop.

Clunk, it went and arrived in the alcove area at the back of the control room to the astonishment of Basil, the Professor and Scrub. The door to the pod swung open and out she stepped.

"Oh thank you Professor," she said, greeting them all and exchanging hugs. "How ever did you do it?"

The Professor just shook his head. "It wasn't me," he replied, feeling a little numb and shocked. "It was Scrub."

"Scrub?" echoed Lady Georgiana in surprise.

"He just couldn't resist that urge of his to press one of those flashing buttons," added Basil, with a relieved smile on his face. "Could you, you wonderful, silly boy."

Scrub couldn't quite work out how he could be silly and wonderful at the same time, but took it as a possible compliment, especially as no-one was shouting at him anymore.

"Thank you Scrub," said Lady Georgiana tenderly to him.

"Oh, ok," replied Scrub, not quite knowing what all of the fuss was about. "I only pressed a button," he said.

"Well you're a very naughty boy," said Lady Georgiana, with a smile whist tenderly tapping him on the nose – which, to be honest, just confused Scrub even more.

Chapter 20 – Back On Track

The sound of the flood filling the waterworks soon brought back to everyone's attention their immediate need of a very quick exodus from the building. Focussing on this task of trying to escape, the Professor began to busily pull up maps on the control desk's computer system to find another way out. However, he quickly found himself surrounded and distracted by the rest of the party; all of whom joined in to offer advice on where any exits or service tunnels might be. He and Basil in particular soon fell into a dispute about which map to look at and where they exactly were. To relieve the problem, Lady Georgiana took Basil back onto the metal bridge to look for other possible exits. Peering over the bridge's edge, they scanned the walls to see if there was a way of climbing down to another level where there might be a door or an archway that could lead to an alternative escape route. The sides of the walls, however, were as smooth as butter and the water level had risen so high that most exits to other corridors were completely flooded.

"We're trapped," said Lady Georgiana.

"Perhaps we could climb up towards the lights and air vents," said Basil, now gazing up at the domed rooftop. They looked for some way to climb the walls to get to the higher level, but even though there was a service ladder built into the wall, it didn't go all the way to the roof. Once again the waterworks building groaned and jerked.

"We don't have much time out here," shouted Lady Georgiana to the Professor back in the control room, who was still trying to get the computer to give him some sensible answers that he could work with. "Let's move back off this bridge Basil," she added. "It's not safe anymore."

They had hardly taken a few steps into the control room when the wall and door that opened onto the metal platform at the far opposite side of the bridge bulged, warped and gave way. From behind it a deluge of water poured out. It rushed across the metal balcony, passed through its grating, then plummeted to the engine room far below. The platform buckled beneath the weight of this unrelenting flood, sending shock waves up and down its framework. Finally it twisted and gave way. Down it went to the engine room below, along with the rest of the bridge.

Basil closed the door to the control room and took one of the chairs from the control desk to wedge it under the door handle.

"That won't do us much good," said the Professor.

"Any extra time we can give ourselves will help," he replied.

"There has to be another exit out of here," said Lady Georgiana. "It can't be a dead end. This is the main control room!"

They searched and searched every corner of the room, right along the walls and under the carpet for any trap doors or service tunnels.

"It's here," cried the Professor, looking at a map of the room and then pointing to the ceiling high up above from where the monitors had come down from. "An air vent in the secondary ceiling," he said.

All gathered beneath the vent to look for it but it was it difficult to see, being shadowed in darkness amongst the TV monitor tubes.

"Up there," he said again, pointing to it.

"And how do we get up there?" said Lady Georgiana.

They all hesitated and then rushed to the chairs that were at the control desk. Having stacked them underneath the air vent, they tried to reach the vent to push it open but were unable to do so. At the same time Scrub continued to gaze through the window at the water in the engine room. It continued to gush in from the many open archways that were located up and down the sides of the chamber. Like a huge frothy bath, it was quickly filling up. The water wasn't clean either, but a murky yellow which smelt like a churned-up stagnant pond.

"We're going to get very wet soon if we don't leave," said Scrub, but everyone ignored him.

"Hurry up!" shouted Lady Georgiana at the two men who were still trying to reach the vent.

"We need the desk," the professor replied. "I'm not high enough to get through."

With quite a struggle they dragged the main control desk to sit under the vent, stretching and snapping some cables in the floor that were attached to the desk's underside as they hauled it into position. After a chair had been placed on top of the desk, Basil volunteered himself to be the first to open the way for everyone. After standing on the chair and pushing the vent to one side, however, he found he could only get the top half of his body through the gap.

"I'm stuck," he called out.

"Scrub, give me a hand to help Basil a push up," said the Professor. "He won't get through that hole without someone helping him."

Scrub climbed onto the desk and together he and the Professor pushed from below whilst Basil tried to heave himself up. The flood had now reached the level of the doorway and could be seen on the other side of the window splashing up onto the glass.

"Hurry up," cried Georgiana, wondering to herself if Basil had been wise in trying to be the first person through the hole.

Keeeeer-thud, the waterworks trembled again. With the flood swelling its way through the last of its empty rooms the building gave a sudden shudder, which caused the control room window to crack and spirts of water began to leak through.

"Stand on Scrub's shoulders!" cried Lady Georgiana in desperation, as she also scrambled onto the control desk to help push Basil from below.

Basil, having finally wrestled much of his tummy through the hole, placed both of his feet squarely on Scrub's shoulders and found that, with Scrub now standing on the chair to give extra height, he could pull himself through into the roof space above; though Scrub wasn't too happy with him when Basil momentarily placed the full weight of his bottom on Scrub's head in the process.

"You next," said the Professor to Lady Georgiana.

The control room window pane finally shattered and the water gushed in. It surged and swirled into the room, filling it at a terrifying speed.

"Use Scrub as a ladder," cried the professor, over the roar of the water rushing around them.

Lady Georgiana didn't argue. Stepping up onto the chair she reached for the roof and, with Scrub's help, managed to push the top half of her body through. After anchoring her elbows on the roof space floor, she put her feet onto Scrub's shoulders and quickly climbed through.

"Pull Scrub up and then get ready for me too," the Professor shouted.

The lights went out as the room became swamped and everywhere was plunged into darkness. Scrub was quickly heaved through the air vent but the Professor found himself cut off from the other three. Standing on the control desk, his survival became like a circus-balancing act as the desk began to move with the water. He fumbled with the chair next to him but lost it to the flood. Then, as the water carried the desk upwards, he became pinned between the TV monitor pipes.

"Professor!" called Lady Georgiana, into the darkness below.

"Are you there Professor?" Basil shouted down. "Are you there?" he called again.

In the darkness no one could see exactly where he was.

"Grab my hand," came the Professor's shrieking voice.

"We can't see it," shouted Lady Georgiana in reply.

Suddenly the small lantern came on and there was the Professor holding on for dear life, still trapped amongst the TV monitor pipes in the swirling flood. His legs scrambled against the current as it tugged at him. Slowly he pulled himself through the pipes and stretched out his hand that held the lantern.

"Grab my hand!" he cried again.

Basil and Lady Georgiana held onto Scrub as he bent down through the hole in the ceiling to pull the Professor up. The current of water slowly lifted the Professor higher towards them and Scrub was finally able to grasp him by the wrist and then the elbows. With a joint heave, they hauled him through.

"Thank you," said the trembling Professor, as he wiped his face with his wet sleeve.

In the roof space, they quickly scanned their surroundings for an escape and, seeing a framework of timber joists and beams that supported the ceiling, climbed between the different trusses. Up and up they went until they reached the roof slates. Using the back of his lantern, the Professor knocked a hole in the roof and from there they pulled down slate after slate to make a hole big enough to climb through.

"Up and through we go," he said. They scrambled through the hole and onto the roof above. It was slanted slightly (probably for weather purposes) making it difficult to move across without slipping and sliding, but move across it they did. Gingerly they made their way to the front of the building where the old scaffolding was, left there many years before when the building was last being cleaned, before it had been closed down. The scaffolding looked very flimsy and weather-beaten. At first they hesitated, but as the waterworks quaked again beneath them, the flood surging right to the top of the building, they mustered the courage to climb down. Descending through its different levels, they quickly got the hang of it and made good progress.

As they picked their way through the scaffolding bars, they could see the great stained glass window on the front of the waterworks next to them. The water behind it was as high as they were, sloshing and lapping up the walls and the great window creaked and groaned with the weight of the flood that was behind it.

"Don't look at it," cried the Professor. "Just climb down."

Down, they climbed through the wooden structure, picking their way through the planks and holes. Below them, they could see a stream of water beginning to pour out from between the cracks of the huge front doors. The ground quickly turned into mud and the scaffolding began to shift and move in the miry clay. Then suddenly, CRACK! The stained glass window began to split open and small jets of water sprayed out pushing the scaffolding away from the building. It swung out and crashed into the crane that was next to it. Basil slipped right off and fell into the wooden window cleaner's box that dangled on a chain from the crane's long arm. The box swung out and then back onto the scaffolding again.

"Into the box!" cried Lady Georgiana. She grasped the chain that dangled from the crane's long arm and, after wrapping her legs around it, lowered herself down into the box with Scrub and the Professor quickly following. There they sat with arms spread out, hearts pounding and clinging onto the box's wooden sides.

"Hold on tight," said the Professor, as they all ducked down in the box, bracing themselves for something terrible to happen.

Off in the distance the police in their patrol balloons had noticed that the waterworks seemed to be alive with activity and they came speeding over towards it, but it was too late. Suddenly the whole building lunged forward on its foundations, stopped and started to tilt. There was a shudder as every brick in the structure quaked. Then BOOM! The front doors blew off and a river shot out from the waterworks' front and rushed down the main entrance stairs, spewing itself out towards the city. The shock waves shattered the stained glass window, spraying a torrent of water through the scaffolding. At that very same moment, the great, magnificent and tired old building leaned forward for the last time, mournfully groaned and collapsed under the weight of the water. Down went the aged monument and whoosh, a deluge of water the size of a tidal wave swept forward, engulfing everything in its path.

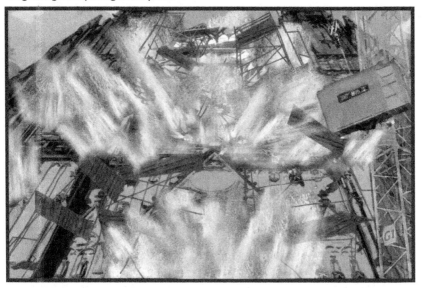

The water carried the scaffolding away and Lady Georgiana, the Professor, Basil and Scrub found themselves catapulted through the air in their window cleaner's box as the crane, hit by the collapsing building and a wall of water, swung its long arm full circle and back to where it started. Then it toppled over under the torrent and down it fell. The woodworm ridden window cleaner's box snapped itself free from the crane's chain and, bouncing and bobbing on the surging waves, shot off with the flood towards the city inner circle. Speeding through the cobbled streets and winding lanes, all that could be heard over the noise of the rushing river, were the shrieks, screams and shouts of the party of four who, with white knuckled fingers, clung on for dear life.

Chapter 21 – Pondweed And Wellington Boots

The evening of the same day found everyone called into the great market square in front of Mr E's palace. It had been a very long afternoon. Police balloons had swooped across the city, scanning for signs of rebellion and searching for those guilty parties responsible for the sudden disappearance of the waterworks. Out of the sky military patrol groups had randomly dropped into the residential avenues of the city and its outer circles. Ransacking homes and overturning business premises, they ran riot through the streets. No one felt safe or knew what was going to happen next. Then everything had gone quiet and, for about half an hour, not a soldier or police unit could be seen. This eerie silence was finally broken by the drone of the city loudspeakers, slowly winding up and cordially inviting everyone to be Mr E's guests in the market square, so everyone was now assembled.

Mr Ritant stood by himself on the platform, gazing with disbelief over the once cobbled ground of the great market square, where a yellowy-brown liquid now oozed. It stank. The substance looked like a fermenting stew as if someone had taken all of the left-overs from teatime, put them through a blender and added a good slosh of stale water. To make the soup complete a scattering of pondweed was added, like a chef's signature dish, complete with bay leaves and garnish. "Pukka," would have been the comment, if it were being made in a professional kitchen by a qualified chef, but the aroma of this particular dish revealed an amateur cook who had no sense of smell. The people of Clearwash City could smell, however, for many a nose was held amongst the gathered crowd who wore Wellington boots and splashed about the in the dirty water; complaining noisily about the flood that had suddenly come rushing into their streets and homes.

"Pray silence for his majestic, noble and most honoured highness, Mr E. Ville of Clearwash City. I give you Mr E," said Mr Ritant, in a very subdued and numbed tone.

Mr E, himself dressed for a rainy day in waterproofs and boots, stepped up onto the stage without any ceremony, sat down on a large iron framed chair and scrutinised the people; who like him were all wearing their Wellington boots and plastic macs. He was in a very bad mood. Earlier on that day he had been breaking one of his own laws by having a very luxurious bath. This was about the same time that the waterworks pipes were shaking, quaking, jerking and squirting their muddy water onto the floor of the main pipe chamber. The same pipes ran deep underground throughout the city and their vibrations shook the sticky mud right along them and up and into the palace. To everyone's surprise the water in the palace kitchens suddenly ran muddy when the servants were doing the lunchtime washing up, but far worse happened moments later to Mr E himself.

Mr E had been lying back in his very soapy, bubbly bath and was half way through singing a song into the bathroom shower head (which he held in his hand like a pop star's microphone) when suddenly out of the shower came a surge of muddy water. It caught Mr E as he sang one particularly long and high note in his song. His mouth was wide open and the muddy water had sprayed straight into it, then all over his face!

"Help!" he had called, coughing and spurting the runny mud out of his mouth. "Somebody help me."

However, the door to the bathroom was locked so Mr E had to scramble about the room by himself, looking for towels to wipe the mud from his eyes, whilst he continued to cough and choke. Back at the market square Mr E coughed again and cleared his croaky throat. He could still taste the muddy residue of the dirty water in his mouth and, every now and then, he managed to dislodge tiny bits of grit with his fingernail from between his teeth.

"My most noble subjects," he now said, leaning back in his seat, microphone in hand and staring out at the people in the market square. "A slight matter has caused concern to me. I have noticed that something has recently happened in this great city of ours, a little disturbance that has caught my attention and may need rectifying."

He looked up into the sky, scratched his ear, sat forward in the chair and then continued.

"I'm sure that some of you will have noticed this little disturbance too; a certain extra unauthorised aroma in the air and a splashing sound coming from everyone's feet as they wade through water one foot deep!"

Mr E stopped at this point and again gazed at everyone. He got to his feet and continued. "Now I know for a fact that we have not had much rain recently so the present state of this city doesn't reflect that reality. I can only conclude that this has been caused by someone meddling with the waterworks, which also now seems to have completely disappeared!"

Mr E began to pace up and down the front of the stage, his eyes glancing this way and that over the crowd, trying to see if anyone was looking guilty. He stopped and walked back to his chair again, gently relaxing into it.

"I know not at this moment in time who the person or persons responsible are, but I'm sure that I am soon to be told by one of you, because if I'm not, then I will have to bring up the little matter of flushing someone, or perhaps some people, down my flusher machine's plughole! So if you value your pathetic little lives, I suggest that you get your minute brains together and come up with the culprits."

Everyone stood in silence. In the middle of the crowd were the Professor, Basil, Lady Georgiana and Scrub who simply exchanged glances, but had nothing to say. They were now wearing new dry clothes but their hair was still a little damp.

"I see," said Mr E, when no one said anything.

Slowly he got out of his chair and walked to the front of the stage. He dropped off the edge and, to the amazement of the guards, jumped over the small fence that normally set the boundary between himself and the crowd.

"Who shall I put into my flusher machine?" he asked, his eyes scanning from side to side across the gathered people. His gaze finally rested on a small group to his right. Taking his time, he looked over each one for a suitable victim. Before he had made his choice, however, one of them, thinking he was 'in-for-it', broke the silence.

"It was him, Mr E," he cried, pointing to his tall, lanky friend standing next to him. "He went into your waterworks and broke it."

Aghast at his friend's betrayal, the tall man looked blankly at Mr E and promptly pointed to the next person nearby.

"It was her," he said, pointing to an elderly lady in her late seventies. "She's the one you want!"

She in turn betrayed two other people nearby who in turn named others next to them. Soon betrayal followed betrayal and a wave of accusations spread across the crowd with voice upon voice informing on innocent and unsuspecting bystanders. People backed off from each other as fingers pointed and tongues wagged. Some found themselves hauled up by the scruff of their necks, accosted by groups of self-interested parties, who together sought to save their own skins by sacrificing the weak amongst them.

"Here's the ones you want!" their voices chanted out.

Chaos and confusion reigned whilst the invisible forces of panic and fear dealt blows to long-standing friendships and family bonds.

Mr E called some guards to him and a volley of shots over the crowd's heads soon brought the people back into silence. When all was still, Mr E, flanked by his guards, purposefully strode amongst the throng. Snaking his way through the mass of people they, like the parting of the Red Sea, quickly moved out of his way wherever he went. Eventually he stopped at Lady Georgiana, noticing that she and her companions were looking a little worse for wear, each with damp hair and faces that were cleaner than normal.

"Lady Georgiana Pluggat-Lynnette," he said, looking her and her friends over. "You don't happen to know anything about this little incident do you?"

"Me Mr E?" she replied, in a tone of surprise. "Why Mr E, I'm shocked that such a thought should come to a man of your standing; that you should think a Lady of the realm would take the time to have knowledge of such a thing!"

"Yes, quite," said Mr E, "but I'm sure that someone of your standing would also be, to some extent, informed about the important goings on in the city? Come now. Who was it?"

"I wouldn't tell him anything M'lady if I were you," blurted Scrub.

"I wasn't about to Scrub," said Lady Georgiana, briefly looking irritated.

Basil almost gave Scrub a kick, but at the last moment refrained himself, not wanting to draw any more attention to Scrub's divulgence of information.

"Oh, so you do know who was involved?" said Mr E.

"I wasn't about to tell you anything Mr E," she continued quickly, "as from my point of view, I don't believe that there's much to tell. It seems this water came here ever so quickly and from who knows where? Anyway, I thought that the water behind the waterworks had all dried up. If there was any left, surely it would be pure and clean? This water is rusty and yellow in colour, the sort of water that would come from a stagnant pond."

"Maybe so," said Mr E looking intently at her. "But the fact remains that the waterworks has gone and we have been flooded. I'm also sure that, as one of my most loyal subjects, you have at least something to share with your leader. For someone so well connected as yourself, being at the heart of the life of so many people here, you must know in some way how this incident happened? You must have an inkling as to who was involved? Come now, don't disappoint and be of good use to your ruler, your…" and at this moment Mr E paused, perhaps hesitated. "Your once so close friend," he said very purposefully. "Tell me, who was caught up in this little sortie?"

"How would I know that?" said Lady Georgiana. "I have been too busy this morning to notice what anyone else has been up to."

Lady Georgiana by rule didn't lie. In fact, everything she said was always the truth. She was just careful what she said and the way she spoke, so that she did not reveal any information she thought unnecessary. In this way she didn't present the full picture of events and so give the game away – everything she said was actually true – just not the complete truth. This was quite a gift, not lying always gave your words more weight.

Mr E stared at Lady Georgiana and Lady Georgiana just looked back at him without any readable expression on her face. He knew that she was more than a match for him in a war of words so he decided to look at Scrub, the Professor and Basil, seeing that each of them were damp, had a severe lack of facial dirt and looked quite timorous.

"Too busy," he continued, and mulled the words over in his head. "Yes, I'm sure you've all been very, very busy."

Mr E turned back to face Lady Georgiana.

"Lady Georgiana, Lady Pluggat or whatever name you go by these days, you don't know how it saddens me to hear that you are empty of information. Perhaps you have also emptied yourself of loyalty to this city too? Therefore, in the light of this and from my most generous character, I wish to extend to you my hospitality. I am taking you into my care. I'm taking you away from this horrible water, which has clearly clouded your head and perhaps your fidelity and devotion."

"Oh Mr E," replied Lady Georgiana, rather hurriedly, "I don't think that kind of honour is necessary."

"Oh it's got nothing to do with honour," said Mr E, in a tone of evil gentleness. "Since when have you or I ever had anything honourable to share together? Always remember," he added, "we're not family."

It that instant both looked at each other, a connection was there from a past history that had been for years locked away. Whatever it was, it was only between them and the silence of the moment kept it there.

"I see you're still wearing that abominable thing," muttered Mr E, as he glanced up at the jet-black pillbox hat that Georgiana wore. It's half net veil was the only thing obscuring their direct gaze and it irritated Erepsin to see it again.

"Of course," she replied. "Why wouldn't I?"

Mr E shook off the moment and stepped a little closer to Lady Georgiana so that he could again take control of the conversation he was having. Every syllable that came out of his mouth was sinister and cold.

"Your company," he said, in almost a whisper, "is just an essential unpleasantness, a necessary evil, so that we, in time, can find out who and what has caused this mess. And I don't think the conspirators are too far away, do you?"

He glanced briefly over at the Professor, Basil and Scrub.

"The sooner I get my answers, the sooner we can talk about the possibility that you may, at some point in time, gain a little more of your cherished freedom. Until then, it will be sadly denied you. You will be staying as my guest, locked away from your damp friends here, in the newest and most affluent, even luxurious, part of my dungeon. I don't know if I've ever told you, but it lies deep beneath the palace. I have especially prepared it for resolving occurrences, just - like - this."

Mr E leaned further forward and lowered his voice even more.

"I call it 'The Hole'," he said, with his nose just an inch from her ear. "A place where there is no daytime and no night, just ever present darkness. And I'm duly informed that it is so quiet and silent down there that you can even hear the very palpitations of your own desperate heart."

Lady Georgiana maintained her statue-like stance without flinching. She remembered her time in the waterworks travelling pod, where she had already been cut off from everyone and everything.

"Just pray that I don't forget I've put you there," added Mr E, when he saw how calm Lady Georgiana was. "I'm getting so absent-minded these days."

Georgiana turned her head to stare Erepsin right in his eyes.

"I have no fear of your dungeon, of being alone, or of death," she quietly replied. "I've already been there."

A brief moment of this truth passed between them. Her strength in this conversation took him by surprise; she wasn't bluffing. Erepsin straightened up.

"Ivan," he shouted. "We have a guest. Escort her, if you please, to her new residence!"

"Err, the entire dungeon is flooded Mr E," said Mr Ritant, "and it will be at least a month before we can get it useable again."

"What!" he exclaimed.

"The only other room I can currently recommend is the palace lounge, where the private family library used to be," added Ivan, in a slightly stressed tone.

136

"Well, lock her in there then!" he yelled back. "And if I don't find out in the next few hours who has caused this mess then you, Lady Georgiana, will become my permanent resident with nothing but a hole to look forward to when it's next ready."

"But that's not fair," blurted out Basil, forgetting to whom he was talking.

"Not fair! Not fair!" cried Mr E, wheeling around to face him. "I'll tell you what's not fair. All of this pond water that's run into my clean supply of drinking water, that's what I call not fair! For the next three days, no one is having any of my water to drink until my supply is clean again. Find your own water to drink, or drink your pond water if you want to."

At this the crowd began to murmur at the thought of having to drink from the dirty lagoon that currently splashed beneath their feet.

"And find your own ointments to rub on yourselves to keep you from being smelly," continued Mr E. "I'll have nothing more to do with you!"

Mr E marched off back to the palace with Mr Ritant tagging on behind him. Three guards came and reluctantly took Lady Georgiana from amongst the people to escort her towards the palace. As they took her away, Lady Georgiana glanced back at Basil, the Professor and Scrub with a look of peaceful resignation on her face, but this did little to relieve her friends' distress.

The crowd slowly dispersed; a little taken aback that Lady Georgiana had been arrested and unsure about how to stay alive without any regular clean water to drink. Once everyone had gone Basil, the Professor and Scrub just stood staring in the direction of the palace gates.

"Nothing to drink?" said Scrub. "What are we going to do now?"

"I'm not sure Scrub, I'm not sure," said the Professor. "And what we'll do without Lady Georgiana, I really don't know."

Basil gazed blankly at the open space in front of him whilst the other two began to walk to the outer circle of the city.

"Come on Basil," said the Professor, over his shoulder. "We have to get moving. You can't just stand here all evening. You'll get arrested if you don't move on. I will gather the rebel committees into my bunker and we'll discuss with them the way forward. Perhaps someone will have a good idea?"

Basil nodded, but still didn't move or say anything.

"Come on," repeated the Professor. "Meet me later at my laboratory and we'll talk about what to do next."

Basil nodded again.

"Off you go home Scrub," said the Professor, in an unusually kind tone towards the young man. "Meet up with Basil again later on this evening and then you can come over to see me in the bunker."

"You mean it?" enquired a surprised Scrub. "You mean, inside your bunker?"

"Yes," replied the Professor, thinking through properly what he'd just said. "Now off you go and Basil will call for you later on."

137

The Professor and Scrub walked away whilst Basil slowly trudged across the market square to his own house.

Chapter 22 – Ancient Wash History

Inside the palace, Ivan led Lady Georgiana up several flights of stairs and through numerous rooms until they finally entered what was called the 'Family Private Lounge'; one of the palace's smaller rooms, this exclusive venue had the reputation of being very comfortable for the few who had access.

"There you go Ms Pluggat," he said, deliberately not addressing her with her proper title as he opened the door. "Here's a place where you can stay and not do any harm to anyone."

"My dear Mr Ritant," said Lady Georgiana, after she had walked into the room. "I must assure you that I haven't done any harm to anyone in the whole of my life and do not intend to."

"Very well," said Mr Ritant, "if that's the way you wish to see things, but I must say I do see things rather differently. It's a good thing that you're in here. Now we know where you are and what you're up to."

"And pray what am I up to Mr Ritant?"

"Well that remains to be seen," said Mr Ritant. "That remains to be seen, but I tell you this, if you are ever caught, then I for one will take great pleasure in seeing you flushed."

With that, he closed the door and locked it.

"Ridiculous man!" said Lady Georgiana, stamping her foot on the floor. "Oh well," she finally said, glancing at her surroundings, "this looks comfortable enough; it's a lot better than a dungeon."

The lounge smelt musky from old books and many a gentleman's pipe. Despite this odd odour there was something hospitable and familiar about it, as if all of its warm and cosy memories hung in the air to welcome each guest into its rich and friendly history. Scattered in groups of threes and fours about the room sat brown leather-backed armchairs with small coffee tables next to them on decorative rugs; often stained from spilt drinks and tobacco ash. Overall, it was a very well furnished retreat, pleasing to the eye, a lot smaller than the main public library, but its snug, relaxing layout showed the room well-ordered and ready for good use.

"I suppose I could do some reading whilst I'm here," she said to herself. "It's always a good thing to enlarge one's education."

She began to look about her at the different books, each neatly stacked on dusty shelves that ran from ceiling to floor, covering the walls. Running her fingers over their spines and glancing at their titles, it was difficult for Lady Georgiana to know where to start. After working her way along one wall, she came to a small seating area where there was a lone armchair. It looked comfortable and welcoming, so she sat in it. Leaning forward, she peered at the books on the opposite wall.

"Hmm, now let me see," she said, beginning to run her fingers along the books and reading their titles. There seemed to be a mixture of comical tales, travel books, general advice and historical records.

B.J.Batty's Book of Historical Blunders was the first.

"No, I don't think so," Lady Georgiana said.

Mrs Hornbeam's Haddocks, Hilltops and Hollows - How to survive a fishing holiday with a deliberately mute husband!

"Hmm - no not that one either," she added with a sigh.

Chasing the Sunshine Across the World – How to Travel the Continent and Not End up Lost, Alone and Wanted by the Local Authorities, by
Mr P. Brain and Mrs C.L.U.Less.

"Definitely not that one," she remarked.

Extreme Backpacking – Finding the Bogs amongst the Trees by S.M.Ells.

"No," she said.

Overcoming Timidity, Shyness and a Nervous Disposition – by
Mr Frank Forthright.

"Oh dear," she remarked, getting quite bored with the reading in front of her. She shuffled in her seat to regain her concentration and then continued to send her finger down the book spines along the row.

Waggon Spotting on the Edge of Civilisation – Going Beyond the Train - by Ivor Anorak and Mr I.M.A.Bachelor.

"No," she said.

Desperate Times and Desperate Measures by Messier Rush du-la Toy Lette.

"No," she said again.

Keeping Healthy by Keeping Calm by M.I. Dickey-Ticker.

Strolling through the Wilderness – by Professor S.P. Hagnum-Moss.

Lady Georgiana was quickly losing interest in the selection of books before her. She persisted down the line to see if there was any chance of a good read amongst them. The next few were atlases of the world followed by various 'Did you know' books of general knowledge. Feeling disappointed, she ran her fingers across the final few. She was just about to give up her search when the book at the end of the row caught her eye. It was a lime green colour with gold-leaf lettering running down its spine and was poking out of the row a little more than the other books.

"Ah, what about this?" she said, sliding the book out. "'The Official and Definitive History of Clearwash City. Well I never," she said. "I didn't know that we even had an official history still written down. This will do nicely."

Back in the main lounge of the royal palace, Mr E had managed to calm himself down a little. In fact, he temporarily found his mind distracted from the day's events. Standing alone, in front of a full-length mirror, he admired himself from head to toe. Running his long bony fingers through his deep, coffee-brown locks of curly hair, he made sure that strand by strand was held perfectly in place by lashings of styling gel. He then pursed out his lips and held up his head to get a good look at his prominent chin. Having examined his eyes, nose, neck and shoulders he stood back to check that his new pin-striped, dark blue suit hung on him correctly. With stiff cuffs and long flowing lines running down his torso and trouser legs, he admired the crease free, immaculate fabrics that clothed him. He gazed at the dust free, stain free 'zone of perfection' he thought himself to be, starting from the top of his head and ending triumphantly at his shiny black, glistening boots.

"Well Mr E, I must say you're looking mighty fine, mighty fine!" he said to himself in the mirror.

Mr E made his reflection respond to his words by saying back to himself, "Oh well now, Mr E, you're too kind, just too kind."

"Not at all," he said back to his reflection again, "I know a handsome and cultured man when I see one and from where I stand, I have to say I am most gratified, most gratified indeed. Is this which I see before me not a picture of... pure perfection?"

"Why Mr E, I do believe you are right," his reflection replied to himself again. "A man of refinement, culture, education and superior breeding. Who could ask for more?"

"Who indeed?" came his own reply.

"And can I say that there's only so much, in my opinion, that any one single city, nay one single nation or world, could take of such wondrous stature and grace and you, sir," he said, pointing at his reflection, "have it all."

"Oh, that's too much," replied his reflection again, looking a little bashful. "Please stop, good sir. Your compliments, though true, are a little too forthright for common conversation."

"Well, you're not in any way common," came the reply.

"True," he replied again to himself, "very true."

"I can honestly say, with my hand on my heart, that I find you to be..." but he didn't have time to finish. This nauseous conversation of self-verbal kissing was sadly interrupted by the quick, half-running, footsteps of Ivan coming down the corridor. Mr E quickly finished his conversation by giving himself a gracious nod and walked over to relax on a nearby settee. When Ivan entered the room, he found Mr E lying on a couch, eating grapes.

Erepsin began stuffing as many grapes as he could fit into his mouth without him choking so that his cheeks puffed out with them – he enjoyed squelching them all at the same time, getting the sensation of pure grape juice running down his throat. Ivan found a nearby newspaper and pulled it open to its centre pages where the latest new laws were listed. In between chews, whilst still continuing to stuff his mouth full, Mr E began to make a different tone of conversation. "I tell you, Ivan, something is going on with the people," he said. "I'm not sure I know what it is but I don't like it one bit."

"I don't think that there's anything to worry about Mr E," said Mr Ritant, in a dull tone. "The people know that you're the only person around here with the long-term water supply. They have to do what you tell them or they'll be ruined."

"That may be so," said Mr E, "that may be so. But still they've never tried something this big before. I mean, a whole building has disappeared and we've been flooded. No, I think something needs to be done."

"Like what?" said Mr Ritant.

"I think that we need to make an example of someone important," said Mr E. "Perhaps…"

"Perhaps what?" asked Ivan, looking around the edge of his paper, sensing that the conversation was getting interesting.

Mr E sat up and scratched the end of his nose. He popped a couple more grapes into his mouth and chewed.

"Perhaps a public trial may be the thing," he said, swallowing and dropping more grapes into his mouth.

"Sounds thrilling," replied Ivan.

"Yes," continued Mr E. "All I need to do is to think up some luscious lies to send in someone's direction. We can soon have the people filled with fear when they see one of their petty leaders on trial again. Let me think on this for a bit."

"Who shall we put on trial?" said Ivan.

Mr E just stared back at Ivan with an expression that said, "Don't ask such a stupid question." He filled his mouth with the remaining eight grapes, shoving them all in at once and then took a swig of his drink to wash them down.

"In the meantime," he said, giving out a large belch and wiping his mouth, "whilst I think about this, let's take a balloon trip across the city."

In the lounge, Lady Georgiana was deeply engrossed in her reading. Once the dust had been blown off the cover, she had quickly flipped through the pages and discovered the fascinating history of the Wash-el Dynasty. They turned out to be an imperial line of kings and queens going back to the dawn of time.

"Really!" she had said, when first coming across this information. "Well, I didn't know that."

The book outlined the King's Law rule of these monarchs over various Wash-el Cities in the North and South of their kingdom and how the cities were designed to be managed and lived in.

"Kings Law," she said to herself, tapping her finger on the book where the text was. "Kings Law," she said again, mulling it over in her mind.

She turned a few more pages and found a royal genealogy that read.

"King Wash-El-Pureté the father of Wash-El-Liberté
King Wash-El-Liberté the father of Wash-El-Camarade,
King Wash-El-Camarade the father of Wash-El-Devoir,
King Wash-El-Devoir the father of Wash-El-Bravoure,

King Wash-El-Bravoure the father of Wash-El-Éclairé,

King Wash-El-Éclairé the father of Wash-El-Juste,

King Wash-El-Juste the father of Wash-El-Ami,

King Wash-el-Ami the last ruling king over the city before its rebellion and decline."

Lady Georgiana continued to intensely scan her new find. This," she said, "will make most interesting reading!"

Chapter 23 – The Smelliest Person Ever

"Hold your arms up straight and don't move," said a megaphoned voice.

Basil had just picked Scrub up from his home and the pair were about to start an evening walk across the city when they were suddenly interrupted. Shielding their eyes, they both froze inside the perimeter of a large circular shaft of light. The beam was so bright that it dazzled the pair, causing them to almost crouch on the ground. It shone down from a large, floating police patrol machine. One of Mr E's sniffer squads had located them and now four large balloons descended out of the sky. Out leapt twelve figures; four of whom quickly surrounded the duo and pushed them to the ground whilst the rest of the posse formed a human chain. Hand over hand they pulled long wire cables out from one of their balloon's baskets, on the end of which were various cuboid devices with sensing instruments attached. Switching on the devices, they walked over to the two men who lay spread-eagled on the cobbled floor and began to probe them with their different smelling mechanisms. First they went over Basil, hovering the various sets of apparatus just above him, sweeping up and down from head to foot. The sensors beeped every time an official smell was located on him.

"Right" said one of the sniffer squad. "We've located four smells of today's lotion and three from yesterday. They're small traces but you'll pass; now what about your friend?"

As soon as they applied their sniffer devices to Scrub... beep, beep, beep, beep, beep, beep, they went repeatedly. The squad all stood back in dumbfounded amazement. Shaking their devices a few times, they tried again. Beep, beep, beep, beep, beep, beep, they went, giving the same result. Moving all around him they systematically ran their sniffers over Scrub and nearly every inch of him had some kind of official lotion smell. They set up other sniffer devices, thinking that the first ones must have developed a fault, but they too beeped and beeped and beeped.

"Incredible," whispered one of them, in stunned amazement.

"Amazing," said another, staring at his sniffer device and reading off its data, "we can even find smells from over a month ago."

The squad gathered into a tight circle, passing their devices between each other to share and compare their corporate readings.

"Look, there's one from last year," said another.

They set up a tripod and attached what looked like a laser gun to its top. "Hold very still," they told him and turned the laser on.

Within moments, it started to send out waves of streaming light that shimmered in ripples across Scrub as he lay face down on the floor. Slowly, as the minutes past, Scrub felt himself heating up under the laser beam's powerful glow, but what he wasn't aware of was the small particles of steam that were now rising from his clothes and wafting up into the atmosphere above him. As these almost invisible droplets floated into the air, the laser beam zoomed over each one, analysing it for a perfect identification. Once it had scanned him all over, they turned Scrub onto his back and the scanning process began again.

Scrub just lay there with his eyes tightly closed, not quite knowing what was happening. Finally the machine stopped and spent a few seconds bleeping to itself and doing various calculations. Then the laser head straightened up and, from some speakers on its sides, played a celebration tune followed by an electronic voice that squawked out the following message.

"Congratulations citizen, on your incredible achievement. We have found more official odours on you than on any other citizen in the history of Clearwash City. Total number of smells, four hundred and sixteen, including the following classic aromas:

La Pong,
Snorky Porky Sniffles,
Old Mice,
Pwoor-du-Potty,
Odourus du Wifus,
Chalice of Slime,
Mystique de-la-Mouse Hole,
Wiesel's Garbage Banquet,
Botany Boghouse,
Leach Lagoon,
Kitchen Smears,
Cheese de-la-Fungus de-la-Stinkus,
Smella Mi Cart-horse,
Putrid Stilton,
Dregs de Canal,
Ghastrus Vulgar,
Odorus Perspire,
Dunghill,
Gooey by Oozey,
Wreakus Repulsideous,
Quagmire Volcano,
Sherbet Smellums,
Pongy Hi Stinker,
Achoo,
Bucket Boudoir,
Drainpipe,
Dungus de-la Cattle Pat,
and Uncle Jack's Bouquet of Bowls, Basins and Bins!

Well done citizen, for attaining the highest standard that the state can expect from any obedient resident."

The team of sniffer squad police all clapped and helped Scrub to his feet; one after the other they vigorously shook his hand, showering him with compliments and patting him on the back.

"Never come across anyone with so many official smells on them as you," said one.

"You're the smelliest person on record," said another. "It's people like you that make our job worthwhile," he added.

Out came a bag from one of the squad's backpacks and, after rummaging through it, a big, bright, red rosette was found and pinned onto Scrub's jacket.

"You're certainly the smelliest person we've ever met," they said. "Well done citizen and keep it up," they chanted together with one voice.

With that, they packed up their things and most of them zoomed off on what looked like small, motorised skateboards to find some more people to check. As the four balloons sailed back up into the sky, Scrub stood motionless in a stunned silence, gently stroking the rosette with the tips of his fingers and quite overcome by his new ribbon. Basil just looked at him, speechless, shrugging his shoulders and shaking his head. He glanced up into the evening sky and breathed out a loud sigh; his breath condensing in the crisp, cold evening air.

"How did you keep all of those smells on you Scrub, when we've all been soaked today by the flood from the waterworks?" he asked. "When I got home I just dabbed a couple of smells on me from the last two bottles."

"Oh," said Scrub, a little embarrassed by the question. "Well," and then he paused. "Please don't tell Lady Pluggat," he whispered, "...as I don't think she'll be happy with me."

Basil just continued his stare whilst Scrub shuffled uneasily on his feet, as if he were a schoolboy about to own up to a bad thing that he'd done.

"As you know," he continued gingerly, "every morning her ladyship kindly pours most of her lotion onto the back of my head, which is really nice of her and Mr E's lotions are so good that the smell stays there all day. So at the end of each day, when I get home, I look for any tissues I can find and wipe my head with them. Then I put them into my grandfather's great big treasure chest; that's where I put all of my most wonderful things. When I want to treat myself, all I have to do is climb into the chest and roll around in it for a bit and that covers me all over in Mr E's delicious smelling lotions. I don't do it too often," he added cautiously, "just every now and again when I feel that I've been particularly good and deserve a reward."

Scrub stood there, looking at Basil with puppy eyes. He felt he had just bared his soul and let out one of his deepest secrets. Basil returned Scrub's stare, trying to get his head around what he had just heard.

"You actually like these smells?" he finally asked.

"Love 'em!" said Scrub proudly, "and because we did such a wonderful thing in getting the waterworks going today I decided to treat myself. Once I got home and into some dry clothes, I jumped into my tissue collection and had a good roll for, err, about five minutes I think. Don't you think it's good to treat yourself Basil, when you've been good?"

Basil turned his back on Scrub and scratched his nose and forehead, not quite knowing what to say or do next. He was about to walk on, to try to forget the whole issue, when glancing over his shoulder he saw that Scrub had already walked off.

"Scrub," he called, "where are you going?"

"I just thought that I would go back to my house and get something," replied Scrub. "I've remembered I need to let my cats out before they make a mess." Scrub returned to his house, just a few doors down from where they were and, after a few moments, came out with a basket under his arm that had a pile of washing in it.

"Scrub," said Basil, without thinking as they walked on together, "what are you carrying that basket of washing for?" Almost immediately after the words had left his mouth Basil wished that he hadn't asked the question - he knew that Scrub's reply could be quite long winded and would not in any way make much sense.

"Well," Scrub replied. "I've managed to get all of my clothes and bed linen wet in all of this waterworks pond water that's everywhere. So, I've washed them in my rain water basin, you know the one that's hidden under my toilet, and now that I've got them clean I'm looking for a place to hang them up to get them dry."

147

"I'm sure someone will one day find that underground wash basin of yours," said Basil. "You can't keep it hidden forever."

"Oh I think I can," replied Scrub confidently. "I've never had anyone stay more than a couple of seconds in my toilet room. They always seem to leave the room far more quickly than when they go in, so I think it's quite safe to hide my basin there and wash my things in it."

"Well, can't you get your clothes dry at home?" said Basil, again wishing to himself that he would stop asking Scrub questions.

"No, I need to hang them up somewhere where there's a bit more wind," said Scrub. "I have used my washing line at home in the past, sometimes for a few days, but I know they will still be wet."

"Scrub!" said Basil, "washing lines are banned! You'll get flushed if you do that."

"Oh, it's OK," said Scrub. "I don't use it any more except at night-time. No one can see my washing then."

"But your clothes won't get dry at night either," said Basil.

"Yes I know," said Scrub, shrugging his shoulders. "I found that out months ago and I know it's true as I've hung all my washing out at night now for the past few weeks."

"So why do you still do it?" said Basil, looking confused.

"To get the washing dry of course," said Scrub.

"But it won't get dry will it?" said Basil.

"Yes I know," said Scrub. "That's why I've got my washing with me now."

"It is?" said Basil, looking more confused than ever.

"That's right," replied Scrub.

"Come on," said Basil, picking up the pace at which they were walking and not wishing to develop the conversation any further. "We'd better meet up with the Professor to try and find a way to get Georgie free."

"You mean Lady Pluggat?" enquired Scrub.

"Of course," replied Basil.

The twosome walked to the end of the grey, dusty street and turned the corner. Passing beneath a huge archway and down a long flight of steps, they found themselves at the foot of a dried up, muddy canal. This they climbed down into and followed for some time until the maze of homes, stalls and shops were left behind. As they continued their walk they entered Clearwash City's industrial zone, or so it was called in its heyday. Now it was lifeless and dormant. After ascending an old goods tramline, which took them towards the outskirts of the city, they began to pass by many old and broken down buildings, alongside which stood a variety of abandoned industrial machines, corroded and long dead.

Huge mills, with their rusted broken water wheels, stood side-by-side, empty and lifeless. There were factories with blackened chimneys and tall towers that looked as if they would topple with neglect. Windows were smashed, roofs fallen in and from the wooden beams of many a broken building came a smell of woodworm-ridden dry rot. Together they broadcast their silent witness to a once lucrative and luxurious past. It brought a sigh of dismay to the heart to see this empty, lonesome place, full of memories from yesteryear but now unoccupied and unfulfilled. It felt as if the place was still seeking some kind of vindication, to ask why it was now treated so badly - that no one should live or work there anymore. "What have I done to deserve this?" it would ask if it could.

After exchanging very brief and muted salutations with several mine workers who were on their way home after a long day at work, they left the industrial area behind and entered one of the city parks. The dirt gravel paths crunched under their feet as the narrow trail wound in and through avenues of brown, dry grassy pitches; often straddled by boulevards of tired bushes and tall trees, sick with thirst and neglect. To the southern side of the park they ambled until they reached a large, imposing rockery. It was empty and bare with bland, lifeless soil crumbling between the rocks and boulders.

Basil stopped next to a wooden sign displayed on the rockery that read, "Herbs and Spices Garden – created by Rupert Brownman." He ran his finger along the edge of the sign as if to say "hello" to an old friend. Casting his gaze over the barren spaces that sat between the rocks, he remembered the inhabitants that used to live there. Lost in thought, he stood motionless, forgetting where he was and entering a world that had long past and gone. He wasn't sure how long he stood there, with Scrub waiting patiently by his side, but however long it was, it was too long.

Basil came back to himself with a jolt as the whoosh, whoosh, whoosh, sound of propelled balloons descended upon them. Out of the sky they dropped until they hovered about eight feet off the ground. Basil and Scrub looked up with their stomachs churning as they saw Mr E leaning over the side of the first balloon. He made a beeline for them both.

"Well Basil," bellowed Mr E, hovering a few feet above them. "What are you doing here at this time in the evening? Can't seem to think why you would need to be in the middle of nowhere right now. Up to no good, no doubt!"

Basil looked down at the rockery sign, then across at Scrub and then back to Mr E.

"Just taking Scrub out for an evening walk," he said. "It's what Lady Georgiana would have to do if she were here; look after Scrub I mean and give him plenty of exercise."

Mr E glanced over at Scrub and then back at Basil. He took the balloon lower down and leaned out so far that he spoke to Basil from just above his head. "Have you managed to find out the name of the person, or persons, who have caused such a ghastly mess in my great city this afternoon?" he enquired in a tone full of accusation.

"Not yet Mr E," stammered Basil, "but we are working on it."

"Not good enough," said Mr E, "not good enough! I need to know who they are! I need to know where they are! I need to know tonight! Do you hear me?"

149

"Err, yes Mr E," said Basil. "I hear you very well."

Mr E stretched right out of the balloon's basket, poking his finger into the top part of Basil's chest several times as he spoke.

"Tell your people that if you don't come up with the names by the end of this evening, I shall bring out your wonderful Lady Georgiana Pluggat-Lynette for a public trial tomorrow morning."

"Trial Mr E?" said Basil, looking very surprised. "What for?"

"You'll find out," said Mr E, with a mean and joyful glint in his eyes. Basil found it rather disturbing that someone's face could actually brighten and shine with the thought of something wicked and malicious. Summoning up his courage, he forced some words out of his mouth in Lady Georgiana's defence.

"But surely she hasn't done anything... wrong?" he said, in a faltering tone.

"Oh has she not?" replied Mr E. "Mark my words you overweight, disloyal relic of the past. I know where your loyalties lie. If I don't get the names of all of those people who were involved in your waterworks plot then Lady Georgiana will find herself on a public trial from which there will be no return. Mark my words, Basil, mark my words. Tonight I will have the names of those people or tomorrow you will have to say goodbye to your good lady!"

Mr E glanced at the sign that Basil was standing next to and then back at Basil who swallowed hard and wished he were somewhere else.

"What's that?!" said Mr E, pointing at Scrub's wash basket.

"It's my red rosette Me E," came Scrub's reply, thinking that Mr E was pointing at the red ribbon that was pinned to his chest. "It was given to me this evening by one of your sniffer squads for being the person in the city who has the highest number of your lotion smells on them, ever! They said there's never been anyone as smelly as me," he added proudly.

Mr E hesitated, not sure what to make of, or where to take the conversation that he found himself having with Scrub (which was quite a common occurrence when Scrub was exchanging pleasantries with anyone). "Oh," he finally said.

"The names Basil," said Mr E, once more turning his attention to Basil. "I shall have those names!"

Then, with the pull of a rope that dangled from his balloon, Mr E and Ivan zoomed off, followed by four more balloons carrying the personal guards from the palace.

With a great sense of relief Basil quickly walked on with Scrub following. They stepped off the main pathway and hurriedly passed between a tightly bunched cluster of Elm trees. Whilst under the cover of this natural canopy they followed an unmarked but familiar trail. On and on they went, striding through bushes, stepping over brambles, under hedges, leaping ditches. They scrambled up and down steep earthen banks, covered with a mantle of thick moss and through networks of small-interconnected wild flower meadows, laden with hardy shrubbery. Eventually they stepped onto a large dried out aqueduct and descended into a great rusty pipe.

150

This they followed until they left the pipe behind and the pair eventually came out of the undergrowth from between the branches of a sickly, overgrown rhododendron bush. A few hundred yards away were the iron gates that led to the woodland garden and the Professor's bunker. After looking upwards and from left to right, to make sure all was safe, they hastily ran towards the gate.

Chapter 24 – Rockets For Breakfast

The Professor's underground bunker smelt of something that had been thoroughly overcooked and burnt to a crisp. Now lit with only candles and a few old lanterns, all that remained after the bubble gum explosion were six charred tables that stood in a line down the middle of the room, about which were a scattering of assorted chairs. On the tables were an assortment of scorched books, papers and pens. Scrub sat at one of the tables sorting through his washing whilst an exhausted Basil sat nearby. He turned his back on Scrub's activities as the Professor brought him what looked like a drink of hot chocolate, though perhaps in reality it may have been something quite different.

It had been a long and difficult evening so far. Not only had Basil and the Professor reported back to the rebel council about why the waterworks expedition had failed but they also had to share the news that Lady Georgiana was to go on trial tomorrow. Once completed, they then had to talk to all the different rebel sub-committees that also existed in the city. These turned up like clockwork at the Professor's bunker every twenty minutes throughout the evening. By the time they had finished they had talked to the:

"Let's get rid of Mr E" committee;

"Freedom for the City" committee;

"Freedom Fighters for the City" committee;

"We Want a Wash" committee;

"Where's My Soap?" committee;

"I don't want to be Smelly" committee;

"Freedom from Smells" committee;

"The Genuine Freedom from Smells" committee;

"The Really Genuine Freedom from Smells" committee;

"Soap Suds for Everyone" committee;

"Who's Up for Washing?" committee;

"Let's All Wash together" committee;

"Let's Get Back to Washing" committee;

and finally

"The Revenge of the Dirty Dish Washers" committee.

It had been exhausting. Each group had to be addressed separately, as they would not talk to, or be in the same room with each other - being in direct competition to see who would gain the honour and praise for setting everyone free. By the end of it all Basil didn't know whether he was coming or going and the Professor was now in an irritable and grumpy mood.

"In the fullness of time..." the last committee had chanted as they left the bunker.

"In the fullness of time..." Basil half growled back at them.

"Why can't they just all agree to work together?" said the Professor, after the last set of people had gone. "If we were actually united in how to go about getting rid of Mr E then I'm sure we would have done it by now. Too many people following their own little schemes where they want to feel important I say! Well they're not using my bunker again for any of their meetings. I've had enough of them."

Basil just nodded and sipped his imitation hot chocolate.

"I'm feeling rather strange," he eventually said.

"Hmm yes, me too," said the Professor, sitting down opposite him and rubbing his tender stomach. "I don't think this waterworks pond water is doing us any good."

"But we have been filtering and boiling it," continued Basil. "It can't be that bad for us. Surely boiling it would make it safe?"

"It's obviously not enough," replied the Professor, scratching his newly growing beard. "We shall have to get a fresh supply of water soon. It won't do our long term health any good to carry on as we are. Some of the people don't have the same equipment that we have and they're already looking really sick. I'm afraid that if Mr E doesn't give us back his supply in the next few days, then it could be disastrous."

"Well it's disastrous for Georgie as it is," said Basil.

"The Professor nodded, looking deflated. For once without any conversation, the two of them just sat there, staring into blank space with nothing but distance in their eyes. Scrub fell asleep, his head in his wash basket amongst the wet and sodden clothes.

Basil broke the silence, "There's only a few hours left for us to get her out of this mess," he said. "Otherwise it's bound to end in her being flushed out of the city."

"So we need a plan of escape," said the Professor abruptly, coming out of his dazed stare.

With these words, he got up and began to walk about the room, pacing here and there whilst looking for inspiration. Eventually he went to one of the back storerooms and came back with charts, books and note pads. Basil watched the Professor search through drawings, sketches and page upon page of writing. Knowing that the Professor's mind was busy and feeling a little useless, he began to tap his fingers on the table in front of him, making them touch the table one after the other in a sort of ripple effect, but quickly stopped when the Professor gave him an annoyed stare.

So Basil sat back in his chair and folded his arms. He could do nothing but sit and look gloomy; being sure that nothing could be done to save Lady Georgiana. Putting his elbows onto the table, he let his head slip into his hands. He wasn't sure if he was trying to think of something to help get Lady Georgiana released or if he was still overwhelmed at her being arrested.

"I have it!" cried the Professor.

"You have what?" said Scrub, suddenly waking from his sleep.

"The answer Scrub, the answer," said the Professor, holding up a drawing. "Basil, in this laboratory I have an old weather rocket stored away."

"A rocket?" said Basil. "A real rocket?"

"Well it's sort of an experimental rocket actually," said the Professor. "Sometime tonight we could smuggle it into the palace lounge and, with the use of a harness, Lady Georgiana could attach it to herself and be propelled to freedom through those high glass windows near the roof. We can pre-programme the rocket to land in one of the nearby deserts where we can send a search party that will find her, hmm, probably within a couple of days."

"That's fantastic Professor," said Basil.

"Thank you Basil," replied the Professor.

"There is just one slight problem," added Basil.

"What's that?" enquired the Professor.

"How on earth are you going to disguise such a large thing as a rocket so that you can get it into the palace lounge in the first place?" Then Basil added sarcastically, "You could always try and disguise it as a very large sausage for her breakfast."

"All right, all right," said the Professor, "I get your point."

"I think that the sausage idea is great," said Scrub.

"Shut up Scrub," said Basil and the Professor together.

"There must be some way of getting the rocket into the lounge though," said the Professor. "Perhaps we could get it through the palace sewers or something."

"You're forgetting one more thing," said Basil. "Georgie doesn't like heights and what about when she lands? It's most likely that she'd be killed."

"Let's go for a walk," said the Professor. "I can't think down here anymore."

Basil and the Professor walked through the city for quite some time that evening, dodging the police patrols and sniffer squads as they went. As the late evening turned into the darkness of night, they made their way towards Basil's house on the edge of the square next to the palace. They stood outside his door for a good few minutes, both of them lost in thought as to what to do about Lady Georgiana. What they didn't notice was that Lady Georgiana had seen them from one of the top floor palace windows and had opened it to call from.

"Pssst," said Lady Georgiana.

"Was that you Basil?" said the Professor.

"No," said Basil.

"Pssssssssssssssssst," said Lady Georgiana in a hushed voice, still trying to get their attention without being overheard by anyone in the palace.

"There it is again," said the Professor. "Are you sure it's not you? Are you deflating or something?"

"No I am certainly not!" said Basil, quite incensed by the question.

"Over here. It's me," said Lady Georgiana, in a muted tone.

Basil and the Professor looked around for a few seconds, trying to see where the voice was coming from. Then Basil saw her.

"Ah, there you are Georgie," he said, and they both walked over to the wall. "We've just been discussing how to get you out."

"Never mind that now," replied Lady Georgiana. "This is more important. I need you to both listen very carefully."

"I am all ears M'lady," said the Professor.

"Me too," said Basil.

Lady Georgiana continued in a low voice, "I have discovered a history book and I think that I've perhaps got an answer for us. Now this is what I want you to do. We need a large flag, a white one. This white flag has to be hoisted and flown from the flagpole of the palace building's central clock tower. You must find a way of getting it up there as soon as possible. Once it is flying from the flagpole, that means that we send out the message that we surrender."

"Surrender to who?" said Basil.

"Never mind that," said Lady Georgiana. "It's too difficult to explain. Now can you do it?"

The Professor looked at Basil who simply stared back, not quite knowing what to say.

"You're quite sure about this Lady Georgiana?" said the Professor.

"Yes I am," said Lady Georgiana. "Do you think that you can do it?"

"Right away," said Basil.

"First thing in the morning," said the Professor. "As soon as it's light. I wouldn't want to go into the palace grounds tonight whilst the dogs are out. Mr E keeps them too hungry for my liking."

"But they're only Jack Russells," said Basil.

"I know," said the Professor. "But they make a real mess of your ankles and anyway, they're so noisy. When they see anyone all the guards instantly know that you're there."

Lady Georgiana just stared at the Professor.

"We'll get it done tonight," said Basil.

"Do try," she replied. "Just come up with a good plan to get the flag up there."

"We will," said Basil. "You can count on us."

Lady Georgiana attempted a smile and closed the window. Basil and the Professor looked at each other, not quite knowing what to make of the last minutes' conversation.

"Well that was odd," said Basil.

"Very strange indeed," said the Professor. "I shall go back and spend the night in the bunker with my staff and work on this project. I'll let you know as soon as we've come up with something so you can come and see us when we get the mission underway."

"And, of course, tell Scrub to go home and take his medicine," said Basil.

"Will do," replied the Professor.

"Was it wise to leave him there all alone in the bunker?" called Basil, as the Professor walked away. "There was a time when you had him completely banned from the place. I was surprised that you even let him in tonight."

"Well," replied the Professor over his shoulder, "after the bubble gum explosion there wasn't much left of anything; nothing that could do any real damage to anyone. So I figured that Scrub couldn't do much harm either."

"True," said Basil.

Just then, however, there was a rumbling sound from the outer circle of the city. This was followed by a muffled boom! Basil looked at the Professor who turned his head slowly in the direction of his bunker. Smoke could be seen drifting into the night sky from that area.

"No!" said the Professor, and he ran off across the square to go back to the bunker.

Basil couldn't stop the big grin that appeared on his face as he watched the Professor speeding off. He turned and walked to his house on the edge of the square and, despite their desperate situation, allowed himself for just a brief moment, a small giggle.

Chapter 25 – The Man With The Wet Washing

The next morning, before Basil and the Professor were up and about, Scrub was meandering through the city with his wet washing, seeking a good place to hang it up. It didn't matter to him if he was caught, he just wanted his clothing dry and its constant dampness was irritating him beyond his patience. After trying four or five times to hang his washing up in different places and being moved on by various members of the city population, he now found himself walking back through the main market square towards Basil's house.

"Scrub, what have you got there?" said a voice behind him.

Scrub turned to see that the voice belonged to Ivan Robert Ritant the city Prime Minister.

"It's my washing Mr Ritant," said Scrub. "I'm trying to find a place to dry it and it's very hard with all this water about."

"Well that's not my fault Scrub," said Ivan. "Whoever let in all of this pond water should have thought of that before they did it."

"But we didn't know that it was going to flood the city," said Scrub, without thinking to whom he was speaking.

"Oh, what was that? And who's *we*?" said Ivan.

"Oh, err I err," said Scrub, not knowing exactly what to say next.

Mr Ritant leant forward and poked his short, fat finger at Scrub. "Who's *we* Scrub?" he repeated.

"Oh, err well, err, I think that err…" said Scrub.

"Yes," said Ivan, still waiting for an answer.

"Can I hang my washing on one of the palace walls Mr Ritant, as I think that it will dry up there?" said Scrub. "I'm trying to get it dry you know and if it doesn't get dry today I'll have to get it dry another day but that's no good as…".

"Don't try and change the subject Scrub," interrupted Mr Ritant.

"What subject Mr Ritant?" said Scrub, shrugging his shoulders.

"*The* subject, Scrub," said Mr Ritant.

"The subject?" said Scrub, trying to look as if he hadn't a clue what Mr Ritant was talking about.

"Yes, the subject," said Mr Ritant.

"Oh err …" Scrub paused for a moment… "About my washing you mean Mr Ritant?" said Scrub.

"No Scrub," said Ivan.

Just then, to Scrub's relief, the Professor entered the square. His worn-out face showed a serious lack of sleep. The night before had been long, difficult and quite fruitless. He and his team had tried two operations to get a white flag up on the palace tower and both had failed.

The first was called 'Operation Dummy' where they had let George fly in a replica of a police balloon towards the palace. It wasn't a real balloon, just a look-alike fabric stitched together and filled with hot air - like a children's bouncy castle. All was going well as George floated on the night breeze in complete silence towards the palace, ready and poised to attach the flag to the pole. As the dummy balloon made its final approach, it was caught and picked up by a sudden gust of wind and blown on the flagpole's pointed tip. The fabric immediately punctured sending George, his flag and his balloon, shooting off into the night sky; just like when you let go of a child's party balloon before tying up the end. George had shot up into the clouds, disappeared from sight and not come down again.

The Professor, watching from a distance, saw the balloon zoom off into the night and let out a big groan.

"Goodbye George," said Basil. "I know you must be upset," he said, turning to the Professor and putting his hand onto the Professor's shoulder to give him some comfort. "He was a good man," he added.

"Good man?" replied the Professor, pulling his shoulder away from beneath Basil's hand. "Good man? Don't be ridiculous. I've got another twelve 'Georges' back in the bunker. It took me two months to construct that dummy police balloon and now it's burst on its first mission and lost in an instant!"

Basil was lost for words.

The second disaster was 'Operation Creepy'. The idea was to use a set of electronic robotic creepy crawling insects. These ant or cockroach like creatures were to carry square pieces of cloth on their backs, being programmed to walk through the city drains and then up through the palace grounds. They would then climb the palace walls, up the clock tower and up the flagpole, assembling themselves together on the pole into a large square. As each robotic ant joined with the legs of another they would, in theory, form a flag shape and the mission would be completed. Quite ingenious everyone thought – and so it was.

The Professor had been very excited about the project and was very hopeful of success. Initially the mission went well and the cockroach robots tiptoed off at high speed, through the city drains and up into the palace grounds. They were excellent covert creatures – now scurrying here, now scampering there - undetected by the guards in the semi-darkness, not even the palace dogs knew they were there. The Professor rubbed his hands together, gleefully peering with delight at the small tracking dots that appeared on his little monitor screen which showed their progress.

"Wonderful, wonderful, wonderful!" he exclaimed to his fellow scientists and helpers. "A brilliant idea from brilliant minds," he added.

All his assistants and helpers in the bunker shared in his enthusiasm, all that is except three or four, who stood glancing at each other, exchanging nervous looks.

"Nearly there now," said the Professor, as he intently watched the little metal critters scuttle their way towards the flagpole. All of the dots on the Professor's screen came together in a long line.

"They're assembling, getting ready to go up the wall and then up the flagpole," the Professor commented.

One by one, all the dots marched forward in single file towards the clock tower. They had just drawn parallel with the palace kitchens, when they all abruptly stopped. There they stood, waiting for something or calculating to make a decision of some kind. The Professor stared at the screen and then tapped it a few times to make sure it wasn't faulty. To his horror, the dots all split up and went off in different directions, some towards the kitchens and others towards the food stores.

"What on earth is going on?" the Professor demanded.

The main problem was that, unknown to him, some of his assistants had, over the years, also spent some time programming these same insect robots - but for very much their own purposes. They had been using them to regularly visit the palace building but not for the purpose of spying or retrieving materials for science experiments. The assistant's aim was simple. To get the robots to search for, locate and then retrieve delicious goodies and treats from the palace kitchens and storerooms. Then they would bring them back to the bunker for a midnight feast when those particular workers were on a late night shift together. This had been going on for years. However, as is the case with all long-term deceptions, there comes a time when the perpetrators get egg on their faces - or should I say, "Egg tarts on their insects."

For, as we have just said, once the mission was underway, the cockroach robots initially did as they were told by the Professor's programming - up to the point of being able to detect food. Once they were parallel with the kitchens, their other programming instincts kicked in, so off they all trotted to the kitchens and food store.

From the insects point of view they had fulfilled their programmed mission within two hours and fifty minutes or so of entering the palace grounds. They had sought out food and then correctly assembled themselves into a flag shape. The flag, however, was not on the palace clock tower flagpole, as the Professor had hoped, but back in the bunker's storeroom where the cockroaches always secretly fed the Professor's staff. The Professor gawped in disbelief as he followed the dots on his screen until they all returned to his bunker, entering via the air vents.

"They're going into the storeroom!" he cried, as a cockroach scurried past his feet with a jam tart on its back.

He ran down the corridors of his bunker and burst open the storeroom door. There, on the table, was the flag with the small robots underneath, attached to each other. Scattered across this white flag, were lots of yummy foods collected from the palace pantry. The spread of sandwiches, buns, scones, jellies, trifles and cakes made a tremendous display of supper on what now looked like a white tablecloth. If the mission had not been so important, perhaps they would have laughed and had a great midnight feast together, but for some reason no one ate any of it, despite hungry tummies.

Now that it was morning, the Professor was desperate to get his mission for Lady Georgiana fulfilled. As soon as he saw Mr Ritant talking to Scrub, he walked quickly towards him, putting on a big welcoming smile over his tired, sleepy face.

"Ah, Mr Ritant," said the Professor, "Just the person I've been looking for."

"What?" said Mr Ritant, surprised that anyone should be looking for him at all.

"I need your permission to do something," said the Professor. "I thought that I had better ask you as you seem to be the person in the city most clued up in matters of science."

"My permission?" said Mr Ritant.

"Yes, your permission," said the Professor, gently tapping Ivan on the shoulder in a friendly way as if they were old pals.

"What for?" said Mr Ritant, standing back a little and not quite knowing what to make of this friendliness that the Professor was displaying.

"Well," said the Professor, suddenly adopting a very serious face. "I want to go to the top of the clock tower to recreate an experiment that will illustrate Newton's Law of gravity."

"Pardon?" said Mr Ritant.

"Newton's Law of gravity," said the Professor. "It's the twenty fifth anniversary today of the city's Science Life Rotary Club and I want to do an experiment that will illustrate this wonderful law to the club members; you know, as a kind of celebration of our collective life together and all of the good that they've brought into the city. I thought that the best place to perform such a prestigious experiment should be the clock tower, it being the tallest tower on the palace site. The future of our young scientists in the city could be greatly enhanced today by this event, not to mention all of the charity work that they do. So, knowing your appreciation of scientific matters and how concerned you are for the future of scientific invention and knowledge in this city – I assume we have your permission to go up?"

"Certainly not," said Mr Ritant, taking another step back.

"Oh," said the Professor, looking a little disappointed. "It would only take a few minutes."

"No," said Mr Ritant, shaking his head, "absolutely not!"

At this point Basil came out of his front doorway and onto the square, completely unaware of the conversation the Professor had just started.

"Ah Mr Ritant," he said. "Just the person I've been looking for."

"Really?" said Ivan, seeing that this was the second person in just a few minutes who was looking for him and the suspicion within him was growing all the time.

"Yes," said Basil. He walked up to Mr Ritant beaming a big smile. "I need your permission to do something."

"My permission?" replied Mr Ritant, sarcastically.

"Yes your permission," said Basil.

"And what would this be for?" enquired Mr Ritant.

"Well I want to go to the top of the tower to do some sightseeing, to see... the beautiful view," said Basil.

"The beautiful view?" echoed Mr Ritant.

"Yes, the beautiful view," said Basil.

"What... beautiful view?" said Ivan.

"Well like, like," Basil found himself a little stuck for words and then he said, "like the cesspit for example."

"The cesspit?" said Mr Ritant.

"Yes I do believe that there are some extraordinary insect species on the cesspit at this time of year and the best place to see them is from the clock tower; got a really strong pair of binoculars you know and that way I can get up close to those amazing creatures without having to endure the terrible smell – or get bitten by any of the little flying critters! Can I go?" said Basil.

"No," said Mr Ritant.

"Oh," said Basil.

"Can I take some of my science students up there to do some experiments on wind direction?" said the Professor.

"What?" said Mr Ritant again.

The Professor launched into a long spiel about the wind and the weather. How the city was undergoing serious climate change and how critical it was that they got on top of the situation. With animated arm and hand movements, he stressed the importance of taking exact readings and how the clock tower was the only suitable place in the city to take those readings from. He went on and on, trying to explain the angles and speed of the wind that came in from the desert and the potential destruction that could come upon them all if they ignored the current warning signs that were all around them.

"...and I must say that, when we're all alive and well in years to come, I'm sure they'll be setting up a statue in your honour to celebrate how your decision today saved us all," he added.

Ivan frowned and opened his mouth to object, but before he had chance to speak Basil butted in.

"Don't forget exercise!" he exclaimed. "Not only is the clock tower good for science but remember, it's a keep fit local resource too. Too many tummies like mine are appearing on the streets these days. I feel in need of some good exercise and I think that the best place to get some is on the clock tower stairs. They'd be such a challenge to these ageing legs of mine but this heart is willing and ready. Perhaps we could charge people for going up, then we could all keep fit and raise money for you at the same time?"

Ivan opened his mouth again to answer but before he could do so, the Professor continued.

"What an excellent idea," he said. "We really do need to make use of the palace's natural resources to help the city population keep fit. Do you know Basil that we could not only do exercise up there but also recommend to the city people that they partake in the 'taking the air' too, for those that have health problems that is. A quick jog up the stairs will get everyone's heart racing and then a good intake of clean air will clear their lungs."

Basil heartedly agreed. He then came up with another suggestion where they might do some sightseeing from the tower and use it to talk about the city's rich history. To this the Professor added an idea about local tours and how the palace's social status leant itself to being used for the purpose of education to help the people appreciate the great value of living in what he called, "this wondrous place."

More ideas flowed between the pair and for the next few minutes they stood on either side of Ivan outlining schemes, concepts and inspirational proposals for using the clock tower to enrich the life of the city.

"Soon everyone will want to be up there," cried the Professor, "appreciating our great city and it will be you," pointing to Ivan, "who has enabled us to do it."

Ivan stumbled for words, glancing between the pair. Then "No!" he said sternly, pointing his finger defiantly back and forth at them both. "No! No! No! No! No! What's all this and why this sudden interest in the tower?"

"Not much reason really," replied the Professor.

"Oh really," said Ivan. "Who do you both think I am? Do you think I'm as stupid as your friend Scrub here?"

"Not quite, Mr Ritant," said the Professor.

"What?" said Mr Ritant.

"No of course not Mr Ritant," said Basil. "We were just..."

"You were just up to something," said Ivan. "That's what you were just."

"Mr Ritant," said the Professor. "How could you think that we were..."

"You're up to something," interrupted Ivan, "both of you. Now be off and leave me in peace and you can't go to the clock tower, either of you. Now clear off or you'll be arrested!"

At this, the Professor and Basil both looked at each other and headed back towards Basil's house.

"Now Scrub," said Ivan, letting out a sigh of relief that they were both gone. "What were we talking about?"

"My washing Mr Ritant," said Scrub. "I'm the man with the wet washing."

"Oh, yes," said Ivan. "Go and put it wherever you like. I've got a headache after listening to those two annoying friends of yours."

"Thank you Mr Ritant," said Scrub.

Scrub went off in the direction of the palace and Ivan went out into the city. The Professor and Basil stopped outside Basil's door, a little unsure what to do next.

"What are we going to do now?" said Basil.

"I don't know," said the Professor.

They both walked over to the wall that surrounded the palace, to the part that was closest to the lounge window.

"Lady Georgiana! Georgie are you there?" called Basil.

He threw a small pebble that rattled against the window.

A few moments later the window opened and Lady Georgiana's face popped through.

"Basil, Professor," said Lady Georgiana, looking happy to see both of them. "Do you have good news?" she asked. "Have you managed to do it?" Her face dropped, however, when she saw how despondent they both looked.

"I'm sorry Georgie, but I'm afraid we've failed," said Basil. "We can't get anywhere near the clock tower. Ivan suspects something."

"We've done all we can but we'll keep thinking," added the Professor, trying to sound positive.

"Well you'll have to think fast," replied Lady Georgiana, "as in a short while I'm told I'll be on trial."

"We'll continue to try our best," said Basil.

"I know you will," said Lady Georgiana. She knew, however, that there wasn't much hope.

Chapter 26 – Bring Out The Guilty Party

The late morning had turned blisteringly hot as the sweltering sun beamed down its fiery, scorching rays; baking the white stone walls and streets of Clearwash City. Everyone felt stifled with the heat which hung in the air like a thick, suffocating blanket. Yet, at the same time, it was all very odd. For even though there was a fair gathering of cloud cover that would normally provide a good measure of shade for the people, none of it got in the way of the bright shining and radiant champion who continually blazed in the heights of the heavens. It was as if a halo of open sky had been carved into the clouds. Not normal, but this went mainly unnoticed by the city populace.

The river that had come out of the waterworks the day before was now almost dried up. It had left behind a heavy greenish-brown residue on the ground that smelt bad, a little like rotting cabbage and the people found it hazardously slippery. Worse than this though, they were also feeling nauseously queasy from drinking the waterworks flood water, which Mr E had forced on them by banning his own supply. Many were becoming very ill and, needless to say, everyone was more than a little irritated by the situation. People staggered from place to place, some of them quite delirious, others violently sick and seeking to find some kind of refuge, not knowing where to go and what to do. The normally lively city now sounded more like a house of the dead and the dying.

It was getting on towards mid-day and the market square filled with people. None of them wanted to be there but the police patrol balloons had spent the previous hour droning their way over the capital, sending out their monotonous and repetitious message; declaring that Lady Georgiana Pluggat-Lynette was to go on public trial and that everyone was most welcome to come. This meant that if you were caught being absent, you'd probably get arrested and flushed to be made an example of.

"Welcome, welcome, welcome," said Ivan, from the wooden platform through the microphone. "Everybody welcome to this most noble and woeful day and here to represent your fear, I give you the great and honourable, Mr E!"

The sound of a great female opera singer flooded out from the city loudspeakers as Mr E appeared at the palace front door. With his guards surrounding him, he paraded with great pomp and ceremony, slowly making his way out and onto the palace steps. Wearing a white toga, a purple cloak and a golden wreath on his head, he descended the stone stairway. The palace kitchen staff walked in front of him, holding great bowls of rose petals from which they scattered delicate flowers onto the floor. Like a Caesar or ancient crowned king, Mr E climbed into a Roman lectica and leaned back in the stance of a great lord, about to be carried down the streets of ancient Rome amongst the riffraff of slaves and peasants. Guards lifted it onto their shoulders and continued along this floral path to the resounding sound of the operatic music. In this way he made his way into the square and finally stood on the wooden platform. There he dropped off his Roman garments to reveal a leather jacket, jeans and the flusher machine keys dangling from his sides – which he took into his hands and shook in delight. The opera singer's voice rose to a crescendo, almost a scream. Mr E bowed to finish the performance.

In front of him was the sickly crowd, now assembled in silence. He was so taken in by the drama of the event (and took such pleasure in viewing the people's subdued frames) that he missed the fact that their passivity was due to excessive illness. It was an oversight on his part, he was just looking forward to bringing them lower still in their servitude.

Standing up close to the microphone he shouted, "Thank you, thank you, most loyal subjects. I must say, that this is a day, which in every way, I have been looking forward to with such intense delight. It's time to say 'Goodbye'."

"She's not been put on trial yet!" shouted the Professor from within the crowd.

Mr E just ignored the comment and continued.

"Oh I feel so good. I feel such a flood of *anticipation*. I feel that there will be such *gratification* when we see the *manifestation* of justice being done. It is all against the one, the one through whom rebellion has come. But today her fate will be set, because she has fallen into my little net. For, as you will all see, I am giving her no pity. Her scheming days are over and gone, for she will be flushed out and we can have some fun!"

"She's not been put on trial yet!" repeated the Professor from the crowd, but his voice was again completely ignored.

Mr E briefly noticed that the crowd was not responding to him in their usual way and were staying unusually quiet. Choosing to ignore this, he walked to the middle of the stage and sat down in his chair. Crossing one leg over the other, he took a glass of wine from the small table that was next to him and, after sipping and savouring the taste, he stood up.

"Bring out the guilty party, err, I mean, the accused," he said.

The front palace doors were opened and armed guards led Lady Georgiana out. Whilst the loud speakers on the palace walls played a dramatic tune, she was paraded through the crowd and brought onto the stage. There she was forced to stand in a wooden dock, looking out at the people.

"Lady Georgiana Pluggat-Lynette," began Mr E, "you stand here today on public trial for crimes against this city. There are multiple offences of various types stacked against you, some of them small and a little trifling I suppose but others are the most cunning and devious I have ever come across in my life! Shocked am I, that someone of your standing in this city could engage and associate with such things! Moreover, because of your standing in this city, I feel that they cannot go unchallenged. Ivan the charges," and with those words Mr E sat down again.

Mr Ritant walked up to the microphone with a sheet of paper in his hands from which he read:

165

"Your Crimes...

Organising undercover groups within the city.

Taking part in unauthorised meetings within the city.

Eating ice cream on a Tuesday."

"Really!" interrupted Lady Georgiana, looking quite astonished that 'Tuesday ice cream eating' was classed as a crime.

"Do you deny it?" said Mr Ritant.

"Well no," said Lady Georgiana. "But I didn't think that it was a..."

"Ignorance of the law is not a defence," interrupted Mr Ritant. "The law against Tuesday ice cream eating was passed last night but backdated to last Monday evening. Now, may I continue?"

Lady Georgiana just stared at him and then said, "Well, I'm sure you're going to go on anyway."

"Good," said Ivan. "So I will continue:

Organising resources against the state.

Wearing makeup for more than three days in a row."

"Since when was that a law?" said Lady Georgiana. "I've not heard of that one before."

"That law was created last night..." replied Mr Ritant, "...and has again been backdated to last Monday evening."

"Oh," said Lady Georgiana. "Well, thanks for letting me know."

"And I will continue," said Mr Ritant, "with the following:

Heading up a rebel force against the city authorities.

Financing a rebellion.

Seeking to get your own personal water supply outside that of the official allocation.

Wearing too many rings on one hand."

"Oh really!" said Lady Georgiana. "No, don't tell me," she said, looking sarcastically at Mr Ritant. "A law created last night?"

"Backdated to last Monday," said Mr Ritant. "And...

Looking after the welfare of rebel troops and...

Reading books in the palace family lounge without permission."

"Reading books?" echoed Lady Georgiana in a mocking tone. Then she added cynically, "A law created last night?"

"Correct," replied Mr Ritant.

"Backdated?" she enquired.

"To last Monday," said Mr Ritant.

"What a surprise!" said Lady Georgiana, deriding the event with a roll of her eyes.

"So in view of all of these crimes you are here today on public trial," said Mr Ritant.

"But you can't prove half of those things," protested Lady Georgiana.

166

"The ice cream, the makeup, the rings and the reading of lounge books we can," said Ivan. "You are completely guilty of those."

"But you can't be serious," she replied. "They're not real crimes and even if they were, they're not worthy of any kind of punishment. Fine me, if you want to and I'll do my best to never eat ice cream on a Tuesday again!"

"All of the laws of Clearwash City are of equal value in the sight of the authorities," said Mr Ritant. "If you have broken the law at one point, then you've broken the whole of the law," he replied. "You are, therefore, a lawbreaker and the whole weight of the law will be used against you. You are guilty," said Mr Ritant and with that he folded up the piece of paper and walked to the back of the stage.

Mr E almost rolled out of his chair and walked over to the microphone with a bounce in his step and a jubilant tone in his voice. "In the light of these breaches of the law," he cried, "I sentence you, Lady Georgiana Pluggat-Lynette, to endure my Free Flowing Foamy Flusher machine!"

Mr E held up his arms to welcome the crowd's applause - to join him in his moment of joy - but no one said a word.

"I said, I sentence you to endure my Free Flowing Foamy Flusher machine," he repeated, but again there was silence.

"But that can't be right," said Lady Georgiana.

"My dear," said Mr E, still puzzled by the quietness of the occasion, "I'm convinced of your guilt, so away you will go."

"That's not fair," shouted Basil, looking very red in the face with anger.

"Yes certainly," said the Professor. "That's not justice. All of this backdating, well, that's against the law."

"Good sirs," replied Mr E in a sour tone, "around here I am the law. And she is guilty, just as you all are."

"Well I'm not standing for this," said Basil, going even redder in the face.

"Then sit down for it!" said Mr E irritably. "Unless you want me to cut off my water supply from all of you for the rest of the week, that is?"

Everyone mumbled and grumbled at the thought of no fresh drinking water. Mr E looked over the crowd again and noticed for the first time that many of them were staggering and wilting. It didn't seem enough to him, however, that this was a proper excuse for their obvious lack of loyalty. The crowd was normally a boost to Mr E's ego, today he got nothing from them, so he launched into a defiant shouting fit.

"You spineless wimps! You disobedient, rebellious fools. Turncoats, you are! Cheaters! Backstabbers! Deserters! You disloyal, double minded and devious renegades! Who told you to be quiet? Who gave you permission to just stand there, you dumb and senseless buffoons? Apostates, that's what you are! Unbelievers! A pathetic bunch of thankless good-for-nothings who don't know what's good for them! So go on - turn your backs on your ruler. Shrug me off. Do your own thing - you half-witted, scheming traitors!"

Mr E paced up and down the stage, red in the face with rage and spitting venomous accusations as he went. Finally, he calmed a little and adopted a more thoughtful, cold and manipulative tone.

"I can see how ill you're all looking after drinking dirty water for just one day," he said, "but I will have compliance from you, unless you all wish to endure my Free Flowing Foamy Flusher machine too?"

"It seems that we don't have much choice," muttered the Professor to himself.

Silence sat still as time almost froze. The people gawped at Mr E in their tormented affliction and he stared back at them with a blackened cloud hanging over him.

"Well, ladies and gentlemen," continued Mr E, in a joyful game-show tone, with a sudden smile and personality change. "It is with a broken heart that I have to bring myself to this most terrible moment in sending Lady Georgiana to her final place of rest. However, not being a man to shun my duty, I have found the strength within me to be up to the task. Lady Georgiana, do you have any last words that you wish to say to the people before you finally meet your end?"

Lady Georgiana remained silent and did not reply.

"I have a speech," said Scrub, almost unable to contain himself and stepping forward from the crowd. "I have written a poem myself, Lady Pluggat, in your honour and would like to read it before you go." And before anyone could say anything he cleared his throat and shouted:

"Lady Pluggat, Lady Pluggat,
Someone so kind and friendly.
You are the real Lady Pluggat,
And you are often very cheery.
You have a very nice smile and nice teeth too,
And I am always happy to see you.
We are all very sad to see you go,
It really is a pity.
But I'm sure that we will someday follow you and
And so we'll see you, in a jiffy."

And with that Scrub folded up his piece of paper, put it back into his pocket and looked at everyone with great satisfaction. In his mind he had said something timeless and really profound. A stillness followed, however, with no-one quite sure what to say next.

"That was, err, very nice Scrub," said Lady Georgiana, not knowing where to take the conversation. "Did it take you long to write?"

"Yes M'lady," said Scrub, "I've been writing it for the past three years."

"Oh thank you," said Lady Georgiana, a little a taken back by the comment. "How, err, thoughtful of you."

"Right, that's it," said Mr E, feeling that the event had run away from him and still baffled by the continued silence of the crowd. "I've had enough. I was so moved by your contribution Scrub that you can both get flushed… together."

"Wow," said Scrub, "Thank you Mr E, that's very nice of you."

"Actually," said Lady Georgiana, turning to Mr E. "I'd rather go on my own and would prefer not to have a familiar smell with me on the way down."

Mr E looked again at Scrub. "Yes, I see what you mean," he said. "Out of the extreme generosity of my heart, you can go first. Ivan, put this *lady* in the flusher cubical!"

Ivan fetched the keys to the flusher machine from Mr E and then tied Lady Georgiana's hands. Some brave souls in the crowd, affronted by Mr E's insults and his treatment of Lady Georgiana, booed and hissed at what they were seeing. A couple of old lotion bottles were hurled into the air, perhaps at Mr E, it was hard to tell, but they only reached the edge of the stage before they smashed. Seeing that Lady Georgiana wasn't wearing an E badge, Mr Ritant quickly slapped one onto her outer coat.

"Just for good measure," he said. "Can't have you leaving us without a sign of your undivided loyalty to our ruler can we," he added sarcastically.

Now flanked by two guards, he escorted Lady Georgiana off the stage and towards the emerging flusher machine.

"I can walk quite easily without your help, thank you," said Lady Georgiana, pulling her arm away from Mr Ritant's hand.

"As you wish," said Mr Ritant. "I was just trying to be helpful."

"Well your help is not something that I need!" she sharply replied.

The crowd surged back and forth amongst themselves, like the churning of the great sea. Bewildered and perplexed they slipped, stumbled and tripped over each other's feet; a mass of chaotic fumbling. Confused by the sickness that filled their minds, they looked like the swell of a tide that didn't know whether it was coming in or going out. Mr E gently sipped a drink in order to prepare himself for the pleasure of seeing Lady Georgiana flushed, but also to glance out at the crowd at the same time to make sure that he himself was quite safe.

"You can't do this Mr E," shouted the Professor from amongst the mayhem. "Lady Georgiana hasn't done anything wrong. You can't prove anything against her."

Mr E went back to sit in his chair, ignoring the cries that came here and there from the crowd and decided to briefly examine his fingernails. As Lady Georgiana walked along, she glanced over at Basil and the Professor to give them one last goodbye with her eyes. Basil stood speechless with tears running down his face.

"Goodbye Georgie," he whispered. He dropped his head, not being able to bear the sight of what was about to happen.

Mr Ritant pushed Lady Georgiana into the glass cubicle, closed the door and locked it. Turning to the flusher machine he began to push buttons here and there to get it ready for the next flushing. Lady Georgiana looked out at the crowd. Taking a few deep breaths, she dropped her head towards her tied up hands. Knowing that no-one was coming into the room after her, she made one last action of defiance by biting through the leather cords that bound her wrists together. She chewed and gnawed and bit at them until the twines broke and her hands were free. Then she lifted up her head and stared out at everyone with her chin held high, defiant to the end.

Ivan put the large key in the machine, turned a few dials, pulled a couple of levers and the flusher machine began to fill up with water. Adding frothy soapsuds, it repeatedly churned the water to get it ready to flush into the cubicle where Lady Georgiana was now standing.

"You can't do this Mr E!" protested the Professor again. "She's innocent!" and others in the crowd began to join in.

Chapter 27 – My Free Range Flushers

The noise from the crowd grew louder and louder as different people took up the Professor's words. "Innocent," they shouted and continued to chant in unison. Mr E was quite taken aback at the crowd's boldness. He had expected everyone to either enjoy watching Lady Georgiana go down the plughole or be paralysed with fear. After a few moments thought, he called some guards over to him and gave an order. The guards all aimed their guns into the air and fired off several shots. With this, silence fell and all became still.

"We will have quiet on this sad occasion," said Mr E, now standing at the microphone. "We must preserve our sense of dignity at such a time as this, for no matter what you say, Lady Georgiana Pluggat-Lynette will go down the plughole today."

He paused for a moment and then continued, "But perhaps I am being a little too hasty. I do have an uneasy feeling about all this. Something is not quite right."

Basil looked over at the Professor and then at Lady Georgiana. There was a glimmer of hope that things may not end as they had all dreaded.
Mr E paced back and forth for a while until he knew he had everyone's absolute attention.

"You see," he said. "Everything I do has to be worthwhile and this, somehow, doesn't seem to fit and fill that delicate, exquisite mould. I must have perfection and this falls terribly short. So I say to myself, 'How can the flushing of Lady Georgiana fill the great hole of disloyalty that we have had in our midst today? What can be done to bring balance back into our gathering?' Upon reflection, I therefore find this event wanting in my sight, for it does not give us the exhilaration that is required when your leader has been booed by his very own people."

Mr E stopped to think, an idea had sprung into his mind and he quietly mused it over. Calling Ivan over, he whispered something in his ear and, after Ivan had walked off towards the palace, he continued his speech.

"For some time now I have been hard at work, saving up a very special surprise that I originally wanted to reveal at the turn of the New Year, something that would have rounded off the season of good will nicely for us all. But now, I believe, it is necessary to share the joy of that event with you all today instead and thus ensure your long lasting loyalty."

He pulled out of his pocket what looked like a small clock. It was about the size of a large, round chocolate biscuit. Holding it high in the air, he wound it up and shook it until it glowed and hummed in his hands. Then he laid it flat on his palm, a pulsating, glowing, tick-tock device.

"Ladies and gentlemen," he said, with a grin and a cheeky smile. "There's something about surprises that always fills my soul with joy. The look of astonished wonder that comes on unsuspecting people is priceless and I'm sure that on this occasion, you will not disappoint. Let me introduce some old friends of this city,

171

now new friends of mine, friends who will always keep you close to my unyielding heart and sweet temperament."

With those words, he pressed the front face of the clock, as if it were a big button. A few seconds later there arose a series of humming noises that echoed throughout the market square. These strange sounds seemed to vibrate and pulsate from the ground and up into everyone's feet. The crowd began to move about uneasily, not knowing where to stand or what was about to happen.

"I will show you," said Mr E, "the meaning of loyalty. I will show you what it is to truly love your ruler, to esteem him and to make him your unwavering delight. I will teach you what it is to choose the right and reject the wrong. I will teach you hope, affection, commitment and duty. I will have your utter devotion and you, when you are mine, will understand what it is to be truly loved by me."

Suddenly a large manhole cover that belonged to one of the market square's drain service access points burst open. Its circular iron lid flipped into the air and then bounced, rolled and eventually flopped back onto the cobbled floor. Everyone stared at the service entrance. The muffled humming noise that had been all around them now openly buzzed its way out of the opening, like the sound of a hornet's nest about to unleash a swarm. Moments later, to the horror of the on looking crowd, a mechanical arm appeared. It waved its hand from side to side for a few moments before anchoring itself onto the cobbled floor to grip the ground. Then another arm came through and did the same. With both hands locked onto the stony floor, the arms heaved – bringing up and out of the drain a crab-like machine. It stood up on its lanky, extended legs, towering about twenty feet high. A single eye shone out from its head, glancing this way and that at its surroundings. Through a glass pane attached to the machine's front, water could be seen churning over and over. On the machine's underside was a thin glass cubicle and underneath the glass cubicle was a wide plastic tube that ran back down into the drain.

"Ladies and gentlemen," cried Mr E, "I give you the sum of all your fears, my Free Range Flusher machines!"

The people gasped in amazement and then cried out in fear as other drainage covers popped open and machine after machine emerged out of the ground. They appeared all around the square, surrounding the people on every side.

172

"Ladies and gentlemen," called Mr E again. "I said Screeeeeeaaaaaammmm!"

The crowds shrieked with terror as more machines kept surfacing out of the ground right across the great square and throughout the city. They began to grab anyone who was near them with their long arms and put them into their cubicles. Then, after spinning their victims round and round, they flushed them through their under tubes and into the drains.

Person upon person was caught by the machines and flushing after flushing took place. The great crowd of people swarmed and fled in all directions but they couldn't get away or out of the square, there were just too many flusher machines. Mr E just laughed as he watched the scene, he was beginning to feel that the day would be worthwhile after all. Finally he pressed the clock again and the machines stopped chasing and flushing the people. Standing on the edges of the great square, they hummed their mechanical tunes and waved their arms gently from side to side, waiting for orders.

"And such is the price paid for disloyalty," said Mr E, gazing out at the crowd and enjoying their petrified faces. "How I wish I could include and embrace you all," Mr E continued, "that none of this had to happen, but you drove me to it."

He walked up and down the stage, thinking as he went. Then, in a moment of gentle loving kindness, he held his arms open wide to them and said, "Honourable friends, I am looking for your loyalty. Friends who wish to share with me a future in this great city of ours; people who will commit themselves to the vision of our shared and most blessed community; reliable ones, who will lift their heads high

173

and not be afraid to face the difficult decisions that we must make amongst us today. We must preserve both our dignity and our future. Will you stand with me, prove yourselves loyal to me? I do not ask for any more, just that we stand side by side in true comradeship, that we jointly face the threats to our world and the attitudes and values of our culture."

Mr E beckoned to the crowd to come close to him and some began to move forward.

"Don't be fools," shouted the Professor. "He'll end up killing us all."

"All I need is a small sign of loyalty from you," Mr E continued. "I have here your keys to freedom; new Mr E badges for you to wear, that will keep you safe from these terrible machines."

Ivan had returned from the palace and brought with him a large box.
Mr E opened it and took out a new badge. Emblazoned across its front was a triple E which he held aloft for all to see.

"Wear them, and as you obey me these Free Range Flushers won't come near you. You can live here again, safely and at peace. Those who are for me come forward!" he cried. Some in the crowd began to walk across the square. "That's right," Mr E shouted. "Choose your freedom."

"He's mad," called Basil. "Don't do it."

Most of the crowd, however, eventually came forward and stood at the fence in front of the platform, which gave Mr E a great deal of satisfaction. He smiled a broad grin.

"Now," he said, in a low and gracious tone. "We will do this properly, then once again I will sustain you with my most precious water and you can know, for sure, that all will be well. All we have to do is to give this rebel, Lady Georgiana, a proper sending off. Once that's done, we can be free again. So join in with me."

And with those words, Mr E leapt off the stage, pulled the keys out of the flusher machine and shook them to jingle out a familiar sound. Then he pushed the larger key back into the flusher machine, rotated it twice and placed his thumb and index finger on either side of a large dial, ready to give it a twist. Then, turning to face the crowd he cried,

"It's time to say goodbye. Goodbye to a betrayer of the state."

He turned to face Lady Georgiana and began to chant, "Flush, flush, flush, flush, flush, flush, flush." Some in the crowd started to join in but others found it hard, their consciences in great turmoil. "Come on," urged Mr E. "Freedom is only a short step away and you too can take hold of it. It is here, standing at your very door. Join us in our song of justice as Lady Georgiana gets flushed away!"

The crowd's voice slowly came together and to Mr E's pleasure a uniform chant formed that steadily grew louder and louder. Lady Georgiana, feeling keenly the betrayal of so many, stood motionless inside the flusher machine. She looked like an expensive china doll, ready to be preserved for a thousand years behind glass.

Despite the invisible sword that now pierced her heart, she felt great compassion for the people chanting her towards her departure. She thought it strange that she should still feel love for them, in the midst of their duplicity, but love them she did. She felt quite at peace and ready to depart.

Ivan pushed a couple of buttons on the machine's front and water began to bubble up from the metal grid beneath Lady Georgiana's feet. The water level rose causing her to gasp and breathe deeply. It was far colder than she'd anticipated. Warmth fled from her ankles and legs, eaten up by the icy spray's cold chill, leaving the lower part of her completely numbed.

"Perhaps this is what death feels like?" she thought to herself.

"I love you Dad," she whispered under her breath.

Once the cubicle was just over half full, the water briefly stopped climbing and the soap suds pipe above Georgiana's head hissed out trapped air, ready to drop its bubbles and foam. Placing her hands flat against the sides of the glass room, Lady Georgiana steadied herself and closed her eyes to mentally prepare for what was about to come. In moments multiple images rushed through her mind, flashbacks of events from the past, achievements, awards, successes, triumphs, trials, troubles, tears, fears, failures, enemies, friends, family and then finally, her own dear father.

Mr E twirled the dial between his fingers, pulled down two levers and the machine at once began to tremble and shake. Its inner engines stirred themselves into life and the lights across the machine's front beamed brightly. With a grinding, a hissing and a deep mechanical cough, cough, cough, its inner workings jolted together and finally formed a rhythmic tune. Whoop, whoop, whoop, an alarm shrieked as more water bubbled up from beneath Lady Georgiana's toes, taking the water level above her waist. Locking her hands and feet against the glass walls in a star-fish shape, like a limpet stuck to a rock, she refused to be moved by the flowing water. The small wheels on the outside of the machine whizzed around at a tremendous speed. First one way and then the other, back and forth for nearly half a minute, until they all abruptly stopped. Then, from a speaker built into the side of the flusher machine, came a deep electronic voice.

"Flushing traveller, prepare for new destination. Direction downwards, lowest level and out," said the machine. "Have a nice trip."

"Whoooooooooopee," shouted the crowd together, though not with the same conviction that they'd performed in the past.

Georgiana felt the sudden jerk of the glass room slowly beginning to rotate under her feet. Opening her eyes again she saw the panoramic image of all that was around her as the room began to revolve. The rotation was slow at first and she caught the eyes of her friends in the crowd with each turn. She could still hear the muffled and dulled voices of the crowd with Mr E chanting her departure. It was strange. For some reason, the voices that spoke against her had lost their power; being inside the glass room made their comments, shouts and taunts meaningless. She was leaving this world by her own will and everything and everyone else who opposed her was shut out from this decision. She didn't want to be where she was, but now that she was there, she was at peace.

On another rotation of the glass room she watched as somehow Scrub began to understand more of what was happening. It dawned on him that this really was a goodbye. He lifted his hand to say a farewell, but too late to make a proper connection, even for him. On another turn of the room she watched as Basil, unable to contain himself any longer, ran across the market square to single–handily begin her rescue. On the next rotation she saw that a band of soldiers had pinned him to the ground to prevent him from getting any further. After another turn there were soldiers scuffling with the crowd and after another turn there was the Professor, on his knees next to Basil, and the people with him; hands on the back of their heads and armed soldiers standing guard over them. All resistance was subdued.

Each turn got faster and faster and then clunk, clunk, the room jolted into a spin. Strengthening every muscle in her body, pressing her hands flat against the glass walls, anchoring her feet against the room's bottom edges, Georgiana continued in her star shape, rigid and taught against the swishing water's flow, trying to stay upright. Above her the large pipe rattled, ready to spurt down its foam and beneath her feet the grill on which she stood trembled, ready for the next and final surge of water to spurt up into the glass chamber.

"This is it," she said to herself. "Dad, I'm coming home."

Mr E continued to wind up the crowd. He was ecstatic and was just about to leap into the air when, BANG, the noise of perhaps a gun or another device being discharged echoed across the market square. In a long arc, an object of some kind flew high over the crowd's heads, until it landed directly on the flusher machine's front panel. It struck one of the buttons like a bullseye and Lady Georgiana found the glass room quickly decelerating its spin, coming to a standstill. She spat out of her mouth the small amount of water that had splashed into it and put her arms around herself, shivering with cold. As the water around her slowed its swirl she could see that in the square, everyone had stopped. The chanting from the crowd had petered out and silence descended.

Standing next to the flusher machine, Ivan picked up the object that had bounced off the control panel and landed at his feet. It was a pebble of some kind. He held it aloft for Mr E to see.

"Who did that?" demanded Mr E.

No-one answered. Mr E opened his mouth to speak again but before he did so, "DING DONG!"

The noise of bells resonated across the city. Then, clap, clap, clap went the sound of cogs and wheels.

Mr E turned in horror to stare at the burnt out palace clock tower, whose mechanisms hadn't chimed since his youth. The majestic clock was coming to life. DING DONG! came the bells again. DING DONG! it sang and then clap, clatter, clap.

"The fullness of time," said Lady Georgiana, from within the flusher machine.

"The fullness of time" said the Professor, as he glanced at Basil.

Person looked at person and a general murmuring and muttering spread through the crowd, everyone wondering what all of this would mean. The damaged tower clock face had more than the normal two timer hands of a standard timepiece, it had many small ones and several small clock faces embedded into it as well. All of them began to move together, round and round they went, turn upon turn. Then they stopped, each one sending out a multitude of chimes, forming a melodic song where each peal, each strike of a gong, each ding, each dong, each clang, each ring complemented the other and together they rang out a harmonious sound that hadn't been heard in Clearwash City for a long time.

In front of the large archway that led onto the market square, two of Mr E's Free Range Flusher machines stood guarding the way out – blocking the way of escape. Within moments, however, both machines collapsed onto the floor, exploding into pieces and sending a column of smoke into the air.

"The fullness of time!" cried a booming loud voice over the noise. The voice was so loud that it bounced and echoed off every building and wall throughout the city. Scrub felt as if the voice had somehow gone within him and shaken his insides. Everyone turned, wanting to see to whom the voice belonged. Behind the billowing smoke something, or someone, moved.

Chapter 28 – Licensed To Wash

Mr E climbed back onto the wooden stage and peered into the miry mist to see who it was that was speaking and had dared to destroy two of his flusher machines. As the smoke slowly began to clear, there emerged a large, white mechanical horse. The metal horse nodded its head up and down and pawed at the cobbled floor with its front hoof, as if it were alive. Sitting upon the horse was a tall, lean-faced nobleman - wearing a royal crested tunic and metal plated armour on his arms and legs. His long white beard and piercing gaze showed him to be a wise, gallant and virtuous gentleman. He kicked his heels and the metal horse walked forward, hissing steam from its mouth and legs as it went. Kethud, kethud, went the metal horse's hooves on the ground.

A personal bodyguard of almost a hundred figures, all wearing monastic dress, followed in a tight unit around the man.

The man continued to ride forward and the crowd parted in awe. Once in the middle of the market square he pulled his horse to a halt, drew a scroll out from his tunic, unrolled it and called out in a loud voice:

"People of Clearwash City, greetings; it has been a long, long time."

The gentleman paused to look about him once more. Over the crowd he gazed, taking in person upon person in his long stare, a mixture of compassion and relief on his face. He continued to read...

"Open your hearts, your eyes and your ears. Take heed. Tremble at this time that is now at hand; the fullness of time, which is here."

Again he looked out at the crowd to make sure every eye was on him and every ear listening to what he had to say.

"Now is the time of your choice," he continued. "Now is the time of your destiny. Now is the brief window of opportunity open to you, when the secrets of your inner thoughts are exposed - and the choices you have already made, revealed. Let your eyes be opened, your consciences cleansed and your minds be washed and purified."

As they listened a great sense of wonder or bewilderment came over the crowd. The herald continued, "I am the herald of the great King who has come back to claim that which is his own. Let there be none among you who are found wanting this day, for King Wash-El-Ami of Clearwash City has returned. So now, make your choice. Bow your knee before he arrives, that he may have pity on you and the deep rebellion of this place can be swept away."

Mr E looked very hard at this new stranger, still trying to figure out what was happening. His own guards hesitated, unsure of what to do.

"Who on earth are you and what are you doing in my city?" Mr E eventually said.

The herald just ignored him and continued to address the crowd.

"Those of you who would accept the King's rule will now have to show your loyalty before he arrives. You must remove the vile E symbol from your clothing and cast it to the ground. I ask that you give me your trust and your belief in my words. For it only takes a mere morsel of faith for anyone of noble heart to step out of this present darkness and into the King's light. Be ready, welcome him, for his love for this city and its people is great and he will reward most generously those who gladly and willingly choose him now."

Mutterings went throughout the crowd at the herald's words, no-one quite knowing what to do or say. Even Mr E was a little dumb-struck by the event taking place before his eyes.

Finally, Mr E spoke out again, "Most noble sir," he said sarcastically. "You have but a few seconds to turn your fancy pantomime horse around and depart. If not, I will not be responsible for the actions of my guards, who are here to maintain the peace and safety of this city."

The herald again ignored Mr E and continued to look over the crowd, watching their reaction to his words.

Mr E spoke again, "My people are loyal and so are my many machines. Now I suggest you and your men take your horse and exit before I get bored with you and you all get flushed away. I am the ruler of this city and here I will stay. I don't feel threatened by your so-called King Wash-El-Ami, whoever he is."

"He is the great king," replied the herald, giving Mr E his attention for the first time, "and He is the ruler of the Wash cities of the north and this is His city."

"I control my guards, my machines and the water supply to this great city. Without me everyone dies. I have over a thousand soldiers who are armed and at my call. You have here but a hundred, as far as I can see. So here I am and here I stay."

"Your pitiful flushing machines and puny outdated weapons will have no effect on me," replied the herald. "Now I say to all you people again, get rid of your allegiance to Mr E for the true King is at the door."

Lady Georgiana ripped off her "E" symbol from her coat and tossed it into the water that surrounded her. Throughout the crowd many followed her example, but not everyone.

"Now," said the herald, whilst the rest of the crowd made up their minds whether to leave Mr E or not. "I will have you, Mr E, removed from your rule. Your time is up and your power is over."

"I think not," said Mr E, standing squarely and facing the herald with a severe and determined face. He raised his hand and the city guards quickly gathered in front of the stage. In moments, they raised their rifles at the herald and fired off a volley of shots. Just as quickly, in one swift movement, the accompanying monks who surrounded the herald discarded their outer cloaks and hoods. (Beneath these garments were what looked like sliver plated, metal scales, covering their bodies from head to toe.) Up they went onto the metal horse, shielding the herald with their bodies; each bullet from Mr E's guards bounced off harmlessly. Then the monks dropped to the floor again and each froze in a combat stance, staring out at the crowed, ready for action, ready for a fight.

"I think not!" said the herald. "The king shall rule here now and he shall have you removed."

"He and whose army?" said Mr E, not really wanting an answer to the question.

"He and this army," replied the herald.

The palace clock tower sounded out a final loud and long "dong!" At this, the herald looked over the crowd, giving those who had not made up their minds yet one last chance to change their loyalties to the king. Then, with a few more people finally dropping their E badges to the floor, he held up a silver trumpet to his lips and blew. The trumpet's sound was a clear, pure note that seemed to reach right across the heavens. It echoed through the sky and, after a short time of silence and stillness, there came from far up above them the deep crash and clatter of rumbling thunder. The thick clouds in the sky seemed to jump within themselves, responding to the trumpet's call. Together they rolled into one another, forming a single, unified blanket that blocked out the sun, casting a deep shadow over the city; dusk in the middle of the day.

Some distance away something shiny and silver fell out of the sky. The people watched its descent until it hit the floor, down one of the city side streets. Another fell and another. All over the city they began to land, a rainfall of objects. After each landed, its silvery body switched itself on and sent out a single beam of light up into the sky. Together, they lit up the city with a dazzling brightness sending out a message – "Here we are, come and find us."

As this was happening, the wind outside the city walls picked up. Howling and moaning its way across the great rocks and dunes, it clothed itself with great handfuls of sand and dirt by scattering the desert's lifeless dust up into swirling clouds. Eventually, as the wind gathered its strength, it turned from a strong blustery gust into the beginnings of a violent, yowling gale. The masses of fine red soil that it now carried in its invisible arms billowed within it and swelled to form a giant screen of debris that added to the general cloud cover's blockade of the sun, casting a darkness and shadowy gloom across the city. Alarm spread amongst the people. Mr E looked baffled, at a loss, not knowing what to do as gusts of wind impacted the market square. Closer and closer the cloud came; looking as if it would completely swallow them up. Until, that is, it held its position just outside the great wall - a vast curtain of wind, dirt and projecting the sound of an untameable noise.

"We're going to die!" cried one person, sending many in the crowd into a panic.

"The end has come," cried out the herald. "Here comes the great King."

Suddenly there was the sound of the roar of many engines. They buzzed and whirred, chugged and spluttered; an ear-splitting noise, as if the desert cloud were about to unleash a hornet's nest. Then, out of the dust cloud they flew, figure upon figure, soldier upon soldier, speeding, zooming, swooping, darting and diving, they kept coming and coming and coming, the army of the great King! Each of the soldiers, covered from head to toe in steel plated clothes, had a buzzing propeller attached to their backs. Like a swarm of locusts they dropped into the city streets and lanes. Down and down they came in wave upon wave of military companies; a band of brothers, rank upon rank, and line upon line until the city was filled with their buzzing, swarming figures.

In his panic Mr E pressed his clock button to bring his flushing machines to life. They hummed and whirred, straightening themselves up to try and grab the soldiers - but the King's army had already landed all over them. Quickly popping small, flashing, metal disks onto their sides, they jumped off and took cover. Within moments the disks flickered and BOOM! exploded, shattering the machines into pieces. Even those machines that fought against the King's army, using their arms to push away their attackers and trying to flush them, didn't last long. There were just too many of the King's men. Down the last few flushing machines plunged, smashing onto the cobbled market floor.

Out of the sky the police patrol balloons also fell, one after the other - like apples dropping from a shaken tree. They hit the ground with a thud, crash and thump; a heavy impact that broke them apart. The King's men, responsible for their fall, descended upon the debris. Pulling Mr E's police force out of the wreckage, they quickly placed them under arrest and soon the skies were clear and an open heaven emerged. The King's army showed no fear, running in unison throughout the city and crushing every last bit of resistance. In the houses or on the walls they went, disarming Mr E's soldiers and taking up their positions to guard their new territory.

Mr Ivan Ritant suddenly found himself surrounded and quickly pushed away from the Free Flowing Foamy Flusher machine. At the same time, two of the King's soldiers removed the keys from the flusher machine, unlocked the glass cubicle door and held it slightly ajar to drain its contents. Once done, Lady Georgiana was brought out. Those who still had their "E" signs on them fled from the city, or ran into their houses or down the drains to try to escape. Others began, in pockets of resistance, to fight back at the new comers, but were quickly overcome by the strength and military skill of the King's forces. Once the fighting was over, the city became quiet and still. The cloud cover in the sky began to rotate back on itself, rolling up into what temporarily looked like a great prophetic scroll, letting in the sunlight again. The windstorm in the desert died down, leaving just a dusty haze, like a brown semi-transparent veil.

Through the city gates came a large carriage drawn by a team of eight horses. Each was just like the herald's horse, made from iron and driven by a power unseen. Nodding their heads with delight in anticipation of the event in which they were involved, they made their way into the market square where they finally came to a halt near the wooden stage. Finally the horses blew out an immense cloud of steam from their metallic nostrils and raised their heads until they were still.

The top part of the royal carriage split open, it hissed with the sound of compressed air, and moved upwards and backwards to reveal the person inside. All in the square stood motionless, gazing at the new King. He smiled at them with his deep, gentle eyes, as dark as wine, full of kindness. His majestic face, though shot with scarring from many a battle (clearly an experienced leader who had himself faced down death) shone with goodness. Now that the fighting was over, the king brought with him a great gentleness that settled on the city.

Lady Georgiana stood looking at this new person and eventually found the courage to speak. "King Wash-El-Ami," she said, with chattering teeth.

The king rose out of his seat and, with the door held open for him, descended the few steps on the side of his carriage. He walked over to Lady Georgiana and, seeing her half drenched clothing and shivering frame, waved his hand for one of his soldiers to fetch a blanket from his coach. One was found and put across Lady Georgiana's shoulders.

"Lady..." the King hesitated for a moment, "Georgiana," he said. "I see that as usual you're right in the thick of things."

Lady Georgiana didn't quite know what to say. "Yes," she finally replied. "Yes I am."

"Pity about my waterworks," remarked the king.

Lady Georgiana looked a little embarrassed.

"It had to come down anyway," the king added with a smile.

He was about to walk on when Lady Georgiana asked, "How, how is it that you are here?"

King Wash-El-Ami glanced over at the palace clock tower and said, "The flag. The white flag of surrender. Wherever there is a white flag of surrender, I come."

Everyone looked up at the palace central clock tower and there, on the main flagpole, was a white flag.

"I have had my team of people dwelling on the mountain heights, working day after day after day, looking and watching. They have continually been my faithful watchmen on the high places. The flag's presence signals that the time is right for me to return, according to that which was written long ago."

The King pointed to the entrance of the market square and there a group of around twenty people stood, amongst whom were
Mr Tremblay and his daughter Anna, who Lady Georgiana recognised as a member of her resistance committee.

"The good Mr Tremblay and his daughter Anna spotted the flag early this morning. Now that I have seen the flag, I have come back," said the King.

"How did that get up there?" said the Professor.

"Who put it up there?" said Basil.

No one seemed to have an answer to this until Scrub, feeling desperately guilty and wondering if all that had just happened was entirely his fault, owned up.

"I did it," he said, confused by everything that was going on around him and bracing himself for a really good telling off.

"You Scrub?" said the Professor.

"Yes. It's my washing," said Scrub. "I wanted to get it dry and I needed to put it somewhere where there was plenty of wind, so I've hung my things in and on the clock tower. My bed sheet was so wet I decided to fly it from the flagpole. I hope you don't mind Mr E, because I put my underwear on the tower clock's hands. I'll take them off as soon as they are dry."

Everyone looked across and yes, there were Scrub's underwear hanging from the hour and minute hands of the clock and his bed sheet flying in the wind from the main mast.

In fact, Scrub had done far more than just hang his washing out. After his conversation with Ivan, he had walked up to the palace to search for an area to dry his laundry. Once he had searched here and there, he finally found himself in a location that was off limits to ordinary citizens, that is, on the palace clock tower stair. None of the palace guards had tried to stop him, for none of them really took any notice of Scrub. They normally saw him tagging on with or behind Lady Georgiana and knew that he couldn't do any harm. It was common knowledge that Scrub lived in a world of his own. Once on the stair, however, he instinctively climbed higher and higher.

Eventually he had entered a room at the tower's very top, a room that was burnt and damaged. Inside were cogs, wheels, assorted machinery, levers, chains, fan belts, pulleys, broken glass and a great clock face that sat at the front of the building. It smelt dank and rotten, but it was spacious. Scrub looked at the damaged bits of metal sticking out of the floorboards and the wheels and chains and pulleys. He didn't know why, but he just stood there, motionless for several minutes, just taking in all the items before him. He seemed to think that in some way they all fitted together. (As I said earlier in this book, if Scrub had thought like an ordinary person, he would have been an incredible inventor, a genius of mechanical engineering.) His imagination soared as he dreamed in his mind's eye about all of the bits and pieces joining together to make a fantastic contraption. Then, something deep within him took over.

Guided by sheer desire and impulse, he looked into his wash basket and pulled out a sock. He instinctively tied one end to a chain that dangled from the ceiling and stretched it to tie the other end to a rod of iron pointing out of the floor. He took another sock and tied two more pieces of machinery together. Taking out his shirt, he ripped it in the middle so that it could reach a little further and tied each sleeve to two levers that sat several feet apart. More socks came out from his basket and he began to join all of the chains that dangled from the ceiling to chains on the floor. His feeling of elation soared as, for the first time ever, he had the space to do just as he wanted.

Now in full flow, he used a belt from his trousers to replace a fan belt on a machine, an old bow tie to re-attach several small sprockets together and a pair of trousers to help transmit the motion between two shafts. On and on he continued going from machine to machine and component to component. He went through more socks, trousers, shirts, underpants and waistcoats, each bit of clothing fitting perfectly so that the machinery all stood up and connected together. A long and intricate job, Scrub worked for nearly an hour, or perhaps it was much longer, until he stood back and stared with satisfaction at the astonishing contraption he'd made. A collection of multi-coloured clothes tied into and between a mass of joined machinery. Scrub felt a deep sense of gratification. He ran his fingers along chains and fan belts and down the clothing he had joined up. It was wonderful, his very own creation.

Scrub didn't know why but he felt that there was still something more he had to do. So he wandered amongst the different parts of the clock tower until he found a small key that dangled on a hook against the back wall. Lifting the key, his merry eyes danced around the room until they found a keyhole in a pillar next to a lever. Walking briskly over to the hole he found that the key fitted, so in it went. Scrub turned it until it would turn no more and something clicked within the hole's recess. He carefully wrapped his fingers around the lever next to it, then pulled it down. Clunk! it went and a shudder ran through the great clock that sat at the front of the room. Without knowing why, Scrub instinctively reached out his hand towards one of his stretched socks and flicked it with his finger.

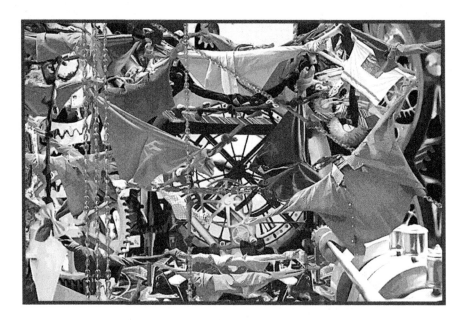

The sock vibrated and this motion rattled a chain to which it was attached which, in turn, rattled another chain that juddered a fan belt and clank, something fell into place. A tick, tick, ticking began and all of the items in the room suddenly moved into action. Chains ran up and down, fan belts went round, cogs turned and wheels rotated; amongst it all was Scrub's washing, also traveling with the different motions. Seeing that he still had his bed sheet and a couple of sets of underwear in his basket, he quickly went up onto the clock tower roof, to fly the sheet from the great flagpole, Then, after dumping his remaining underwear onto the two clock hands, he returned to see his mechanical creation working again. The pleasure within him soared through his soul as, not only did he have a working machine on his hands, but he figured the constant movement would help make his clothes dry too. This pleasure began to fade, however, when a voice like Lady Georgiana's suddenly rang through his head.

"Scrub, didn't I tell you never to touch anything you don't understand!" it said.

Feeling desperately guilty and, not wanting to get into trouble, he left the palace; telling no one about his wonderful and amazing machine. Imagine Scrub's surprise, therefore, when in the market square later on, instead of being scolded, he was in fact a hero.

"Scrub," said the Professor, looking at the white flag sheet, "you're brilliant. How did you get your bed sheet wet in the first place?"

"Better not ask," said Basil, laughing and shaking Scrub by the hand. "Who knows where he sleeps!"

"You are wonderful Scrub," laughed Lady Georgiana, giving him a gentle kiss on the forehead.

"You're marvellous," said the Professor.

"Oh," said Scrub, looking confused, "Thank you, but I only hung my washing out."

"Stephanus Cadmar Roberto Uriel Bannerman," said the King, talking to Scrub. "You did not just hang your washing out. You did nothing of the sort. You fulfilled your calling and your destiny."

Scrub felt pleased with himself, but as usual didn't quite know why.

"But that's against the law!" blurted Ivan Ritant, as he was being escorted back to the stage surrounded by King Wash-El-Ami's men.

"You can't do that Scrub, you're not licensed to wash. It's against the law."

"Not anymore," said King Wash-El-Ami.

One of the soldiers walked up to the King and reported,

"The city has been secured my Lord. All resistance has been removed."

At this, the personal guards surrounding Mr E looked at each other and slowly fell back. One by one they began to move away from the crowd, dropping their rifles as they went. Then they turned and fled.

"Oh dear," said Erepsin, more to himself than anyone else.

"Yes it is 'Oh dear'," said the King. Pointing his finger at Mr E he shouted, "Seize him."

At this, the King's men leapt onto the stage and apprehended the dictator. Everyone who was left in the city square cheered, except Ivan Ritant of course, who was just looking very shocked and numb at what was happening.

"Can we flush Mr E?" asked Basil, looking very hopeful and rubbing his hands together.

Chapter 29 – Oh Scrub, Shut Up!

"Not just yet" answered the King.

Mr E was brought down from the stage and made to stand in front of King Wash-El-Ami, who looked him over.

"Mr Erepsin Ville," he continued, "I have been following your activities very closely and I believe that you are very fond of getting others to try on your quite disgusting lotions. Perhaps, before you leave us today, you should try a few of them yourself. I always think that leaders of people should set an example by doing first what they ask of others. Don't you agree?"

The crowd in the square met this comment with great delight.

Mr E was completely silent as a crate was brought from the palace laboratories containing an assortment of bottles. Many of them were opened and there wasn't any shortage of volunteers from the resistance movement to help Mr E and Mr Ritant wear a good dose of each bottle. A cheer rose from the crowd each time one was emptied over the pair.

Once Mr E and Mr Ritant were covered in smelly lotions and the smell was so bad that even the crowd was having a problem staying near them, the Professor shouted, "Can we smell them?"

"Yes we can," they replied, and all laughed.

"And now," said King Wash-El-Ami, "before we take this villain to the Free Flowing Foamy Flusher and end his vile reign, there are some people I would very much like you to meet."

The king signalled to the herald who blew a second time on his trumpet. The great, fading cloud in the desert seemed to part in its middle and, like the opening of a door to another world, a great crowd of people walked out. Through the main gates they streamed and made their way into the city inner circle. From the throng in the market square, shrieks of joy and surprise rose up as people began to recognise their lost loved ones who had been flushed over the years by Mr E. All over the city friends and family greeted, hugged and kissed as their reunions took place. Amongst them were George and finally Sir Frederick James III, along with his brother Alfred. George and his fellow scientists shook hands, even the Professor was pleased to see him, whilst Lady Georgiana and Sir Frederick embraced like a separated brother and sister.

"Now!" said the great King. "I think it's time this city said goodbye to its tyrannical ruler. Oh and by the way," he said, looking Mr E squarely in the eye. "After you've been flushed, you'll find your surroundings very hot indeed. The desert is a burning, lonely place and there won't be any of my people out there to rescue you." Then he cried out. "Off with this vile man."

"No!" shouted Mr E. "No you can't do this to me. Help me Ivan! Help me!"

"Yes Ivan," said the King. "Do follow your master. You can go with him too."

Mr E and Ivan Ritant were both led off to the Free Flowing Foamy Flusher's glass room and locked inside. The keys were inserted into the flusher machine and, the large dial twisted and a few levers pulled. The machine came to life. It hummed, clunked, hissed and spluttered - its inner engines stirring themselves into action. With a grinding "grrr", a hissing "shhhhhhh" and a deep mechanical cough, cough, cough, its workings jolted together and finally formed a rhythmic tune. An alarm sounded. "Whoop, whoop, whoop," it shrieked as water bubbled up from beneath Mr E's and Ivan's feet and the room gradually started to fill with water.

"Traitors are you all!" cried Mr E defiantly.

No one watching seemed at all worried. Stripped of his authority he was just a man and all the threats that poured from his mouth were hollow and empty. The water rose higher and higher in the glass room whilst Mr E and Ivan, out of breath from yelling, gnashed their teeth in powerless aggression.

The small wheels on the outside of the machine whizzed around together. First one way they went and then the other. Back and forth they whizzed for nearly half a minute until they all abruptly stopped. Then a deep electronic voice spoke from a speaker built into the side of the flusher machine.

"Flushing travellers prepare for new destination. Direction, downwards, lowest level and out," said the machine. "Have a nice trip."

"Whoooooooooopee" shouted the crowd as one voice together and then laughed. The small glass room slowly turned round and round and round and round. Clunk, went another cog. Clunk, clank and then clunk again, taking the room into a spin. Faster and faster it went, speeding up with every turn. From the glass room's ceiling bubbling soapsuds poured down through the large top pipe and the rising water now gushed and spouted upwards from holes in the floor, causing Mr E and Ivan to topple over in the flood. Soon the small room was spinning and humming at high speed with a whirlpool of water inside. Somewhere, between the splashing water and the soapsuds, a foot or an arm or hand of Mr E or Ivan could still be seen, before vanishing again amongst the water's frothing suds.

"You ungrateful bunch of vagabonds!" Mr E shouted, briefly pushing Ivan's head down into the water to try and make some more space to breathe, before he too was pulled down again into the swirling current. For some reason, however, everyone responded by letting out cries of "Yippeeeee," whilst jumping up and down with delight.

"In the words of Mr E himself," shouted Basil, and he began to chant the words that they had all heard every time Mr E had flushed someone out of the city. The crowd joined in:

"Round and round and round we go,
Faster and faster the water does flow.
It gushes and froths with pure delight,
It swishes and sloshes till flushing is right!"

Everyone rushed forward, all of them eager to be the one who pulled the chain to finally flush Mr E and Ivan away. At least twenty hands from the crowd grasped hold of the long chain as it was hauled down under their weight. Then there was a clunk and a great gurgling noise, which echoed through the air as if a giant plug had been pulled from a bath. This was followed by a swilling and swirling and then, "Sluuuuuuurrrrrp." The descending water gurgled and the glass cubicle emptied itself, flushing Mr E and Ivan away.

"And off they go!" cried the Professor, everyone laughed and cheered.

"Well that was a good one," said Basil.

The crowd all responded, "Loads of bubbles that time, don't you think!"

Lady Georgiana walked over to the platform, ascended its stairs, walked over to the microphone and turned to face the crowd. She quietened everyone down and then, looking directly at the King said, "On behalf of the inhabitants of Clearwash City I should like to welcome you, most noble and highly honoured King Wash-El-Ami, as the rightful ruler of this city".

Everyone cheered.

"However," continued Lady Georgiana, "as you can see, we are in a dreadful state. Our city is filthy and so are we. We are thirsty and ill. Can you help us?"

The King smiled. "Do not fear, Lady Georgiana and people of Clearwash City," he said. "My heart is for you all and always has been. You have found out, by now, what happens when a city throws off its constraints and tyrants rule. This is and always has been my city. I care for those who live here. You are all already clean, having responded to the words of my herald, having rid yourselves of the vile Mr E and now having received me back again. Soon you will all be washed and well-watered. All I need is my rightful place on my throne."

"Throne?" said the Professor. "What throne? There's never been a throne in this city."

The Professor looked at Basil who in turn looked at Lady Georgiana and she returned their confused gazes. The King walked to the stage. He held out his hand towards Lady Georgiana and she walked across to meet him. However, when she took his hand to help him up the steps, he instead helped her off.

"Better stand away from the stage. It will be safer that way," said the King with a smile. He then turned and took some small pebble-like items from a pouch at his side. Flinging them onto the wooden stage, he shouted with a strong and loud voice in a language that no-one understood. Sentence upon sentence he spoke and then he stepped back a few paces.

The scattered pebbles seemed to move. They jumped a little and each split in two, from top to bottom, doubling their number. What looked like short legs sprouted out of the split pieces and up they popped onto their little feet. They scrambled about on the stage and then climbed on top of each other, like ants, to form the shape of a small hillock. Once they were still, they split apart again and collapsed into a heap. New legs shot out from the split pebbles and they reformed into a hillock once more. Again they split apart, grew legs and reassembled themselves. This process went on and on, over and over, multiplication upon multiplication until there were so many of them that the stage collapsed under their weight. The crowd gasped, some cried out, but the King turned and raised a gentle hand to calm them, giving an assurance with his smile that everything was alright.

The insect-like pebbles continued their work of assembling and splitting. The Professor stood fascinated by the process, but even he had lost count of the number of times the pebbles had multiplied. Finally, once they reached a certain number, they assembled just once more; clicking together one after the other as they locked themselves into place. Bit by bit a large shape appeared forming into a most majestic throne with many steps leading up to it.

"My throne," said the King to the crowd, and with those words, he ascended the steps.

The King reached the top of the stairs and turned to face everyone. "It's good to have you all back," he said. "Life is mystery," he added, "and just as the wind blows and you know not where it comes from or where it is off to, so springs of life appear wherever my reign is, bringing life and cleanliness everywhere."

At this, the king sat down and smiled. His throne seemed to hum. The humming turned into a gentle pulsating vibe and the tremor ran down the steps and then directly under the feet of the gathered crowd. The ground began to rumble and at first, some panicked.

"What's happening?" said the Professor.

"Don't know," replied Lady Georgiana.

"It's an earthquake!" cried Basil.

Just to the right of them, on the edge of the square, a fountain of water suddenly burst through the ground. Up it shot into the air, spraying everyone with clean, fresh water. Then another burst and another. Fountains began erupting all over the square and throughout the city. The new water gathered itself into pools and streams as the fountains continued to spring up and pour out their shower of life-giving rain. Streams ran everywhere, babbling and bubbling with a chattering enthusiasm. Soon the main city street had become a river and the river a torrent of water. It rushed and gushed through every avenue, every highway, boulevard, lane, pathway, track and side-alley, washing everything clean as it went. After a time the water from the streets receded until all that was left was a wide and lively river, a persistent swishing waterway - heading down the city's main street and continually pouring through the main gates and out into the desert, bringing life wherever it went.

All over the city, the people began celebrating the new water, jumping into it to wash themselves clean.

"This is the most wonderful sight that I ever did see," cried Basil above the noise of the crowd, whilst wading through the water.

"Yes, I think you're right," said the Professor, who was standing next to a fountain, jumping around and getting very wet. "It's wonderful. Have you ever tasted anything like it?"

Scrub sat down next to a bubbling fountain to drink deep of the new water. It was rich in a way that he didn't know water could be. Cool, refreshing, thirst quenching, yet gave you a desire to drink more; the more you drank, the more you felt cleansed from deep within.

"Perhaps this is what Lady Pluggat meant by not just using soap on the outside - but being clean on the inside?" he thought.

Lady Georgiana stood by herself, quietly watching all the people splash and play in the new water. She enjoyed so much their boisterous delight. A great wave of relief and completion poured over her. Tears welled in her eyes and she didn't know whether to laugh or cry. All she could feel was a fresh river flowing out of her own soul, washing and cleansing her from the inside. The striving within ceased. No more need to struggle and fight for freedom. No more need to prove herself. No more need to make amends for the past. Just glad to be where she was, who she was and glad for the peace of the city. Tilting her head on one side, she removed the jet-black pillbox hat that she'd worn for so many years. It had become part of her uniform; a daily reminder of the battle within and the struggle without. The wind blew through her hair and the spray from the fountains felt so refreshing as her head became drenched with this new holy water. Loosening her grip, she felt the hat fall from between her fingers and a whole host of history fell with it. The river at her feet picked it up and carried it away on a never ending stream. Then, lifting up her head and letting the gentle splashes of the fountain's rain fall on her face, she opened her mouth to let the water in. In that moment she regained something she thought she'd lost and felt she'd never recover, that sense of home.

Everywhere across the capital, the celebrations of freedom started. Without any organisation, parties spontaneously happened and even the most mundane jobs, such as washing clothes, became an adventure for everyone to join in. Never before had so many washing lines appeared and people enthusiastically enjoyed hanging out their frocks, socks, coats, skirts, shirts, costumes, vestments and assorted garments. You could hang anything out, without embarrassment, for it was all clean for all to see.

No one questioned the rule of the king, and who would want to anyway? Clearwash City was clean again and deep down everyone knew it was back on the road for a further adventure of a lifetime, though no one quite knew what. It would just happen when the time was right.

That evening Sir Frederick, the Professor, Basil and Scrub all assembled at Lady Georgiana's large manor house to join her for a celebration evening meal whilst King Wash-El-Ami settled into the royal palace.

"Well, I'm glad to be back," said Sir Frederick.

"And I have never felt so happy in all my life," said Basil.

"I'll second that," said the Professor.

"And I've never seen the people so happy," said Lady Georgiana. "I'm sure the celebrations will be going on way into the early hours of the morning."

"At least we can all sleep in tomorrow," said Basil. "Never again will we have to get up early to buy those stupid and smelly lotions of Mr E."

"Oh that sounds too wonderful to be true," said the Professor, slurping his soup.

"I believe I shall be heavily involved in some serious fishing by that time," said Sir Frederick. "I hear there's lots of good catches in this new river. Goes on for miles you know."

"And I shall be having my third bath by that time tomorrow morning with real lotions and suds galore," said Lady Georgiana. "It's so wonderful to be clean again."

Everyone agreed and tucked into the next course of the meal, but as they ate Lady Georgiana noticed that Scrub was looking quite solemn and thoughtful. It probably meant that he was still thinking about something that had been said earlier, so she said to him kindly, "Scrub, whatever is the matter? You look a little sad, what's wrong? Thanks to you we are all free, clean and healthy again. Surely you're not sorry to see the end of Mr E and Mr Ritant are you?"

"No, Lady Pluggat," said Scrub. "I'm not sorry to see them go and it is nice to be healthy and clean again."

"Then what is the matter?" said Lady Georgiana, who, along with the others, looked quite concerned.

"Well," said Scrub thoughtfully, whilst stroking his big, bright, red rosette that was stuck onto his chest by one of Mr E's sniffer squads.
"I suppose, I just wish that Mr E had passed on to me his lotion recipes before he went."

"Oh Scrub," the friends jointly replied, with affectionate smiles.
"Shut up!" they all said together, and everyone laughed, even Scrub.

THE END

- -- - - - - - - - - - - - - - -

Book 2
The Fall of
Clearwash City

Timothy J Waters

Chapter 1 – A Scarcity of Sound

Clearwash City sat in the middle of a most inhospitable desert and shimmered in the baking heat. Basking in the sun's dazzling brightness, she momentarily roused herself from her deep slumber and yawned. Stretching out her stone limbs in lazy surrender, she relaxed her rock-like members in the brilliance of the morning light. It was hot! The oven dial pointed to a fiery roast and all around the air was a-stir; a moving, swaying, rippling mass that wobbled in the scorching breeze, stimulated and enthused by the engulfing temperature. Sitting beneath this blistering hotness the city closed her tired eyes and dozed. All seemed peaceful and very quiet. Having dissipated the night-time chill with her radiant, fiery beams, the great golden globe looked down from the firmament above and smiled. It gave her great satisfaction to see every part of the wide blue expanse saturated with her goodness; to see once again her dominance established in the heavenly realms and her reign unchallenged. Now she poured out from on high her sweltering kindnesses onto the many houses, streets and market squares below that belonged to the great metropolis. Like a weaned child under the care of an attentive mother, the city mumbled a half-hearted greeting to the world and then, after muttering something briefly under her breath, rolled over to continue her slumbering. Relaxing in the muggy warmth, she felt safe in the overbearing caresses of temperate, affectionate cordiality.

To the baked streets that were used to this kind of extreme heat, all seemed comfortable, agreeable and most satisfactory. To the human eye, looking on at the many dwellings and habitations scattered across the city, all was in place, an environment that was both neat and correct, kept with an immaculate fine-tuned efficiency, micro-managed down to the smallest detail. The city buildings were clean, well-ordered, and the many parks and open spaces showed off a landscape that was lush and green. The historical turnaround looked complete and at last sustained. No smog, no smoke and dirt it seemed was a thing of the past. Cleanliness was the word that came to mind, shouted from the rooftops even, and if cleanliness (which is next to godliness) was the aim of the day, then this was a successful city; a locality that fulfilled its divine call and put into practice that which it vigorously and religiously preached.

Looking across the skyline at the houses, parks, market squares, malls, mills, hills and canals, you could see that it was a place of no nonsense and no compromise. It was as if a dedicated army of fanatical cleaning technicians made sure that every spot of every surface was washed, polished and shone. Purity was now the new romance. For those in charge it was the latest and greatest expression of heart-throbbing eye-candy; a coalition of habitations, industrial workshops and public spaces that together cast a charismatic allure, hypnotising the visitor with its perfect edifices, shapes and architectural masterpieces. A wonder to behold, it all worked like a neatly fitted jigsaw to form a seamless and impeccable picture. If it

196

were an anthem, then it would sing out its tune in perfect harmony. If it was an engine, then it would have purred with pleasure; a perfectly balanced, precision made, well-oiled machine. This was success on a scale rarely imagined, let alone realised. To any that saw the big picture, who understood the grand utopian plan, they could feel nothing but the tingling satisfaction of a romantic and idealistic vision fulfilled.

This too was the perspective of the burning sun who watched from on high in the expanse of the sky and followed each day her faithful course across the heavens. But this champion of the heights lived so distant above the capital that her evaluations and assessments were obviously limited. Just as a dictator only sees the broad picture painted before him (standing on his balcony to overlook the cheers and applause of his troops, officials and specially selected populace; not seeing those places off limits to the dictatorship's propaganda machine, the realities of poverty and starvation, oppression and fear) so too it was from the bright shining sun's standpoint as she daily watched the scenes unfold in Clearwash City. "All is well," would be the sun's repeating mantra from her far-off vantage point – but these things can only be clearly seen from the ground. As always the 'devil was in the detail' and this 'devil' had run riot in the city streets for many weeks and months, perhaps years.

One of those 'on-the-ground' details lay just outside the city's front gates. There the historic remains of a great riverbed ran its deep channel into the hardened rock where a gushing waterway had previously carved out a passage of life years before. Now only trickles of water meandered and tiptoed over those smoothed pebbles and rounded stones where once a torrent had flowed. The eminent and illustrious river was subdued. The thirsty desert had drunk for so many-a-season of the river's great banquet of abundant supply that at one time it was actually rumoured to be ready to yield up its territory to the continuous flood – but now the sand was back and the ground panted for just a sip of water.

Back in the city, blubbering pools of wet mud briefly appeared each morning throughout the streets and lanes where once fountains of water had spouted and flowed (these ever-emerging muddy overflows were quickly cleaned up by an army of volunteers nicknamed the S.P.L.O.D.G.E. team, 'splodge' meaning the 'Sanitisation and Purification of Leaking and Oozing by Disinfecting with Germicidal Engineering'). Memories of those crystal-clear powerful and gushing sprays were now faded, and perhaps it was just a dream or the beginnings of a legend that they once fed the city with fresh, vibrant and clean water. It was so sad to see such strong springs of life reduced to a mere whimper. In their place large industrial pipes had been used to cap these untamed sources and the water was now restrained and piped in a more civilised way that allowed the population to control their flow; though the water pressure was not what it used to be and sometimes a mere dribble was all that they got from their new business venture. This wasn't, however, the most disturbing thing about Clearwash City. Disappointing might be a

197

word chosen to describe the lack of bubbling brook and absent watercourse but deficient would be a better word to describe the derelict human life that existed within the confines of the city walls.

It was rush hour, time to be busy, but instead of hustle and bustle a muted noiselessness draped itself over the subdued capital. Like a miasma of gloomy desolation, this heavy silence splayed itself across the airwaves like a saturating and polluting smog that would not shift or move, even though it was a bright and hot spring morn. Amidst the great heat, you could still feel the chill of the quietness and hush as if it were an eerie calm preparing the way for a great thunderstorm, a tempest or typhoon. So invasive was this hush and stillness that it pervaded not only the parks, canals, avenues and gardens, but the back alleys and market squares too - everywhere where humanity should be, and yet was not.

Even the wind was lost. Normally this rousing gust of activity found its blustery bearings by passing in-between and around a busy humanity. It loved to run from person to person, from child to adult, from families and friends to groups of boisterous teenagers. All together they created a variety of gaps and narrow spaces that forced the breeze to squeeze here and there as it made its daily journey across the city. Human bustle made life in this place interesting, colourful and fun to navigate. Now, chasing its echoes down the winding lanes and cobbled corridors, the solitary breeze whistled its way through the streets looking and searching for signs of life. No coats to tug, no hats to blow off, no children to laugh and play with – it tarried for a moment on its broken hearted and lonesome path to cast a glance at the disappointing emptiness. Then on it continued, finally reaching the outskirts of the city walls, untouched and unmoved by those it sought out.

It wasn't that the absence of any noise itself was a problem or that the stillness and quiet was somehow unexpected, it was something else; this peculiar, subdued tranquillity that now hung in the atmosphere showed a locality holding its breath. The city suffered not so much from a shortage of noise but rather a scarcity of sound. The lack of clamour from workmen and the non-existent din of a crowd revealed a city in starvation; a famine of racket, uproar, tumult, shouting, agitation, hubbub and hullabaloo.

This strange singularity of deprived commotion gave off a silence that was so deafening it demanded being listened to, so loud that you had to strain your ear to hear anything at all, for there was indeed nothing to hear. Nothing, that is, except perhaps the odd chirp from the early morning bird who sought to tell everyone that he'd been up for hours and that, if they were not very careful, he would be the only one to show his face that day.

Sound had packed its bags and left, a withdrawal of noise that was the embodiment of abandonment. Where it had gone and why, was a question anyone could ask, but there wasn't anyone to ask. Perhaps the answer lay in the presence of a corpulent, portly, invisible lady, a woman of drunken pleasures, called 'motionlessness' who sat in the main square. Next to her was her sister called 'dearth'. Together they made up the new ideological order of the day and their presence ensured that all hopes and dreams that would normally stir the human soul to life on such a fine morn were dulled and sedated. Noiselessness now ruled over the activities of what might be called the 'living humanity' that existed throughout the hours of daylight. Living the population might be, but 'human' or indeed 'humane' is not a word that should be used to describe their deeds.

For the citizens of Clearwash City were all dreamily shut away behind closed doors. Cosy, clean, contented and chilled, the good life was here and no-one was going to take it from them. Like a mind drug, shrouding vision and insight, the silence that had infiltrated the lives of these people, the general populace, was comforting. They slept so peacefully and every morning it was the same. It didn't matter that your sleep had been slightly interrupted at dawn when doors were kicked in and soldiers made their arrests and those few voices of dissent were marched off to who knows where. Betraying others the night before, to prove your loyalty to the new regime, would guarantee a supply of food, unlimited exclusive commodities and entertainment for hours; followed by a sleep-in that subsequent morn which imitated the life of a spoilt millionaire. Party, sleep, rest and more perpetual play to follow, a cycle of quick immediate pleasures, exhilarating and thrilling, bringing instant gratification to the soul. The body, however, worn out by this constant activity, could chill and find its rest throughout the following hours of daylight, getting ready to do it all over again when evening came. So the night life was found to be better than the day, for it held the keys of happiness and contentment; strange that this had become the final conclusion of the city's enlightened citizens. Education, it seemed, didn't hold the keys to wisdom and insight, just to a dictatorship of what is called 'current thinking' which pays no homage to the realities of the life that surrounds us. Now, for the people of Clearwash City who were drenched in the new ideology, the day had nothing to offer them but the song of blank vacancy that played itself out to the background beat of snores from an exhausted people.

There was a sound, however, that did sometimes slip into this blank space of empty life. It meandered its way on the breeze, across the open air, in what was once a more affluent part of the city (now considered a little old fashioned and frumpy); a cheery tune, highly at odds with the rest of the dulled quiet that surrounded it. The city's stillness tried to suffocate this irritatingly happy intrusion but the melody persisted, undeterred and unrepentant – despite the strong disapproval that surrounded it. The tune's delightful message leaked into the atmosphere from the back of a grand mansion. To be precise, through an upper attic window, left slightly ajar. Behind the window, a small room, and the source of the charming jingle, a horn of an old and rusted record player that magnified and fed the agreeable sound into the air. The player's receiver head floated gracefully along its prescribed path on the grooves of the vinyl disk like a beautiful skater performing a well-rehearsed routine; that is until it bounced up and down where the record had warped slightly and the tune being played wobbled in protest. The lively notes that did manage to get played correctly, however, soothed their way through the room's stillness, leaving it enriched by its joyous sound.

The furnishings within the converted attic space were comfortable enough, two leather backed armchairs facing each other opposite an open hearth that hospitably housed the remaining embers of a night-time glowing fire. If there had been a normal peacefulness in the air you would have thought the environment homely, sociable and even jolly. Indeed, to the stranger's eye, the first impressions of the room would bring ideas of sweet friendship and cordiality. Outside, however, the descended silence had nothing to do with serenity.

At a table, set just behind one of the armchairs, sat a lady of the realm. The sharp and pointed expression etched across her face hid her normal gentle features that were so familiar to the people amongst whom she lived. She was a woman with a task before her, one that she would rather not do. Taking a few moments to mentally prepare herself for the job at hand, she briefly stilled her mind and then picked up a silver quill, dipped it into a small bottle of ink, and penned the following:

"Lady Georgiana, daughter of Lord Stephen Pluggat and Lady Melanie Lynette,

To the people of Clearwash City, set free and made clean by the King's liberty and grace. To those whom I love, who have so grown in my heart and who I now hold with such tender care and great affection.

My dear friends,

It is with great anguish and turmoil within that I write for you this short account of those things that have so recently been fulfilled amongst us. I do this now so as to not lose my voice in the midst of this present chaos. In writing this, I am very aware that it is not only a short history of a season past that I record, but also my personal farewell to those of you that remain once I am gone. For I sense and feel that my time here is drawing to an end and that I shall soon pass through and beyond the veil that separates our world from the next."

- -

Keep an eye out for the next books
being written in this series:

The Fall of Clearwash City
The Silence of Clearwash City
The Ransom of Clearwash City
The Purge of Clearwash City
The Hope of Clearwash City

Find out more at www.clearwashcity.com

- -

About the Author

Tim Waters stepped out onto his new literary horizons in the mid-1990s. He began to run annual "custard slinging" Summer clubs with his wife for children aged 7-12 and, as a result, found himself writing short plays for the children to watch. After writing,

- Enter the Jungle
- Invading the Ocean
- Way out in the Wild West
- The Knights and Ladies of Camel Knot Court
- Search for Stone Valley
- Splash into Spaghetti

...he decided to write a play called "The Waterworks of Clearwash City." (The following year he wrote Surfing the Supernova). The young audience so enjoyed the waterworks wacky adventure that he decided to turn it into a book. Over the years Tim has developed and moulded the storyline into a mature text ready for people of all ages to read. As a bit of a perfectionist Tim loves to use words to paint pictures of the book's world in the reader's mind by adding great descriptions, clearly illustrating the surrounding sights, sounds and smells. At the same time he makes every paragraph as tight as possible so that the story flows well, making it an easy read. It is this attention to detail that marks Tim's style and purpose as a writer.

As a young child Tim's favourite stories were those written by Roald Dahl and C.S. Lewis and later in his teenage years by J.R.R.Tolkien. He also grew up on the comedy of Laurel and Hardy along with other classics such as Dad's Army. Somewhere between all of these, along with other childhood sources, are the many influences by which he has written his drama scripts and hence this book. He wants his fiction work to be available to all of the family so that each age group can appreciate his daft and hopefully interesting stories at their own level. Tim strives to write in such a way that each individual can take something unique away with them from their read and hopes that people can begin to pick up the secondary meanings in his text, whether a comic reference or a serious point made. It has taken years for Tim to discover his unique writing style and this book represents his "growing up" over that period. He hopes that his next books will take a little less time to write.

Tim enjoys being a husband and a dad. He likes watching Sci-Fi adventure movies, playing the guitar, watching films too young for his age, painting, drawing and dining out at "All you can eat buffets." It is not wise to play Monopoly with Tim as he turns into a different person. Apart from this flaw in his personality he's not too difficult to live with - and so he reminds his wife on a regular basis.

His full first name is actually Timothy but if you meet him, however, please call him Tim as he normally only gets called Timothy when he's in trouble with his wife or family. He really hopes you like this book and also looks forward to creating new reads for you as and when he can.

- - - - - - - - - - - - - - - - -

To help Tim, could you please leave a review of this book on Amazon where you purchased it.

- - - - - - - - - - - - - - - - -

Georgiana's Attic

Georgiana's attic is the fictional hiding place of a wise and courageous heroine, Lady Georgiana Pluggat-Lynette. Surrounded by vintage treasures that remind her of happier times, she recounts on paper the exploits of a group of unlikely rebels. In their attempts to keep Georgiana's beloved Clearwash City free from tyranny they discover that friendship is the key to victory. You can find out more about Georgiana's attic and the items that are on sale there at https://georgianasattic.com.

Printed in Great Britain
by Amazon

14005863R00122